C000201932

the
mess
we're
in

By Annie Macmanus and available from Wildfire

Mother Mother
The Mess We're In

the mess we're in

annie macmanus

WILDFIRE

First published in 2023 by
WILDFIRE
an imprint of HEADLINE PUBLISHING GROUP

1

Cataloguing in Publication Data is available from the British Library

Hardback ISBN 978 1 4722 9712 9
Trade paperback ISBN 978 1 4722 9713 6

Typeset in Dante MT by CC Book Production
Printed and bound in Great Britain by Clays Ltd, Elcograf S.p.A.

HEADLINE PUBLISHING GROUP
An Hachette UK Company
Carmelite House
50 Victoria Embankment
London EC4Y 0DZ

www.headline.co.uk
www.hachette.co.uk

For O and R. Never forget you're half Irish.

'I'm a fountain of blood
In the shape of a girl'

– Björk, 'Bachelorette'

'There is, in Ireland, a deep connection between dancing
and displacement.'

– Fintan O'Toole, *We Don't Know Ourselves*

CHAPTER 1

ANOTHER CHANCE

A low, throbbing, faraway sound, pulsing at the edges of my consciousness. Slowly, the sound shifts, the throbs taking form, separating into the bumps of a bassline. It's familiar; the way the notes climb up and fall back down again, and that sample at the top of the octave. I know this song. We've been playing it all night. It sounds dull now compared to before, all flat and clogged up somehow, but I recognise it, which means I'm back in my brain again.

I open my eyes slowly. I'm slumped against the radiator, my chin on my chest, my legs skew-whiff on the carpet in front of me. The room is a haze of smoke. Light streams in from the window behind, spotlighting Hamo, who is spreadeagled on the sofa, his mouth clamped shut and lopsided, as if he's had a stroke in his sleep.

Olly is perched on the edge of a stained armchair, staring at the television, smiling to himself while his joint slowly burns out between his fingers. His hair has been shorn badly, a home clippers job, without any care taken around the ears. Earlier in the night, I thought he was beautiful. I told him his smile should win awards all over the world.

My fist is clenched around a small glass bottle. I loosen my grip so that it falls out of my fingers on to the carpet. I laughed at them when they started doing the poppers. I shouted *TIMBER* as they toppled over, one by one, like felled trees. I was sure the amyl nitrate wouldn't work on me, some vague memory of a failed attempt in the past, so I made a big show of taking two lengthy sniffs from the bottle, one in each nostril. *I'm grand*, I said. *Look at me. Not a bother.*

Then it all went blank.

I pull myself up with the help of the radiator behind me and cough. The record spins on the deck in the corner. The coffee table is covered; overflowing ash trays, empty beer cans, half-full glasses with cigarette butts floating in the liquid, like tiny dead bodies. A semicircle of space on the side nearest the sofa holds a row of messily chopped lines of cocaine. Hamo stirs and adjusts his legs.

– What time is it? I croak.

Hamo swallows as his eyebrows raise in suggestion. – You can sleep here.

I try to push out a smile. – Nah, I'm going today, remember? What time is it?

– It's seven, says Olly, without taking his eyes off the telly.

2

I look down at the lines of coke on the coffee table. – One for the road?

Hamo blinks slowly and sticks out his hand, which is already clutching a rolled-up five-pound note. I take it and bend over, holding my top close to my chest so he can't get a look at my cleavage.

– See yiz next time! I say, before they can remember that there will be no next time. Not in this place, anyway. Hamo leans over the table to snort a line as I leave the room.

Standing on the porch, I feel dizzy, as if I've just stepped off a boat. *Deep breath, Orla. Up through the nose, out through the mouth.* The street is silent, curtains still drawn. A black cat slinks through a gate across the way. I step down to ground level and set off towards my house.

It's muggy already this morning; the clouds are smudges on smudges, charcoal on paper. The birds chitter-chatter above me as I walk; warm melodious warblings that ring pleasurably in my ears. I feel fizzy. Adrenaline pumping through me. If I walk fast, I could be asleep by eight and get a few hours before I have to get up and pack the rest of my stuff. I follow the black railings around the perimeter of Montpellier Park and pull my Discman and headphones out of my bag.

Goldie – Timeless.

When the synth arrives at the start of the first song, it's like snow falling: a blanket of calm in my head. Everything in my vision has more mystery and depth to it. I pull my shoulders back, stick my chin out into the damp morning air. I'm in a music video now, mouthing along to the words, roaming the poxy pastel streets of Cheltenham for the last time.

It takes fifteen minutes to reach the cluster of shops at the top of our road. There's the wheelie bin sitting sentry outside our house, filled to the brim with bottles. Inside the front door, the hall smells of incense and allspice.

Neema is standing over the sink in the kitchen. She turns when I walk in. She has eyes like a fawn; big, brown, wet things that make her look permanently as if she's about to break down in tears.

– Hiya, I say, pulling off my bag, and add, – Before you say anything, yes, I'm just getting in from Hamo's.

– Aha, Neema says with a half-smile. – Was it fun?

– Was it fun . . . I repeat, pretending to think really hard. – We did a load of MDMA, which was fun. The poppers were not a good idea.

She nods, knowing and wise, sage-like, as the kettle clicks behind her. – Want a chai, darling? she says, doing her best Indian grandmother. She enunciates every letter of the word, ending in a pronounced 'geh' – darliingeh, the second syllable always half an octave higher than the first. I love it when she calls me darling. It's a short song, a work of art. I nod.

– Please. What time's your brother coming?

– He said two, but he's always late. I'd say more like three . . . Orla. She jumps over to me and grabs me by the arms, leaning into me, her eyes bulging out of her face. – I'm excited.

Back in my room, I undress and stand in the tiny space of my bathroom to wipe away my make-up. My head is thumping already. I pull on my pyjamas and sit down on the edge of my bed to take my first sip of tea. It's warm and sweet and slightly spicy, and it evokes a powerful surge of loving feelings towards Neema. I want to write her a note and put it under her door:

Thank you for your tea. And your big non-judgemental eyes. I love you.

By my feet, my cork board is balanced precariously on top of my packed bags, photos and flyers still tacked to it. My sister Anna grins out at me from one of the photos, wearing reindeer antlers on her head at The Phoenix in Dublin, a pint of cider in her hand. Beside her is the photo I love of Ma and Da before it all went wrong; they're dancing together, locked in the embrace of a waltz at Cousin Niamh's wedding. I took that photo. They were both playing up to the camera, Da singing along to the words, probably a Beatles song to get him looking so into it, Ma grinning, her face all flushed from red wine.

The faint choppy rhythms of Neema's UK garage compilation start up from beyond the wall. I take the last slurp of my tea, climb into bed and push in my ear plugs.

I must think about nice things. Moses.

I'm glad I got to say a proper goodbye to him last night.

The lights came on in the student union bar, exposing us in our sweat and drunkenness, and I pulled him into a hug and then held him by the shoulders with my hands, forcing him to look at me. I tried to tell him everything with my eyes; that I've fancied him for a full year, that I'd love if he would kiss me sometime, anytime, right now, even – but he just stood there smiling at me, that smile that makes my heart do a little jig in my chest, until I said, – Give us your number then.

Thank God he wanted to take mine too.

I get up to go to the toilet, and I can't help but see my face in the mirror as I walk past. Big eager eyes on me. Pupils still enormous. I look like Gwen Stefani if she had a weight problem and a face like a potato. As if I have any sort of a chance with Moses.

Nice things, Orla.

Back in bed I close my eyes, and now I'm cross-legged on the living room carpet at home, tucked in between my da's legs as he plays his guitar and sings his evening recital. Ma and Anna are clattering around the kitchen, but in here it's just me and him, warmed from the orange bars of the fire, and his light, easy baritone filling the room. He loved the sound of his own voice alright. And I loved the feeling of the songs washing over me; the pictures they formed in my head. The Don McLean song 'Vincent' was my favourite. I'd be rapt, my head whirling with imagery, as he sang of flaming flowers and starry nights and shadows on the hills.

I never understood that the song was about Vincent Van Gogh when I was small; I just thought that it sounded like an apology, and I wished that someday I could be important enough that someone would want to say sorry to me in the way that my da said sorry to this Vincent man in the song.

When I became old enough for Da to teach me how to play the guitar, he used to rub the hardening skin on my fingertips, and say, – You're a real player now, Lorley.

I rub the top of my fingers against my thumb now, under the blanket. The skin is smooth and soft. My callouses are long gone. I try to imagine his guitar in my arms, how the fretboard would feel as I push my fingers into the shape of a G and then an A minor, then a C and a D and then back to G again.

A car horn beeps suddenly outside my window, startling me, my eyes opening in the surprise of it, and I see myself. The absolute state of me.

I am a twenty-one-year-old woman, strung out on MDMA and cocaine, lying in bed in broad daylight, pretending to play a guitar.

Neema's door clumps shut. I listen to the crank and groan of the pipes as she starts up the shower down the hall. She'll be in that baby blue bathrobe she wears, that drags on the floor behind her. There'll be even more grooming than usual for the day that's in it. I close my eyes to test out how tired I am. I need to sleep so that I can feel good for the journey. I need the fizz in my head to go flat.

God, please let me sleep.

I want to draw a line between yesterday and today. I never knew a year could drag as heavy as this year in Cheltenham has. It was like wading through water. But today; today is a new start. Today is my chance to start England all over again.

CHAPTER 2

FALLIN'

I expected more drama on arrival into London. Some sort of cityscape. Some big, imposing emblem of Englishness. Apart from a small cluster of high-rises looming in the distance, it's mostly flat as we come off the motorway; grey, non-descript buildings hump-backing away from us on both sides. Thin cloud hanging low overhead. Or is it smog?

Neema is squashed up beside me in the cabin of the van, a packet of tobacco open on her lap, rolling a cigarette. She rummages in the compartment under the CD player to find a lighter; she lights the roll-up, passes it to Kesh, and starts to make one for herself. It's a warm, balmy afternoon, and the windows are down a few inches, allowing the air to swirl through the cab of the van, and the smoke from Kesh's cigarette to swirl out. Kesh drives with two hands on the wheel, eyes darting between the road and his rear-view mirror. There's a quickness to his movements that echoes Neema's, a kind of sprightliness. When I met him and the rest of the band back in April, he had his hair cut into a shaggy Mohawk, and kohl smudged around his eyes. I was excited because there was a review of his band, Shiva, in that week's *NME*, where they had described him as 'an Asian Jeff Buckley on amphetamines'. There's no hint of his rock-star status today, apart from the R.E.M. logo on the front of his T-shirt.

– This is Acton, he says, pulling up at a set of traffic lights. – We're not far from Ealing and Southall, which is South-Asian central. I wanted to stay away from there, so we ended up in Irishtown instead. There's loads of Irish pubs.

– Jesus, there's no escape from the Irish, I say. – We're like a virus.

– A friendly virus, Neema says, and points at two men crossing the road. – Oh, look. Brown people. Finally.

I grab her hand. She smiles and puts her other hand on top of mine briefly, before pulling away to tend to her cigarette. Kesh jolts the gearstick forwards, pushes his foot down on the accelerator. Radiohead's 'Kid A' album is on the CD player; Thom Yorke sings in maudlin tones over an acoustic guitar. As the van picks up speed, the song takes a turn into minor chords, all edge and menace. We drive past a petrol station, a pub, a park with a playground on the border by the road, children shrieking and shouting, two mothers leaning against the railings, staring vacantly into the throng.

– Neema, will you remind me to phone my ma when we get there, I say.

– Sure, she replies.

Kilburn High Road is long and shabby. We crawl along with the traffic, past big, old art deco buildings, betting shops and bars, a jeweller's shop with a sign for Claddagh rings in the window. There's a big fruit and vegetable stall on the corner, and as we turn right on to a long, tree-lined street full of towering townhouses, Kesh says, – This is us.

– God, what a pretty street, I say.

– It's a lot grimier up close, murmurs Kesh, his roll-up hanging out of his mouth as he manoeuvres the van over a speed bump. The road runs down a hill and up again, to where the houses are smaller.

– There it is, says Neema, pointing at a grey pebble-dash house, a black door with the number 74 on it. It stands out from the exposed red brick of the other houses up and down the street. The front porch is held up by white columns. A wiry shrub grows out from under a grey satellite dish on the roof.

Kesh parks the van and we drag our bags and dump them on the porch, then go back for more. When the porch is full of our stuff, Kesh unlocks the door, pushes it open and helps us carry everything into the hall, where the smell of weed is strong.

– Eeeeeeey, the new arrivals. A voice comes from a room off the hall.

11

– Thanks for the help, guys, Kesh calls back, rolling his eyes at us and gesturing for us to follow him into a long, drab room.

Richie, the drummer in Shiva, unfolds himself from an armchair. He turns to us, scratching his head, which is shaved short. His lanky frame is counteracted with a baby face: full lips, dimples under the stubble, a small silver hoop in his left ear. After a slight pause, he walks over and reaches down to hug us both.

– Welcome to the mad house, he says, in his sing-songy Liverpool accent, crunching the 'h' in house so it feels like a whole process, the utterance of that one word. He's clearly stoned out of his box.

Frank, the bass player, pushes an overflowing ashtray out of the way to make room on the coffee table for his plate of chips, then stands up from the low sofa. His hair is a shoulder-length triangle of thick corkscrew curls. His hug is firm and followed through with a fixing of green-grey eyes on to mine and a small nod. He's a good bit shorter than me. Two band members shorter, one taller. *Thank God for Richie.*

– I'll show you to your room, Kesh says, picking up one of our bags in each hand and heading for the stairs. There's a nervous energy to his steps, like he can't afford the time to put the soles of his feet entirely on the ground, so he charges around on his tiptoes instead. We follow him up past the first floor landing and up another flight of stairs, to a tiny landing holding a single door. – This is you, he says, walking into the room and dumping the bags on the carpet. – I'll go and get the rest of the stuff.

Neema and I stand in silence, breathing heavily from the climb. The back wall of the attic is full-height, but the ceiling slopes down to knee-height at the front of the house. There is a Velux window in the ceiling, already tilted open. The room is bare apart from two single beds that sit against each wall. It feels claustrophobic compared to the high-ceilinged spaces in the rest of the house. I walk over to the Velux and stretch on my tiptoes to see out. Through a window across the road, a man stands over a hob, stirring something. I can hear the hum of traffic from the High Road. A low siren bleats in the distance.

– Here you go, says Kesh, puffing into the room with my cork board and a black sack of Neema's shoes. – That's the last of it.

– Thanks Kesh, Neema says.

– You coming down? Kesh asks.

– Yeah, Neema says. – We'll unpack later.

Back in the living room, it's hard not to stare. Dirty brown curtains fall off the curtain rings on the rail at the window. A small black-and-white photo of a band hangs in a frame above the sofa. I lean over for a closer look.

– That's Black Sabbath, says Frank. – Classic photo. They'd just invented heavy metal there. Look at Ozzy.

I examine the photo. Ozzy sits second from the left in the

line-up: big angelic eyes, skin boyishly smooth in contrast to the others, who all sport heavy moustaches and long hair.

– He looks so innocent, I say.

– He is, says Richie. – That was before he lost it to drugs and started making shit albums.

Kesh walks in with two plates piled high with fat chips and puts them down on the coffee table in front of us. – We planned ahead, he declares, delighted with himself.

– Ah, thanks, Neema says. – I'll go and get condiments. Is there some for you too, Kesh?

– Yeah, he says.

– I'll get them. She walks out of the room, and Kesh flops down on the sofa next to Frank.

I feel the eyes of my new housemates rest on me.

– Is it okay up there? Kesh says, eventually.

– Oh, sure, yeah. We'll be fine up there, I say too quickly, because I'm trying to distract myself from the hot feeling rising up from my neck into my face.

Frank stands up, talking over his shoulder as he walks across to the corner of the room. – We're excited to have girl housemates. The last guy was a nightmare. Didn't say a word.

– Well, you won't have that problem with me. I can talk for Ireland, I say, and laugh. But my laugh is too loud and forced, and I swallow quickly and focus on Frank, who is lifting a white wooden door that was propped against the wall, and standing it in front of the window.

14

As he comes back to his chair, he looks at me and says, –
The curtains don't work, so we use the door instead.

I try to make my nod agreeable, and direct my eyes towards
the television, where everyone else is looking now. Tony Blair
is on the screen, shining his toothy grin at a clapping crowd.
Kesh crosses his legs in his chair and starts to build a joint.

– Cheers, he says as Neema walks in and puts a plate of
chips on the arm of his sofa.

She looks at the TV as she sits down beside me. – So it's
final?

– Yep, says Richie. – He's in for another term

We all stare at the TV until Kesh asks, – What's the plan
for tonight?

Frank and Richie look at each other before Richie speaks
up. – I said we'd meet Gwen at The Oxford Arms.

Kesh nods and says, – Do you two want to come?

Neema pauses, shaking an excess of salt over her chips,
then looks at me and says, – Yes please.

Later that night, after several bottles of wine, a dessert
of skunk spliffs and a frenzied dressing session in the loft,
Neema and I walk up to the High Road with the boys
to get the bus to Camden. I walk carefully, my senses on
high alert from the skunk, seeing every shape and shadow,
hearing every sound acutely. We stop at traffic lights and
wait to cross the road, where a pub called The Bell Inn has
its doors propped open to the street, slot machines blinking

coloured light through the windows. There is noise from every direction. The fading light is tinged with pink, the air thick with fumes from the cars that snake up the road as far as I can see. At the bus stop, buses come and go, but ours isn't here yet. Kesh stands at a remove from the rest of us, hands in the pockets of his baggy combats, eyes hidden behind wrap-around sunglasses.

Richie air drums with his hands as he talks to Neema and me. – Buses are cheapest, then Tube.

– But Tube's free if you jump the gate, says Frank with a smirk on his face. His hands are wedged into the back pockets of his jeans, which sit tight on his squat legs.

– How d'you jump the gate? I ask.

– It's all about timing, Frank says. – You have to slip in behind someone, but you have to do it smoothly or you get noticed.

– I don't think Frank has paid for one travel card since he's lived in London, says Richie, and we all look at Frank, who shrugs his shoulders.

– One advantage of being short, I guess, he says. – Richie, you wouldn't get away with it.

A group of boys rushes past us, chattering excitedly in a language I don't recognise.

– Who's the Gwen that we're meeting? I say, to stop myself staring at the boys any more than I already have.

– Gwen's our PR. She works at the label. She's good fun, she is, Richie replies.

Our bus arrives, and we settle into the two rows of seats at the back. Kesh has one arm slung over the back of his seat, his ankle resting on his other knee. Richie sits on the edge of Kesh's seat. He seems always to be moving, his long limbs shooting off in different directions all the time. He is the tallest, but Kesh is the most conventionally handsome, with that chiselled face, all sharp corners, counteracted by soft nut-brown eyes.

Frank sits on the seat across from me. In profile, his nose is hooked, his mouth small. He's tried to tie back his fat curls without brushing them out, giving him a lumpy head. I don't know if it's his sleepy-looking eyes, but he's doing a great job of looking like the most bored man in the world. I try to engage him. – So, what's Kilburn like?

He blinks a little and then goes to speak, but before he can, Richie cuts in from behind us. – Frank's an amateur historian. He'll tell you the whole story. He nods at Frank as if to say, *You can start now.*

Frank looks at me, then around the bus. He speaks in a low voice, so I have to lean in to hear him. – You can trace the origins of Kilburn High Road back as far as Roman times. It began in St Albans and led all the way down to Hyde Park.

His words have these long, lovely curves in them. I can't remember where he's from, but it's somewhere in the south-west. He speaks slowly and methodically.

– A lot of the Irish people here call it County Kilburn because of how many Irish settled here in the fifties and sixties, he continues.

17

– Why'd they come to this bit of London? I ask.

– I presume it was because it was so cheap to live here and it's so close to Camden. I read that Camden was the furthest place they could walk to from Euston station with their suitcases which is why loads of them settled there.

– Really? I say, and he shrugs and smiles, showing me his crooked front teeth as I try to imagine trainloads of young Irish following each other through the new and dangerous streets of London, walking in their good shoes until their feet ached.

– This is us, Richie says, as the bell shrills under his finger.

Neema and I follow the boys down the steps and off the bus. We walk towards Camden High Street in silence. Camden Town is legendary. Home of The Good Mixer, Graham Coxon's favourite pub. Home of Dublin Castle and the Electric Ballroom. Home to London's goths and punks. We pass an old woman, covered in grime, crouching against the wall, smells of weed and urine coming off her. *If Camden was a woman.* We walk over a bridge to see the canal curling out from below, and a cyclist tearing down the towpath at breakneck speed.

I steal a glance at my friend. I am unfamiliar with this Neema, who strides through Camden in her fake-fur coat and her high-heeled boots, as if it's hers for the taking. It's as if moving in a pack bolsters her, or maybe it's being close to her brother? I have an odd perspective-tilting sensation as I walk beside her, of shrinking, my surroundings stretching into a vast, endless expanse around me. If this is just one town in London, how many more are there? I focus hard on the dull clop of Neema's high heels on the pavement.

The Oxford Arms is filled with smoke and loud, forceful voices. Heavy rock music pounds through the speakers. Richie manages to manoeuvre us into a corner banquette before dragging Frank to the bar, which is packed two-deep.

Kesh's eyes are flitting all over the room as he talks.

– We're playing a gig on Friday night, just up the road. To launch the new single.

– You have a single out? I say to him.

– Yeah, it's called 'Brick by Brick'. Second one from the album, he says, dragging his eyes from the pub back to us. His accent is different from Neema's, less pronounced northern, more vaguely English. Neema told me that he was sent to a private school outside Bolton, whereas she was sent to the local state school. Which was ironic, as she was the one who'd pursued law, and he'd decided to be in a rock band.

I don't know what to do with my hands, so I'm grateful when Richie and Frank plonk our drinks down and I have something to hold. Frank squeezes in beside me, and Richie sits at the edge. Kesh picks up his pint and directs his words to Neema and me over the top of it. – Welcome to London, you two.

– Cheers, say Frank and Richie, and we all clink glasses. I must look like a fucking eejit, the amount I'm smiling. I take a big gulp of my pint.

– Eeeeeeeey! Richie stands up and shouts at a woman who is pushing through the crowds of people, walking towards us.

– Alright you bunch of bastards, she says, arms outstretched. They all greet her with hugs.

– Gwen, this is Neema and Orla, Richie says.

She exclaims loudly: – Neema, look at you. The famous little sister. And hello, Orla, she says to me, as if I'm a long-lost friend. Her accent is thick Glaswegian. Her hair is crimson coloured and cut in a shoulder-length bob, and her eye make-up is heavily black under her fringe, in stark contrast to her pale and pockmarked skin. – Shift up you lot, she says, and we all squeeze tighter together as she sits down beside Richie. – Cheers. She holds up her drink and makes a big show of looking at us, right in the eyes. Big gulp and swallow, and then she puts her drink down. – Youse ready for the weekend? she asks the boys.

Kesh nods and the rest follow.

– I've got a shit load of people coming down. It's going to be good, Gwen says.

– As long as we don't get compared to Muse again, I'm happy, says Frank.

– What are your fans like? I ask Frank.

He opens his mouth to answer, but Kesh is there first.

– Little misfits and weirdos. He says it affectionately, and at the same time he starts jumping up and down in his seat. – No way, they're playing my favourite Incubus song.

Frank stares at Kesh, and then turns to me with an eyeroll, his pupils briefly disappearing under his lids. – Kesh is obsessed with Incubus.

I nod, and fix my eyes back on Kesh, who has been hijacked by the music. He slams his palms down on the table in time with the drums of the song and joins in, singing the words loud enough for us all to hear.

He shouts over at Frank and Richie. – You should have come with us to see them at the Astoria last year. Mate, they fucking blew my mind.

Gwen buys a round of sambucas for us all, and she and the boys tag-team in telling us stories of the band's escapades. They are accounts of total hedonism: Frank and Richie up for three days straight; Kesh falling asleep in a shopping trolley outside a supermarket after a house party because he was too tired to go anywhere else; the tour manager, Shane, squatting in a disused nursing home, and later sleeping in their basement at 74 Mill Road for a whole week without the rest of the band knowing.

– What's it like in the basement? I hear myself saying, wondering if there's any more room down there than in the attic.

Richie answers. – It's not a place to live in. It's full of rubble from a renovation that was done before we moved in, and it's got no heating. The toilet is outside and it's disgusting. I can't believe he managed a week there, to be honest.

I think of the basement window I saw on entering the

house earlier, how it was completely covered in stacked-up paint pots and material so that no light could get through it whatsoever.

– Maybe he could move in permanently if he didn't mind it, Neema says.

He'd make a good guard dog for our stuff, Richie replies. – There's always burglaries on our road.

– What would you expect him to do, bite the burglars? I say.

– Let's be honest, he'd scare them away with his hairstyle, Richie says, lifting his pint to take a sip, and Neema and the boys laugh.

– What's his hairstyle like? I ask.

– He has a rat's tail. It's short all over, and then there's this long, greasy tail at the back, says Richie. He is geed up now, in full performance mode, acting out the scene of the burglars seeing Shane. – It's no use, lads. Everyone turn around. I can't rob a house belonging to a man with that hairstyle. We've got to leave immediately.

Gwen leans in over the drink-sodden table, her gravelly laugh cutting through the din. Her throat catches and she descends into a fit of coughing, but she keeps laughing through the coughs, and that makes us all laugh even more. As her coughs finally ease, she shakes her head with her hand over her mouth, and croaks, – More shots?

– It's my round, I say, jumping up from the table. Squeezed

between bodies at the bar, I try to stop grinning, to fix my face to look more casual at this scene – this pub in Camden, this band that I live with now – as if this is just a typical evening for me instead of the first night of the rest of my life. Then the barman catches my eye. I lean forwards. I'm a Londoner now. I'm a voice in the noise. I'm ready.

– *Hello, DDT Alarm systems?*

– *Hi, Mam.*

– *Orla. Jesus, you had me worried sick.*

– *Sorry Mam, I meant to ring you yesterday but we ended up going out.*

– *Well, I was imagining all sorts of disasters. I was up half the night.*

– *Mam, you know I have a mobile phone now. You can call me on that anytime. I emailed you the number.*

– *Hmph.*

Pause.

– *Well, you made it anyway.*

– *I did. Got here yesterday early evening and then we went to Camden.*

– *Have you a bad head on you?*

– *Very bad.*

– *Are they nice? The band. Is the house nice?*

– *The band are nice. The house is really big. There's one room that has all their gear stacked up to the ceiling. All their instruments and amps and stuff. That's where they record their demos. The kitchen is really small and dirty, you'd hate it. Oh and there's only one toilet.*

– *Jesus Christ, I couldn't be doing with that. (Howrya Gary? Yes, just put them on there and I'll get to them in a second, thanks.) And have they a washing machine?*

– *Yeah, thank God. And a washing line in the garden.*

– *Listen, I need your address. Give it to me now.*

– *What are you sending me?*

– *A card for your birthday.*

– *It's not for a month, Ma.*

– *I don't trust the postal system. I can't have you not getting a card on your birthday.*

– *How's Anna?*

– *She got a promotion in work. She's on the marketing team now.*

– *More free Heineken on the way, so.*

– *And she's got a new fella from Blackrock. Alan, his name is. He comes and collects her in this fancy red car; you can hear it all over the estate. Thinks he's bleeding Ayrton Senna.*

– *Oh, I bet she loves that.*

Pause.

– *And Ma, are you okay? Like, in general? Not too . . .*

– *I'm grand!*

Pause.

– *You're not to be worrying about me. It should be the other way round.*

– *Well, I'm just checking.*

– *I'm going for dinner with the girls on Friday. And I've found a painter to do the house.*

– *Very good.*

– *And I've an idea for the shed.*

– *Speak up, Ma. Why are you whispering?*

– *I'm going to turn the shed into a gym.*

– *But it's Da's shed. He might need it.*

– *It's sitting there empty, Orla. We might as well put it to good use. (Ah, Mr McGivern come on in, he'll be ready for you in two minutes.) Orla, I've got to go now. Ring me soon, okay?*

– *Okay, bye Ma.*

CHAPTER 3

VOYAGER

A queue snakes out the door of the post office at the top of Mill Road. At the fruit stall on the corner, the rainbow colours of the fruit gleam bright under the sun. The man behind the stall nods at me as I walk past. I nod back, gesture at the oranges and say, – I live down the road. I'll buy some on the way home.

He raises his eyebrows in a bemused expression, and I feel silly explaining myself to this man. I walk quickly on, turning north on to the Kilburn High Road.

Kilburn. Kill. Burn. Two violent words stuck together. This is my home now.

Up in the loft room, Neema and I have tried to contain most of our clothes on two low clothes rails that run along the bottom of each of our beds. My bedside table is an upturned cardboard box. My stereo sits on the ground beside it, dangerously close to the door. My shoes live under the bed. It has taken a bit of getting used to, this close proximity to Neema. I enjoy watching her morning make-up routines when I'm half asleep in bed. The meditation of it. Patting and brushing and blending. She can change a whole outfit without showing any flesh. And I can't get over how lightly she treads. I take up so much space in the room, compared to her; my big, broad shoulders knock into things. *You'd fare well in a scrum*, my Uncle Hugh used to say to me when we had to go and visit his family, while my cheeks burned red with embarrassment.

I'm trying to keep my side of the room tidy, for her sake.

Even in the morning, Kilburn High Road is dense to the senses. Music blaring and engines revving and all sorts of people milling about. I have to force myself not to stare at the faces. They remind me of a line in the Tribe Called Quest song where Phife Dawg lists all the different types of women he likes: black, yellow, Puerto Rican and Haitian. As if people were pick 'n' mix sweets. He wouldn't fare well in Ireland, old Phife Dawg. It would be white mice all the way.

The boys went to a label dinner last night, so Neema and I ate in front of the TV downstairs and then retired to the loft. I sat cross-legged on the carpet and Neema rolled the joints, her feet hanging off the side of her bed, encased in furry rabbit slippers. She has this poster on the wall of her side of the room of the Hindu goddess, Durga, wearing an enormous bejewelled gold crown and sitting astride a tiger. Each of her eight arms holds something different in it. From my place on the carpet, I could make out a shell, a bow and arrow, a staff, a chalice. At the tiger's feet were offerings: flowers, candles, plates of luscious fruit – and, at the same level, Neema's head, which was bowed over her hands as she crafted a cone shape from her rolling papers. She'd just got off the phone with her mum. When she's agitated, Neema has a way of talking with her whole body. Her limbs bounce like a puppet on a string.

– You'd think me going to law school in September would mean she'd stop giving me shit about getting married. No chance.

– And does she give Kesh shit, too? I asked.

– Yup.

– And will Kesh do it? Get married, I mean.

– He's so far away from that life, she said, looking at me over the rolling papers as she folded them over gently to seal them, carefully pressing down along the wet paper with her thumb. She spoke again then, – I hadn't realised how much weed he smokes. Like, it's all day, every day.

– He's a hard worker though, I said, thinking of Kesh, who had spent all that day in the gear room, fiddling on the band's four-track recorder, recording demos, and Frank's deep sigh as he dragged himself off the sofa after Kesh yelled at him to come and help. I said, – If Kesh doesn't get married, does that mean there's more pressure on you?

Neema sucked on her joint and talked through her exhalation. – I feel it. I feel like, especially from my mum, it would make her life so much easier if I could just do it, like all the other girls do it. Mum is really religious, so it's . . . She stopped talking as the hash clouded her thoughts. Above her, Durga stared out from her sun-beamed perch, face set in an expression of total peace. Neema closed her eyes briefly before speaking again. – So, it's wrapped up in that.

– I just can't imagine having to get married now, I said.

Neema shrugged, taking another pull on her joint and disappearing behind a cloud of smoke. – Welcome to my life.

We turned off the light at 1am. Neema wanted to get some sleep; she has an interview at a temping agency today. I lay there for what seemed like hours, my head a whirl of fog, trying to figure out how long I can live here before I run out of money, and how I'm going to find a job, until I heard the sound of the front door two floors down, and the mutterings and footsteps of the boys going to their rooms.

Now, I cross Brondesbury Road and walk through the blue gate of Kilburn Market. There are stalls selling tools, cheap school shoes, towels, bed sheets.

– Video, CD? A man gestures from behind a stall filled with VHS tapes and CDS. I shake my head and pass an ebony-skinned woman with an enormous chest folding swathes of colourful material as she chats to another woman across the way. As I walk on, the big-chested woman lets out a peal of laughter, that echoes through the stalls beyond. It's a lovely sound.

I've been listening a lot at 74 Mill Road. When the boys

are in, there is music coming out of different rooms all day long, and feet thundering up and down the stairs. I'm getting to recognise who owns the sounds: Kesh treads lightly but always slams the doors; Frank is a stomper. He blasts that Scottish band Mogwai when he wakes: big dense layers of guitar rumbling up through the floor of the loft from his bedroom. Richie's laugh is deeper than his speaking voice, and it comes easily and often. I like hearing his Liverpudlian greetings to family and friends when he's on the phone in the hall: *What's the crachhhh.*

Kesh sings and plays through the days. I should be used to live music in the house, from my da singing and playing his guitar every evening all through my childhood. But where my da's recitals seemed to blend into the sounds of the house and fill up my senses in a gentle way, Kesh's voice sears the air. Neema had played me Shiva's debut album in Cheltenham, so I knew his voice was unique because of how high it was, but hearing it so close up, it's very different. There's a reediness to the falsetto that makes my skin crawl.

God knows what the neighbours must make of this madhouse. The boys are practising today, in the living room, working through a few new songs, Kesh had said. So, when Neema left for her interview, I got out too. I'm looking forward to not feeling like I'm in the way in every room I'm in.

I turn back on to the High Road and walk north. The people of Kilburn are thirsty. I pass an Irish pub every fifty yards or so: Biddy Mulligan's, The Kingdom Bar, Sir Colin Campbell. I walk past a pub called The Golden Egg, and as I glance into the darkness, I see an old man standing at the bar, dressed in a mini skirt over a pair of sparkly leggings. Frank's low voice arrives in my head: *A lot of the Irish people here call it County Kilburn.* The man dressed as a woman could be one of them. If they came in the fifties and sixties, they'd be in their sixties and seventies now. I wonder if he is glad he stopped here.

A staccato bassline punches through the subwoofer of a black car, eclipsing every other sound for a brief moment, until the lights turn green and the traffic crawls forward. I follow the cars past a petrol station and Kilburn Tube station, until the buildings become residential and more spaced out. I turn around at a road sign marked Shoot-Up Hill.

About halfway back to Mill Road, I pass a pub with a sign in the window, an A4 piece of paper with words written so small that I have to step right up to the window to read them.

Bartender wanted. Must have experience. Enquire within.

The windows are made of stained glass, making it hard for me to see through into the pub. I take a step back to the edge of the pavement to have a look at the place. The strip of windows is at head height and covers the breadth of the front façade. The walls are dirty white, and a faded red sign above gives the name of the place: Fahy's Bar. A mobility scooter is parked neatly to the left of the front door. I look down at myself. I'm wearing wide, flappy blue jeans, my trainers and an old T-shirt with the neck cut out. My handbag sits across my hips. I wonder if I should take out the ring in my nose. *Fuck it. We're in London. There's all sorts here.*

I walk in.

It takes a few seconds for my eyes to adjust to the darkness and allow me to make out the shape of the place through the fog of cigarette smoke. It's a square room, dominated by the bar, which sticks into the middle, nearly slicing the space in half. There are benches lining the walls, with tables in front of them, as if the bar itself is the main entertainment. The high strip of windows strengthens this perspective, the light shining straight on to the shelves, refracting through the glass bottles, creating coloured patterns on the paintwork behind. I move my eyes along the bar, the old wood panelling, the stools peppered around the edge. There are no staff in sight. I feel eyes on me and focus on the shadowy shapes sitting on the benches around the edges of the room. It's all old men in here, some of them talking at a low volume so as not to compromise the church-like quiet, some of them staring at me, slack-jawed. I can feel myself blushing now. *This was stupid.* I turn to walk out, and just as my hands are on the door, a voice calls out, – Can I help you?

I stop and turn to see a woman behind the bar. *Fuck's sake. I have to talk to her now.*

– I'm here about the job, I say, and in the ensuing silence, continue, – The bar job.

The woman gestures with a nod of her head and I follow

33

her round to the back of the bar, where she lifts the hatch, walks out and takes her time to size me up.

– Do you have any experience? She's Irish. Short grey hair. Sharp face. Glinty eyes. *If Ireland was a woman.*

– I've worked in lots of pubs. Back in Ireland. Waiting tables and bartending, that kind of thing.

– Well, there's no waiting tables here, she says, pulling her chin into her neck. She adds, – Where are you from?

– Dublin, I say, forcing a smile. – My name's Orla.

– Orla? she repeats.

– Orla Quinn.

She is still inspecting me as if I'm a chicken she's about to pluck and roast, so I carry on, in order to quash my discomfort.

– I'm twenty-one. I've just moved in down the road, so I'm looking for something to keep me going.

– Are you a student? she asks suspiciously.

– No. I've just finished college actually.

– Are you looking for other work? she says.

I hesitate, then lie. – Not at the moment, no.

– Well, she says. – We'd better try you out. You can do the Thursday night shift. I'll need you here at four o'clock. Then she narrows her eyes and cocks her head and adds, – It's important that you look smart.

– Right, thanks. I'll see you then, I say, before bolting for the door.

I pause outside to blink in the light and heat of the High

Road. On the way home, I stop off at the chemist and buy hair dye. Truffle chocolate, the colour's called, as if my hair will be a luxurious dessert. I have my ma's dense, wiry hair. She has always bleached hers into submission, so I did the same from when I was sixteen. It's time for a change.

CHAPTER 4

PURPLE PILLS

– Finally, we're in the middle of things, I say to Neema. We stand huddled together at the end of the bar of The Barfly in Camden, clutching our drinks and looking out over the room.

– What do you mean?

– I mean *this*, I say, gesturing around the bar with my hand. The last of the sun streams through the long windows, lighting up the motley crew of drinkers in all their mismatched glory. Ripped jeans and PVC and mohawks and shaved heads and piercings and tattoos. – This is what I thought England was going to be like. I thought there were going to be *scenes*, Neema. You know, like in *The Face* magazine. Cool Britannia, Britpop, jungle music, trip hop. All these *scenes*.

Neema is looking at me now, smiling. – And then you arrived in Cheltenham.

I talk right into her face. – Neema, what *was* Cheltenham?!

– I know, Neema says.

But I'm still talking in her face. – Bland as fuck. And what was with the obsession with pheasants? Pheasants bleeding everywhere. On cups and plates and bags, and anywhere they can put a picture of a pheasant . . .

Neema intercepts, serious now. – You need to look at last year as a stepping stone. It was a way to get you to London.

– True, I say. I take a sip of my drink and add, – I'm excited to see Shiva.

– Wait till you see Kesh on stage, she says with a darkening of her expression.

– What does he do?

– Just jumps and crashes about. But it's always a bit much. A bit much for me, anyway.

– Have your parents ever seen him?

– On stage? Not in Shiva. He was lead drummer in temple when he was a kid, so they saw him do that. But they'd hate watching him in Shiva.

The pub is filling up now, and a good few of the patrons are downing their pints and looking at their watches. I nudge her with my elbow and say, – We should go up and get a good spot.

Upstairs, the venue is small, with the bar at the back, the stage no more than a platform raised a foot off the floor.

– Trust me, you don't want to go too near the front, Neema says.

37

We find a space halfway back.

– It's Shane with the rat's tail, Neema says, gesturing with her chin towards the small, serious-looking man in the sound booth at the back of the room.

There are Shiva fans talking at the front of the stage. The misfits and weirdos. I see Shiva's logo on the back of a T-shirt, tour dates listed below. A skinny Asian kid with sticky-out ears stares at the empty stage. Beside him, a group of girls chatter, sporadically checking the stage for signs of the band. As the lights go down, a plump girl squeals in excitement, causing them all to giggle. A song pipes through the speakers: crackling vinyl, a woman's voice, sounding sad and beautiful.

– It's from an old Bollywood film, Neema says into my ear.

There is a spotlight on the front mic stand on the stage. As the boys come out, the crowd cheers. Neema shifts on her feet.

There are a few seconds of silence where we all get to take them in. Kesh grips the mic with two hands and stares out over the heads of the crowd, twitching and possessed, his electric guitar swaying on the strap from his shoulders. Frank is watching Kesh through his curls, fingers poised over the strings of his bass, and Richie is clutching his sticks, serious, staring at his own hands, as if priming them for what's to come. Then, without warning, Kesh folds his body over his guitar and starts shredding wildly, Richie's sticks click together as he counts them in, and the sound is huge, so

38

huge and crashing that it's hard to make out any musicality in it, but the kids at the front are pushing each other around, knocking into each other as Kesh and Frank fill the tiny stage with jerky movements. I try to keep my face neutral, aware of Neema beside me.

It takes three songs for my ears to properly adjust to Kesh's falsetto. He's pushing too hard with his throat, so he's on the edge of a shriek all the time. Every so often, feedback rings from the speakers, causing the crowd to collectively wince. The boys do a good job of looking completely indifferent when this happens, as if it's all part of the show. Back in the sound booth, Shane is frowning at the knobs.

Kesh seems troubled, as if he's trying to figure something out in his head. Frank is looking very serious now. Richie, so solemn before, is the only one who looks like he is enjoying himself, his face twisted into a gurn of concentration and pleasure as he moves. I like watching him shift in his seat between songs and wipe the sweat off his brow. He's part of the band, but he feels detached too, as if he would happily sit up there on his own without an audience and play for hours with the same enjoyment. I would like to drum. I would like banging out my frustrations into fills and rhythms.

They've been playing for nearly half an hour when the lights fall away, leaving a single spotlight on Kesh. His shirt is gaping open, allowing us full view of the rivulets of sweat dripping down his chest. He softly strums an acoustic guitar and clenches his eyes shut. His voice is cracked as he sings.

You can put me in a box and I'll break down the walls
Brick by brick by brick
You can put me in a box and I'll break down the walls
Brick by brick by brick

As he spits out the words, Frank and Richie start playing again, and Kesh's singing becomes more and more intense, his face more pained, with each utterance of 'brick' ascending higher and higher until he reaches the top of a long, soaring note – after which he jumps wildly all over the stage, knocking into Frank, who seems to be ready for him, shoulders braced. As Richie ends with a flourish, everyone cheers and claps. I look at Neema. She is staring at the floor, and I put my arm around her shoulders, pull her towards me and give her a reassuring smile.

Kesh changes to an electric guitar for the last song.

– This one's called 'What Will They Think', he says. – Thanks for coming. We're Shiva. See you soon. He wipes the sweat from his brow with his sleeve, then launches into frenzied double-time strumming. Richie comes in next, followed by Frank. After the last chorus, Kesh steps forward and pulls his electric guitar over his head. His eyes are wild as he swings the guitar around his head and crashes it on to the floor of the stage with a loud thud. Then he's swinging it again. The stage is so small that I worry he's going to catch Richie or Frank with the body of it as he thrashes it through the air. The rows of people at the front push back for their own safety.

In the final few seconds of the song, Kesh turns to the drums and starts whacking the guitar on to the main kick drum. It makes a huge, chaotic noise. Richie steps off the stool, still drumming as the drum kit topples over, and the boys pick their way over the kit and the guitar to clamber off stage. Feedback screeches around the room. I realise that I'm squeezing Neema's shoulders with my hands. I join in with the clapping and whooping and fix on a smile as Neema turns to me and says, – I told you.

The dressing room stinks of sweat and smoke and whiskey. As we walk through the door, Kesh hugs me tightly and I'm immediately soaked in his sweat. He holds Neema by the shoulders and says, – Well, sis?

– I need a drink, she says and everyone laughs.

After that performance, it's strange to see them smiling again. Kesh looks at me and asks, – What did you think?

– It was amazing, I oblige. – I think people really loved it.

I speak emphatically because it's the truth. I'm not sure if I enjoyed what I just saw, but I *was* amazed by it.

– Neema? Richie says, holding out a shot of whiskey to her. She downs it and winces. Then it's my turn. There's a knock on the door and a tall, clean-cut man comes in. He wears brown desert boots and a buttoned-up khaki shirt.

– Okay, he says. – Okay. You guys just smashed it . . .

The boys jump up like puppies. Richie asks, – Who was there?

The man rubs his hands together. – The BBC Radio guy loved it. They're going to discuss it next week. The XFM guy seemed really positive as well, he said he's gonna call Redstar this week about a session. It felt good, guys.

They all cheer, except for Kesh, who is sitting in a chair in the corner. He silently punches the air with his clenched fist.

The man holds the flat of his palm up and everyone goes quiet. – Kesh, man. We can't keep smashing guitars.

Frank gives the thumbs-down and shouts, – Booooooo.

The man shakes his head at Frank and then looks at Kesh. – We can't afford it.

Kesh speaks to him earnestly. – I promise I'll try not to next time.

– Girls, this is our manager, Damian, Richie says, gesturing at the clean-cut man. – Damian, this is Neema, Kesh's sister, and Orla, our new housemate.

Damian reaches out to shake our hands. – Great to meet you, he says, and turns back to Kesh. – Kesh, Alex from Redstar is outside. Is it okay if I let him come see you guys?

– Sure, sure, bring him in, says Kesh.

Damian leaves quickly after that and Alex appears, big bushy beard on him, beer belly protruding through an open shirt.

– C'mon, Neema says to me. – We'll wait for them downstairs.

★   ★   ★

– Now we really mean business, says Frank, as he plonks four glasses of a piss-coloured drink down on the table in front of us. His shirt is open at the chest, exposing a dark rug of hair. He's all pumped-up, triumphant. Different than in Mill Road.

It's hot in the bar, air dense with smoke. Gwen joins us and then leaves to go to another gig across town. The boys introduce us to people. We shout hellos over the music, and we drink more of the piss-coloured drinks, which turn out to be tequila, vodka and Red Bull. A girl stands up on the table next to us and then falls off, smashing glass in the process, and there is a huge collective jeer from the patrons of the bar. Neema helps her up.

Neema and I go to the toilets for a bump of cocaine. – How much can we do? I ask, as I squeeze the cubicle door shut behind us.

– Not too much, Neema says. – Frank gave it to me. She scoops the powder out of the wrap with the corner of her bank card and holds it up to my nose, then scoops up another mound for her. – Hey, Kesh says we're going to a party after this, she says, her eyes dancing.

My phone beeps and I pull it out as Neema folds up the wrap. – Neema, I say, staring at the text. I hand the phone to her and she reads it out loud.

– *Orla, it's Moses. I'm coming to London in a few weeks. Want to meet up?*

I take the phone and stare at the text again.

43

– This is very good news, she says. Then, as if she can read my mind, she adds, – Don't you dare answer it now. Wait until tomorrow.

I will myself to forget about the text, but it's hard, knowing those words are sitting there in my phone, and thinking about what they could lead to.

When we get back to the bar, Richie is waiting at the door, gesturing at us impatiently to follow him outside where Kesh is hailing a taxi. As we climb into the black cab behind Richie, Kesh tells the driver to take us to a place called Angel.

– We're going to The Castle. It's a recording studio but we rehearse there too. They do raves there, he explains to us, teeth clenched in concentration as he pokes around in his pocket for something. He takes a little plastic packet out of his hand, opens it, takes out some ecstasy pills, glances briefly at the driver, and hands them out to Frank and then Richie. Then he breaks one in half and Neema, smiling, sticks out her tongue as if she's at the doctor's. He puts it there and we all laugh.

– I would like a whole one please, I say to Kesh, causing Richie and Frank to laugh.

Kesh looks at Neema and says, – Can she handle it?

Neema looks at me with an amused expression and then nods at Kesh, so he passes me a whole one and I swallow it down with a slug of warm water from a bottle. I look over at Neema. She's squished up against Richie, his arm running along the back of the seat behind her. She shakes her head and smiles at me at the same time.

The party venue forms part of a road of tall, terraced townhouses, completely unremarkable from the outside but for the muted thumps of dance music coming from the basement. The boys hug the girl on the door and lead us into a room with amps and speakers stacked up around the edges, and a makeshift bar in the corner. After we get our drinks, we descend two flights of stone stairs to the basement, where the sound system has been set up in a booth at the back of the stone-walled space. Old office chairs are scattered around the edges. The DJ is playing breakbeat, and the drums sound satisfyingly crunchy and crisp. I move towards the bass bin until I can feel the bass reverberate around my chest. I start to dance. The boys have collected people on the way down, they're all shouting at each other over by the wall, but I'm happy here on my own. My skin is starting to feel tingly now that the E is taking effect.

I move slowly, close my eyes, sway from side to side. I was seventeen when I first went to a proper night club and took ecstasy. The force of the sound felt like jumping into cold water: there was initial shock at how loud it was, but then it was in my chest and in my head, powering me from the inside out. I saw two girls from my year whom I'd never spoken to before, and they greeted me like an old friend, like I had entered this secret world that only we knew. And then I danced.

I danced so hard, the sweat fell off me.

I remember walking up George's Street in Dublin with my pals afterwards, the E still coursing through me, feeling completely weightless, as if I was floating. I weighed myself when I got home; I had lost four pounds in one night. The muscles in my cheeks hurt from smiling. I felt shiny and new, like a snake shed of its skin.

After that night, I needed to chase dance music, to find a way to exist in it all the time. Preferably at a volume so loud that I could feel it in my chest.

Like now.

My feet are moving of their own accord. I let them lead me in side steps around the stone floor. The DJ has put on a track with pianos in it, and I can feel my arms pumping with the bass drum, my legs stepping back and forth, back and forth. The boys laugh in a huddle in the corner, Kesh hanging back against the stone wall; his eyes flick backwards as he rushes. And now Neema is walking over and taking my hand and laughing as I hug her. Neema dances with her hands close to her chest and pointing upwards, her index and middle finger pulled close together. Her face is set into a small, contented smile. Her eyes close now and again.

There are other people here, shuffling around us, and we shuffle with them. Frank joins us, dancing with his hands up in front of his face as if he's a boxer, sparring.

– You need to take your hair out of your face, I shout at him, and take a bobbin from my pocket. I spin him around and pull his hair into a short, thick ponytail. I get a hug and a double thumbs-up as a thank you.

I don't know how long we stay there, but it's long enough for the rest of the boys to come on and off the dance floor, and for hugs with strangers, and for Kesh to snog a girl in the corner and for me to have to vomit suddenly, by the wall.

Now, I am floating up some flights of stairs, my hand clasped tightly in Neema's. Richie and Frank are in front of us. We follow them through a fire-escape door and on to a roof. The night air is wet with a light, soft rain; it feels like a caress on my skin. Neema pulls me to the wall at the edge of the building. Below us a cluster of cars sit outside the entrance to The Castle, waiting for pick-ups, tail lights fuzzy in the drizzle.

– Wow, look at London, Neema says. Her hand squeezes mine. We both take deep breaths through our noses and exhale into the damp night.

– It never ends, I say, scanning the sprawl of rooftops stretching as far as I can see in every direction.

Neema takes out a packet of chewing gum and offers it around.

– Smashed it, Neema, says Richie softly as he takes a stick.

– Richie, Neema says as she unwraps her gum. – Orla wants to get work experience in the music industry. Do you think she could have a meeting with Damian?

– Sure. I'm sure he'd meet you for a coffee, Orla. I'll ask him for you.

I don't even have time to gawp at her because Frank is talking now. – Who wants a cigarette? he says.

– Me, I say, hungrily, and lean in to get mine lit. We all stand side by side, chewing and smoking into the drizzle. I am tingling all over.

– We live here, Neema says between chews. I look into her eyes. Neema holds my stare with her own. She's talking to me with her eyes, saying, *It's all happening now, Orla. This is the life you were dreaming of.*

And with my eyes I tell her, *I feel it. I really do.*

CHAPTER 5

UPTOWN GIRL

I'm getting better at not staring at people on the Tube. I look at hands and I look at shoes, sometimes at the books and magazines people are reading, anywhere but into someone's eyes, God forbid. Today I can smell the faint lemony whiff of shampoo from the woman sitting next to me. I forgot how loud it can get in the carriages.

Before I started making weekend trips to London from Cheltenham last year, the only time I'd visited was when I was eight years old. I don't remember anything about that visit, except for taking the Tube. When you grow up in Dublin, a subterranean train is as thrilling as a Disneyland rollercoaster. I sat beside Ma and as the train gained momentum I listened carefully to the rumbles and creaks and the rattle of the doors, and when the train picked up speed and the rumble grew into a roar, my excitement turned into terror. When the force of the roar grew bigger, into a sort of prolonged, deafening scream, I clung to my ma and screamed along with it, my tears wetting her sleeve, until we disembarked.

MIND THE GAP.

I step down on to the platform and join the flow of people walking to the escalators. I am to meet Damian in a pub in Soho called The Blue Posts. Outside Oxford Street station, I'm hit by the grease and spice smells of a Chinese noodle stall. There's a sticky sort of heat rising up off the concrete, with no breeze to temper it. I walk down Argyll Street towards the Tudor façade of Liberty. *A shop called Liberty. A place called Angel.* All these dreamy names, free and full of hope.

There's music in my headphones.

Nas – *Illmatic.*

Big boom-bap beats and moodiness, jazz samples and a young Nasir Jones giving me poetry about life on the streets of Queens, New York City. I'm more familiar with the postcodes and place names of New York than London, because of all the rap I listen to. I used to argue a lot about rap with the lads on my course in Cheltenham. They were all West-Coast fanatics – Dr Dre and Tupac. I was all about DJ Premier and Guru and Tribe and Biggie and Nas. Nas, who made the best rap album of all time when he was nineteen going on twenty. And what have I done? Scraped the points for an English degree in Dublin, where I had seven hours of lectures a week, all the better for partying, which is pretty much what I did for the three whole years. Then I got out. The cars slow down and stop for me at the pedestrian crossing. I try to hang my shoulders loose as I walk. To keep my eyes straight ahead.

According to Anna, Ma had a great spiel for when I left. *Oh, we've lost her to England,* she used to say, as if England beat Ireland in a bet and I was the prize, when the truth is I couldn't get out of Ireland quick enough. *She's off to the world of academia. Post-graduate course* – stressing the 'post-graduate' with a lowering of her chin and widening of her eyes – *in music.* Conveniently leaving out the technology part. *Yep, she gets it off her father.*

She still thinks my college was all stone buildings and gowns and string quartets.

I stop and squint into my *London A–Z* map book, then turn right down Poland Street and left down D'Arblay Street. I'm wearing a black short-sleeved shirt dress that stops at my knees, and some black sandals. I took my time over my make-up this morning, tried to keep my hand movements firm and fast like Neema does. I'm still not used to my brown hair. I left the dye in too long; the darkness of it pushes out the paleness of my skin. I've tried to clip it back as neatly as possible.

Damian Glass. He has a name like a rock star. I wonder if he ever wanted to be one.

A new song arrives in my headphones, a sampled xylophone sitting alongside the beat. I like that the bass line doesn't arrive until Nas ends his first line. Last year in

Cheltenham, I got to record whole songs from scratch. I would lose days on the computers in the library, making rhythms on the music programmes. I wanted to build those beats that swing effortlessly, beats like DJ Premier's on this album.

Boom. Bap. Boom-Boom. Bap.

I didn't think it would be so hard. Now I know it's about the space between the beats. The bits you don't hear. My course teacher, Mr Langham, described it as negative space, but for me, it's positive space. That space is more important than the beat itself in a way. You need it to breathe, to assess, to ready yourself again. You need it so you can hear the next beat in the best possible way, anticipate the approach of it. The space is as loud in its own way as the beat itself. I'm mad for the beats too. I love a cool, crisp snare drum. And that tinny full stop of a closed hi-hat. The best beats are the ones that transcend quantitative measurements and feel like living, breathing things. That's what you're looking for. Fluid, effortless movement.

The Blue Posts reminds me of the pubs in Dublin, all faded velvet cushioning and big windows and brass. It's full when I walk in, a mix of aul' fellas, blokes in suits, and casual media types. I see Damian in the corner, talking loudly on his mobile phone. I stand near him and allow him to see me and wave as he talks, and then I go and stand at the bar. I turn around and spy that he has a pint, so I decide to get a half for me and another whole for him.

It takes a full five minutes for him to finish his call. Eventually, I hear him say, – Orla.

I bring our pints to the table. – Hi, Damian. I got you another one just in case, I say.

He replies, – Are you trying to get me drunk in the afternoon?

There's not enough humour in his eyes for me to know how to react. I shrug, pulling out the old Irish stereotype. – I'm from Ireland. It's what we do.

He allows me a small smile. Even in a black T-shirt and jeans, he looks groomed compared to the boys of Shiva at Mill Road. Clean-shaven, with a hint of musky scent. His bare arms are pale and freckly. A fat gold chain-link bracelet adorns his left wrist.

He takes a sip of his pint and says, – Cheers.

I'm unsure whether it's a thank you or a toast, so I clink his glass with my own and say, – You're welcome. Cheers.

– So, Damian says, – Richie said you're looking to get into the music industry?

I shift in my seat, take a slurp of my pint and say, – That's right. I've come to London to shag me way to the top and live the high life.

He raises his eyebrows over his pint. He's not amused. I backtrack, – Ah no, I'd love to get any experience really, I say hurriedly. – I'm starting work at Redstar for a couple of weeks next month, so that will be good.

– And do you know what you want to do in the industry?

53

– I, well.

I pause here and look at the ground, and then back to his face. I feel the weight of potential in this exchange. The places it could lead to. He's waiting for me to continue.

– To be honest with you, I want to make music, I say.

– Right, he says, nodding, as he crosses his right leg to rest on his left thigh. He looks across the pub and smiles. It's not a kind smile. Then he pulls his gaze back to me and says, – So you want to be an artist?

– Eeeeh, I say, tilting my head as if I'm just figuring this out now, here, on this bar stool. – Not necessarily. I play guitar, and I've just done a music tech and production course.

– So, who could you compare your music to?

– I've only just started making beats, so it's all very basic. But I have some tracks I made in college, and there's one with me singing on it. I love rap. And soul. And singer-songwritery stuff. And I love dance music. Ultimately, I think I'd like to write songs, proper songs, but with an electronic backdrop.

Damian looks puzzled as he nods slowly, his eyes drifting around the pub. Then he drags his gaze back to mine again. Jesus, this is hard work for him.

– Do you sing? he asks.

– I do. I've been writing and singing songs since I was twelve. Just as a hobby, I suppose.

He cocks his head sideways at me, as if to examine me in a new light, and asks, – What's your voice like?

– Ah, here, you'd have to hear it yourself. I wouldn't want to compare it to anyone's.

– Well, what singers do you like?

I'm straight back at him. – Björk. PJ Harvey. Róisín Murphy. Liz Fraser and Shara Nelson, you know, who sings on 'Blue Lines'? Oh, and I like Joni Mitchell and Carole King, and classic soul, like Gladys Knight and Aretha Franklin, and Lauryn Hill, obviously . . .

He nods into his pint as I trail off, takes a gulp, smacks his lips and says, – Well Orla, if you'd like me to listen to your music, I'd be happy to give you my thoughts.

– Okay. That would be great. I'll get my demo to you, I say too quickly, and then add, – And if there's ever any work going, you know, in your office, or if you know of anyone who's taking anyone on . . .

– I'm afraid I don't have the resources to be taking on anyone else at the moment. But yeah, I'll keep an eye out, for sure.

I nod enthusiastically. He looks at his watch and directs his words at it. – Sounds like it would be good for you to spend some time honing your sound.

– Yes, this is my problem – because I need access to a studio, you know, to do that. I can't find any computers in the public library here that have music production programmes.

He drains his pint and stands up. – I'd just keep writing songs. Everything starts and ends with the quality of your song. Once you've got songs, then it's about finding a producer who can work with you.

– But I want to produce my songs as well.

– That won't work. You'll need someone experienced. Send me the tunes and let me have a think. He looks at his watch again and says, – I've got a meeting, so better run.

Is that it?

He reaches out his hand and allows me the full force of his eyes for the second that my hand is in his. – Good luck, he says, with a cursory nod, before walking out of the pub.

Behind me, a table full of lunchtime drinkers bursts into laughter. I see a glimpse of the back of Damian's head as he walks past the window and then he's gone. I finish my drink and try and get my head around his words. *That won't work.* Was that whole year in Cheltenham learning how to produce songs a waste of time? Outside the window the sun beats down on to the cobbled streets of Soho. A man lifts his sunglasses to peruse the magazine stand at the newsagents on the corner. I was going to phone Da to tell him about this meeting. I wanted him to think that I was progressing over here. I see his face in my head and quickly shift myself in my seat so I'm facing inwards, towards the bar. I try to focus on the murmur of voices. The strike of a match as a cigarette is lit in the corner. *Just keep writing songs,* Damian said. I want to make them too.

He left the full pint that I bought him on the table. I pull it towards me.

CHAPTER 6

BLESS THE ROAD

It's the tail-end of a mid-summer's day, one where the air is weighed down with water but there is no relief of rain. July has turned into August. I'll be twenty-two the week after next.

This is my second week and sixth shift at Fahy's. I'm getting to know the rhythms of the place: the slow tick of the old-fashioned clock on the top shelf of the bar; the tidal flow of the patrons, arriving after work and drawing out before close. I prefer to work in the daytimes, because Pat pretty much leaves me to my own devices. The hours go more slowly, but there's a dreamlike quality to the time here, and I'm never alone.

I'm getting to know Pat. She grew up in Clare, in an actual thatched cottage with whitewashed walls, like Peig Sayers. She left Ireland when she was seventeen, and now she lives in the flat above Fahy's with a man called James. He has an illness of some sort, which means he's nearly always convalescing. The few times he's come downstairs, there's a deliberate nature to his movements, as if he needs to plan them out in his head before he begins. He never stays long.

Pat's got a way of looking at you intensely with this questioning expression before she speaks; she does it for just long enough for you to lose any sort of confidence you'd had in what you were saying. She likes to be busy. She'd swipe the glass out of your hand before you'd even swallowed your last gulp. She changes kegs as if they're as light as shoeboxes.

On my first shift, she hovered around me like a bluebottle.

– This isn't just a service job, she warned me. – You're more a therapist than anything else.

I looked around at the room, taking in the patrons sitting on the green-covered banquettes facing the bar on three sides.

– Is it always just men here? I whispered.

Pat gave me a look of mild amusement and said, – Mostly. The women come at the weekends more.

– And what do you do if you need to kick somebody out?

– I turf them out, she said, matter-of-factly.

– Have you never been injured?

– I had two black eyes once. That was from a woman, mind.

On that same first shift, she was bent over the shelves behind the bar, rummaging for something, when I'd asked, – Do you do things here? Like entertainment?

She'd stood up straight again and pointed at the large TV

sitting on a bracket on the wall opposite the bar. – There's your main entertainment. All they want is the horses, or the Gaelic football, and the hurling when it's on.

The horses are on the television now, getting lined up to race, nodding their long heads in agreement with each other. I've sprayed and wiped the bar three times already today, so I check for empty glasses and then go to the precarious pile of CDs in the corner by the stereo. Pat usually has a crap radio station on in here, turned up high, but I like to play the CDs.

It's a different world of music in this place, but the songs suit the faces I see when I hear them. It's all Irish artists: Christy Moore, The Dubliners, The Chieftains, The Clancy Brothers; The Pogues in the evenings, when the door is propped open and the regulars blend into bigger, noisier groups of drinkers.

Today, I choose Mary Black's album *Speaking With the Angel*. Another woman's voice in this room wouldn't hurt.

Old Eamonn is wedged into the corner banquette by the door of the toilets. The owner of the mobility scooter out-side. *The most regular regular*, Pat calls him. Mayo Dave and Gerry are here at the bar, Fahy's very own Bert and Ernie. They sit a stool apart with their pints of Harp. Dave is a retired lorry driver, a huge lump of a man with a face like corned beef and a taste for a Jameson with his pint at a certain time of day. You'd be lucky to get three words out of him in a whole shift, and when he does speak, he sounds like he's just got off a tractor in Cavan, or Mayo I suppose, given the name. Gerry talks for both of them. He's an old elf with a Cork accent; leathery pink cheeks, neat grey-white hair, his shoes always shined. Gerry is married to an unfortunate woman whom he calls 'Herself'; he only mentions her to play the long-suffering victim of her nagging.

He's talking to me now in his sing-song voice. – If you've got a degree, why aren't you working as a doctor or a politician or something?

– Well, I want to do something in music, I say, standing up to serve a man on the other side of the bar. I feel Pat's eyes on me as I work the till and give him his change. She still doesn't trust me not to mess up.

When I'm back in my place, Gerry says, – Sure, isn't there plenty of decent music back home?

– I want to make electronic music, and there's loads of it here. That's why I came.

He drains his pint. – Is that what the huns listen to nowadays, is it? He starts to wheeze with laughter; on seeing me shake my head, he laughs even more. I swear he thinks he's so funny he nearly falls off his stool laughing at himself. Ever since he found out that I was raised a Protestant, he teases me relentlessly. Any excuse to call me a black hun and he's in there like one of those horses on the TV, straight out of the gates.

I wonder what my sister Anna would make of Gerry and Mayo Dave. She came to visit me at Easter time, when I was still in Cheltenham. She wooed all the boys with her capacity for drinking and piss-taking, and couldn't get over the fact that none of my friends had known that the Irish language existed before I spoke it to them. She lectured them with her hand on hip, her head cocked to the side.

– Fucking right we have our own language. It's called Gaelic. We have our own language and our own currency, our own female president, our own terrible taste in pop music, and our own fucked-up religious baggage. We have twenty-six of our own counties, too.

She turned to me then, and I dutifully reeled off the counties in the order that we'd learned them in school: – Louth, Meath, Dublin, Wicklow, Wexford, Kildare, Carlow . . .

Anna loved playing up to being horrified at their ignorance, and targeted Olly for her put-downs because he was the one who'd started it all off by asking her if she knew any of Westlife. Of course, she ended up in bed with him, and I had to sit up with Hamo smoking weed until the early hours, when I finally dragged her out of bed. We couldn't get a taxi because she was too drunk. All the way home, she sang Robert Palmer but changed the words to: *Might as well face it, I'm addicted to dick.*

– And you've no boyfriends yet now, Orla, says Gerry, pulling me back into the room. It's a statement rather than a question, as if the fact was preordained. I pick up a tea towel and a glass and start to wipe.

– No. There's a fella coming up to see me in London soon, though, so who knows. His name's Moses.

I like to roll the shape of his name around my mouth. Mo pronounced *mow*, as in mow the lawn. But the Dublin way, where the whole vowel is rounded into two sounds, is *Mo-uh-zuz*.

And Gerry starts to laugh his wheezy laugh again and says, – Moses. He pauses. He's cooking something up, staring at the bar with intent. – Did you find him in a basket floating in a river?

I roll my eyes and he's off again, wheezing. Mayo Dave laughs with his shoulders.

– Does he like to burn bushes?

– Jeeesus, I groan, as Mayo Dave brings his pint to his mouth.

When he gathers himself, Gerry says, – We'll have to find you a good Irish man.

I shake my head at him as Pat comes around the bar towards me and says, – And why does she need a man at all?

– Thank you, Pat, I say, leaning back against the bar. I add, – And why would I move from Ireland to London, if I only wanted to hang out with Irish people and fall in love with Irish men?

Gerry's all het up now. – And what's wrong with a good Irish man?

– Well, I say, catching the eye of old Eamonn limbering up to the bar, his belly hanging out the bottom of his jumper like a prolapse. Pat gets to him first. I say, – Nothing. But there's nothing wrong with English men, either.

THE MESS WE'RE IN

The men retreat into their pints. The door is propped open, allowing for a long shard of dusty light to reach halfway across the carpet before it's swallowed up by the gloom. I watch Eamonn's Guinness as it settles, the bubbles turning into black. I catch his eye and give him a nod. He nods back, his chin disappearing into his three other chins, and looks away. Pat tops the Guinness and jumps into action, lifting the hatch and heading off on her sweep of the tables. She can hold five empty pint glasses in each hand. As if she senses me watching her, she turns and gestures with her chin towards the glasswasher.

   – Orla. There's work to be done.

– *Sister Orla.*

– *Anna.*

– *I hope the good Lord is watching over you this evening.*

– *Jesus, what is it with you pretending we're nuns?*

– *Well, hello to you too.*

Pause.

– *What's up with you, Anna?*

– *What do you mean, what's up with me?*

– *I mean, what's up with you? Why aren't you saying anything?*

– *Sure, amn't I speaking now?*

– *Yes, but normally you ask all the questions and I answer them.*

– *Maybe I've had a long day at work, Sister Orla.*

– *Maybe you have, but why are you calling me with nothing to say?*

– *Jesus, Orla, maybe you could say something for once in your bleeding life.*

– *Okay. How is your fancy new boyfriend?*

– *Split up with him, didn't I? Wanted to keep me options open for me holidays.*

– *Are you serious?*

– *I'm too young to be tied down, Orla. Plus, I met his mother. He thinks the sun shines out of her arsehole. She didn't take a liking to me, and the feeling was mutual.*

– *Fair enough. And how is Ma?*

– *Drunk every night. She rings me to make sure I'm bringing wine home from the office, like I'm her drug dealer or something.*

– *And do you drink with her?*

– *Sometimes.*

– *Is she getting up in the morning?*

– *Yeah, she's still up and out to work at the same time, but she's had to change her route to the office because she doesn't want to go near Stillorgan.*

– *Because of Da?*

– *Yep. It's fuckin' annoying, to be honest, Orla, because I used to go to Stillorgan a lot and I can't now . . . Da told me they cycle to UCD together now, him and Flatface.*

– *What?*

– *I know.*

– *But it's on them to be awkward, not you. It probably hasn't even crossed his mind that you might have to change your routes and your plans.*

– *I know. I reckon I'll start going back there soon. I just don't know what I'd do if I saw them together.*

Pause.

– *Is Ma going to be okay when you go to Mallorca, do you think?*

– *I can't fuckin' babysit her, Orla.*

– *Alright, alright, it was just a question.*

Sigh.

– *If you're so concerned for her welfare, come home when I'm gone.*

– *I've just got this job, so I can't up and leave now for a week.*

– *Course you can't.*

– *What's that supposed to mean, Anna?*

– *It's pretty obvious that you've been avoiding Dublin like the plague ever since Da shacked up with Flatface.*

– *Fuck off out of it. I was always coming to England. I can't afford to just POP across the Irish Sea on a whim, Anna.*

– *Okay, okay. No need to get your knickers in a twist.*

– *I've to go, anyway.*

– *Why?*

– *Frank watches this soap called Family Affairs and he's got me into it, and now I have to watch it every day. It's just started.*

– *Well, excuse me, getting in the way of your busy soap schedule. I won't tell Da that nugget of information.*

– *Bye, Anna.*

– *Does the soap tell you how to have a functioning family?*

– *BYE, ANNA.*

CHAPTER 7

BECAUSE I GOT HIGH

I wake up on the morning of my twenty-second birthday, alone in the loft room. The rectangle of sky visible through the skylight is coloured in flawless blue. It will be hot later. I lean out of bed and rummage around the loose cassette boxes on the carpet, looking for my demo. I climb out of bed, insert the tape and press play. Neema told me to ask Kesh to bring it to Damian when he was going for a meeting with him last week. *He'll have to take it seriously that way*, she said. I wrote him a letter to go with it. As the first song comes on, I try to imagine what it would sound like to someone cynical and experienced like Damian Glass. I called the project *Metamorphosis*. Three songs based on the life cycle of a butterfly: a slow, shuffling funk instrumental for the caterpillar; a warm techno thing for the pupa; and a breakbeat piece with vocals I did myself for that big reveal of the butterfly bursting out. Now, I hear all the bad bits the loudest, but there are a few moments where all the parts click together and the songs feel fully realised.

In the house, doors are being opened and people are going downstairs. I go to sit on Neema's bed to check the small alarm clock that sits on her bedside table. It's eleven. Neema will have been up ages. From here, my side of the room is a mess. I must get some shelves for my books, at least. Mounted on the wall to the right of Neema's bed is a framed photo of Kesh and Neema's family, the Tiwaris. In it, Neema is a young girl, with a sweet, unaffected smile; her mother looks regal and serious; Kesh stares straight into the lens, solemn and enigmatic, magnetic even as a child. Their dad has a receding hairline and a jovial expression on his face, as if he's trying to hold in a laugh.

Will my da call me today, on my birthday? Will he remember without Ma to remind him? His voice arrives in my head.

Orla, I've met someone. It was just after Christmas last year. *She works at the university too.* I looked her up on the University College Dublin website. She had a big pale forehead and lips pursed like a fish.

I'm going to be living with her now.

I imagine them in the kitchen of her place in Stillorgan. Clean but untidy. Piles of books on the table. A cafetiere. They laugh a lot. He does impressions of the other lecturers. She can quote Keats and Yeats. He gets a kick out of her intelligence. I try to picture them cycling to the university together. Da's never owned a bike in my lifetime. No wonder

Anna and Ma are avoiding Stillorgan. Now I see my ma, blotchy-faced and drunk on her own in the living room at home, one leg crossed over the other, huddled into the corner of the couch. Eyebrows raised, blinking at the TV, chin pushed into her neck.

– Orlaaaaaaa, Neema calls from below. I jump off her bed and run down the two flights of stairs.

Neema is waiting for me in the living room, still in her pyjamas, plaid pink, a silly grin on her face. There are balloons bobbing around the carpet. On the coffee table is a plate of toasted crumpets with candles stuck into the holes. She picks up the plate and holds it up to my face, rushing through a tuneless rendition of 'Happy Birthday'.

– Ah, Neema, I say. – You shouldn't have. Even though I'm delighted she has.

– Make a wish! she says.

I blow out the candles. *Please let him like the demos.* Then I reach for Neema and hug her tightly.

– Twenty-two, she says. – Do you feel different?

– I actually do, I reply.

We spend most of my birthday in Hyde Park. All three boys come. It's so hot you can see the heat rays wavering off the concrete path as we enter the park. London heat is more intense than that in Dublin; more concentrated, more claustrophobic. I've had to cut two pairs of jeans into shorts already this month.

We walk down the main drag, past Saturday tourists snapping their cameras, past people rollerblading and walking their dogs. Benches upon benches of faces gratefully tilted towards the sun. It's strange to see the band exposed like this, out of their natural habitat of Camden or Mill Road. Pale and already stoned. They're like insects when you pull up a rock from soil, dark and scurrying back to the shadows.

– Try and get as far away from people as possible, Richie says, looking around him, all sketchy. So, we walk until we find a shady spot under a tree, looking down over the lake. As Neema and I lay down a blanket, Kesh produces a six-pack of beer and passes one around to each of us.

– Cheers! I say, and we all clink cans. Kesh sits down, crosses his legs and immediately starts to craft a cone shape with his rolling papers. He wears wrap-around black sunglasses and a silver chain that looks like it could be a bicycle chain around his neck.

Richie takes his football out of his backpack and starts playing with it in the grass beside us. We watch him in silence, as he effortlessly suspends the ball in the air with his head, knees and feet.

After a minute or so, Kesh looks up from his joint, squints at Richie and says, – He could have been pro.

Richie, not missing a beat, turns to us, catches the ball, and says, – But instead I discovered rock and roll. He pulls his mouth wide and sticks out his tongue, like Gene Simmons from Kiss. We all laugh.

Kesh says in a dry tone, – I think he's more suited to rock and roll.

We take turns to join Richie in kicking the ball about. He takes his top off after a while; his chest is pale compared to his arms, with very little hair. His back gleams with sweat. Neema bounces around him, kicking the ball with real enthusiasm. Kesh is a natural athlete like Richie, able to go from standing to sprinting in a second.

As the afternoon passes, the sun beats down harder, and all the while, spliffs are rolled and passed around. After a long stretch of playing football, I flop down on the blanket between Neema and Frank.

– I'm not fit enough for this shit.

Neema looks at me and then turns back to watch Richie and Kesh heading the ball to each other over the grass. Frank is closest to me, sitting up, pulling on his joint. He wears a bucket hat pulled over his head, and his ponytail sticks out the back in a circular frizz. Unlike the other boys, he keeps his T-shirt on. His legs are stretched out in front of him, thick with muscle and covered in dense, dark hair.

As if he senses me looking at him, he looks down at me and says, – Here, handing me the joint.

I shake my head and say, – I can't move.

He smiles and leans down over me and puts the joint in my mouth. I gratefully suck on it until he takes it away again.

– More? he says, and I shake my head and give him an I'm-fucked-enough face, which makes him chuckle again.

71

I lie back on the blanket and watch the clouds glide from one side of the sky to the other above us. I like the presence of Neema on one side of me and Frank on the other. The weed makes me feel every tiny blush of breeze on my cheek. When I close my eyes, I see bright, throbbing colour: cerise pink, turquoise, yellow, back to pink. Everything is soft and cushioned underneath me, as if my bones are made of cotton wool. In my mind, I replace Frank with Moses, imagining him beside me now, leaning back on his hands, smiling his big, quick smile. I'd walk my fingers over the blanket and entwine them in his. Then he'd lean down and kiss me slowly, his fingers sitting lightly on my belly, and then slowly moving up my T-shirt so that his hand is encasing my ribcage . . .

– Watch out!

Whhhhhhummmmmmp.

– Oocchhh! I scream. My hands go to my head, and I open my eyes to see the worried faces of Neema and Frank leaning over me.

– Oh my God, are you okay? Neema says, pulling me up to sitting.

I can't speak at first, because I'm still in shock and the weed is making me so slow, but after a few seconds of rubbing the side of my temple where the football hit me, I nod and say,
– Thanks a bunch, Kesh. Great birthday surprise that was.

Kesh is here now, his concerned face shifting into laughter.
– Fuck, Orla, I'm so sorry.

– You should have seen your face, Frank says, and he does an impression for me, all screwed up in shock, which has me laughing.

– Okay, I'm going to buy you a go on the pedalos to make up for it, Kesh says. He's shielding his eyes with his hand, looking down to the lake where the pedalos are.

– Kesh, are you ever able to just sit still and relax? Frank asks.

– Never, says Neema and adds, – You know, when he was a little kid, my dad called him Rocketman.

And Kesh launches into an impression of his dad. – Ey. Rocketman. Can you just. Sit. Still. While I tie your laces?

And we all laugh some more. Kesh doesn't laugh much at all, but I can see he is content by the smile on his face, and that's enough for me, that they all seem glad to be here with me on my birthday.

In the queue for the pedalos, a small boy sucks on a lollipop and stares at Kesh. Kesh ignores the child. I make funny faces at him behind his parents' backs. Richie gazes out at the lake, looking worried.

– Do you like water? Neema asks doubtfully.

– I like water, but I don't like swans, he replies.

– They can be vicious, says Frank, looking out towards the water.

– Cheers, Frank, Richie deadpans.

– Only if you provoke them, Frank adds. And then he

elbows me and whispers loudly, – They hate Scousers, apparently.

When Richie rolls his eyes, Frank laughs his stoned laugh, the one where he throws back his head and croaks. He gives me the impression of a reptile, or a baby bird waiting to be fed.

Richie gathers all our cash and hands it to the man at the front of the queue, and when the man pulls two pedalos up to the edge of the water, we all stand there looking at each other, like the stoned eejits that we are, until the man grows impatient and points at Neema, me and Richie, directing us into the first pedalo, so that Kesh and Frank are left to go in the second.

Richie and Neema take the pedals, and I sit up front. Neema sits, ruler-straight, all regal, the breeze blowing her hair round her shoulders as she and Richie find their groove with the pedals and we start to move, smoothly and steadily, through the water. The heat is heavy, but the proximity of the water tempers it, and the breeze provides a lovely coolness on our faces.

– Jesus, this is the life, says Richie.

– It's glorious, I agree. And then, as my stomach growls, I root through the pile of bags at my feet for the sandwiches we bought from the kiosk. I tear open two packets and give a triangle of sandwich to Richie, then Neema, and then I take one for myself. There's a contented silence as we all chew our food. We move towards the far side of the lake, away from the cafés. There are speckled brown ducks following each other in circles by the water's edge. And there are swans now, six of them, coming up behind us.

– Orla, what are you looking at? Neema asks me.

I swallow my bite of sandwich and point over Neema and Richie's shoulders, and they turn around in tandem, still chewing, to see the swans, closing in on the pedalo in a V-formation, as if in some sort of tactical swan invasion.

– Fuck, says Richie.

It takes seconds for the lead swan to glide right up beside him. On the same level as us in the water, the thing is enormous, with cold matt-black eyes. Neema and I start to scream as the swan leans its long neck over the side of the pedalo and snatches the sandwich out of Richie's hands with its beak.

Richie yelps. There's two more of them now, on each side of the boat.

– They want the food, they want the food, Neema shouts, pointing at the plastic bag by my feet. – Okay, okay, I yell, grabbing the bag and wobbling across to the side of the pedalo, but just as I go to open it, I lose my footing, drop the bag, and nearly topple over. I scream then, a big hysterical Quinn scream, causing the people walking the path by our side of the lake to stop and stare, as I crouch down again to grab the bag.

– Open them, Neema shouts, her legs pumping the pedals, so I rip open the last three sandwich packets and throw the sandwiches into the water, and there is a flurry of feathers

75

and splashing as the swans rush to scoop them up, and then we are speeding away from them. I hear laughter in the wind, and look up to see Kesh standing up on his pedalo a distance behind us, Frank holding on to the sides, as the pedalo rocks dangerously in the water.

– Are they gone? Are they gone? shouts Richie.

– Yes, they're gone, I say.

– Oh my God, my legs, says Neema, who has stopped pedalling and is rubbing her thighs. The boat slows down in the water. I'm still crouching down in front of Richie and Neema, holding on to the side of the pedalo.

– I can't fuckin' believe it, I say, and then yell in the direction of the swans, – They were bacon and brie sandwiches, you fuckers! And cranberry!

Richie's face has lost all its colour.

– Are you okay? Neema says to him.

He nods, attempting a smile, and then, looking at me, says, – Orla, you nearly fell out of the boat.

And Neema starts to laugh that breathless, tinkly, stoned laugh that sets me off immediately. We're all in fits then, letting out big, hysterical honks of laughter until I'm wiping tears out of my eyes from beneath my sunglasses.

– Stop it, I'm going to piss myself, I manage eventually, clambering to the front of the pedalo. The laughing has me feeling loose and light, like I could float above the water.

Richie and Neema slowly guide us on; they don't speak, but they pedal in rhythm with each other, and it seems to satisfy them into a sort of trance. We glide towards a stone bridge where tourists gather, their camera lenses flashing as they try to capture the perfect frame of London in all its summer glory: the glittering lake; the city skyline behind it, shimmering in the heat; domes, spires and monuments reaching up to the blue. As if you could ever really capture this place in a photo. This place where I live.

— *Happy birthday, Orla Quinn!*

— *Ha, thanks, Ma. Oh, my God, tell her to stop singing.*

— *Anna, she says 'stop singing'.*

— *Happy birthday to youuuuu . . .*

— *Thank God that's over. Thanks, Anna.*

— *My present's in the post, sister.*

— *Yeah, right. I'll believe it when I see it.*

— *Anna, here, give me the phone back. So, where've you been, Orla? I've been calling you all day.*

— *Oh, we went out to Hyde Park for a picnic. We went on the pedalos. It was gas.*

— *And how do you feel being twenty-two?*

— *Well, it's good not to be twenty-one any more. Like I can get on with being an adult now.*

— *Ha! She's in London two months and she's calling herself an adult.*

– *Ma, are you speaking to Anna or me here?*

– *You. Calm down. Did you get the card?*

– *I did, thanks.*

– *How's the house?*

– *It's good. You'd hate the dirt, though.*

– *I don't know how you live with three men.*

– *You should see Frank's bedroom. It's like a municipal dump.*

– *Orla, you need to watch out for vermin. I'm serious. And Neema, how is she?*

– *Neema is good. She's got a temp job to take her up to when law school starts, so she's trotting off to work in her pencil skirts. Then she gets paid to go to law school. She's got it nailed to be honest.*

– *You must be running out of money, are ye?*

– *No, I'm good for a bit, Ma. I'm not actually spending that much money.*

– *Mmm, okay.*

– *And what about you, Ma?*

– *I'm doing grand, love. Pounding away on me exercise bike.*

– *When do you do that?*

– *When I get home from work. Then I have me dinner in front of* EastEnders.

– *After all those years of shouting at us to sit at the table, Ma, you eat on the sofa now?*

– *Turns out it's very relaxing, Orla.*

– *Ha.*

Pause.

– *Da hasn't called me yet.*

– *Right.*

Pause.

– *He'll be looking to speak to you today, I'm sure.*

– *Have you spoken to him, Ma?*

– *Me? Spoken to him? I'm not going out of my way to speak to your father.*

– *Fair enough. It's your life, Ma.*

– *And what's that supposed to mean?*

– *Just that . . . well . . . he's just gone off and done exactly what he wants. Maybe you should think about doing the same.*

– *Well, I can tell you right now, Orla, I'm not ready for a new relationship.*

– *No, Ma, I don't mean that. I mean, get out there, go travelling . . .*

– *He's filing for divorce. I got the papers through today.*

Pause.

– *I can't believe I'm after telling you, Orla; I didn't want to you to find out today. I have to find a new solicitor, because he's using Mr McGeehan. Bridget has recommended her uncle, so I'm off into Dawson Street tomorrow to meet him.*

Pause.

– *Orla? Are you there?*

CHAPTER 8

QUEEN OF MY HEART

The band leave for their tour this morning: two weeks of small shows around Ireland, Scotland and Wales, leading up to the Reading and Leeds Festivals. Gwen is accompanying them for the first dates in Scotland. She stayed over last night. I heard her snores when I crept down for a glass of water in the middle of the night, and peeked into the living room to see her curled into a circle on the sofa, like a sleeping dragon, an overflowing ashtray still smoking beside her.

Now, I find her in the kitchen, wearing a black Blondie T-shirt, skinny black jeans and boots with silver buckles. The red of her hair has faded into the colour of smoked salmon, a brown stripe of roots emerging from the line of her parting.

– When are you leaving? I ask.

– Jesus, am I that bad a house guest? Her voice is gravel.
– Get me the milk would you, Orla?

She busies herself opening and closing cupboards,

looking for the instant coffee. She doesn't seem remotely bothered by the dirt of the kitchen. She shrugs it off like she seems to shrug off life, as if it's something to get through, rather than enjoy. I hand her the milk and watch her from behind as she pours it into every cup apart from Richie's; he takes his black. My mind travels to an image of my da's hands, spooning three sugars into his cup of tea. The slow, careful stir of the spoon, and the one single tap on the side of the cup.

– Are your parents still together? I ask.

She turns and looks at me quizzically for a brief second. In the light from the kitchen window, I can see every tiny crater of the acne scars on her cheeks.

– Yes, unfortunately, she says, and adds, – My mum is an arsehole. She opens the cutlery drawer and pulls out a teaspoon to stir the coffees.

– And your dad?

She emits a long, slow sigh, as if dredging thoughts and feelings of her parents to the surface of her mind is heavy labour. – My dad is soft as they come. I just can't stand her, so it's never fun going home.

I nod as she picks up the tray and turns on her smile like a light switch, shining it right at me as she says, – Instead, I go to music festivals.

And she's off out, leaving me standing in the smell of her musky perfume and cigarette smoke.

★   ★   ★

God knows why, when we've the whole of London to choose from, but I arrange to meet Moses and his friend Carlos at Fahy's bar. It's a gorgeous summer evening, warm air strengthening the smells of bleach and cigarettes in the bar, dust motes dancing in the dim light. Carlos is from Argentina, with doughy arms and a boneless-looking face, in stark contrast to Moses, whose torso is so slight that his head looks disproportionately large on his shoulders, like a Punch and Judy puppet. In the context of this room, with all the auld men with their lumpy noses and spider veins, he looks startlingly beautiful.

– Is that your Moses? Pat asks, looking over at him in the corner banquette. He sits, ear cocked to Neema's mouth as she speaks to him. Carlos sits opposite.

– Yep, I say, pulling the Slim Jims towards me, – and that's my best friend, Neema.

I point to her and, as if she can feel the weight of our eyes on her, she looks up and grins and waves. She's been watching me constantly since I told her the divorce news. Big, round owl eyes on me, every which way I turn, asking me if I'm okay every half an hour.

– Very good, says Pat, sizing them up over my shoulder. I can't tell if she's glad we're here or not. It's a Sunday night, so she'll have plenty of time to stare at us and read our lips. She always seems to know what people are talking about.

I open my mouth to tell Pat about the divorce and then close it again, gathering the four glasses in my hands and heading back to the table. When I sit down opposite Moses, we catch eyes.

– So, are you still in Cheltenham? I ask, as I push his drink towards him.

– I've been at home all summer, going a bit mad to be honest, he says, and continues, – I'm actually moving here; moving in with Carlos.

– That's amazing, Neema says, and I'm glad she says it, because even though I want to cartwheel around the bleeding bar at this news, I have to play it cool.

– Anyway, Moses says, and gathers himself to sit more upright. – Happy belated birthday, Orla.

He holds my gaze as we clink glasses. As I look away, Neema is giving me the eye, as if to say, *You're in there*, and I give her a look that tells her to fix her expression back to normal. He's talking again . . .

– And how are you guys getting on? Orla, are you making any music?

– Music? I say. – Oh no. Nothing there. I work here about four shifts a week now. But I met up with Shiva's manager, and I've sent him my songs to listen to.

Neema cuts in. – She's doing work experience at Kesh's record label in September.

– Nice. What's the label again? asks Moses.

– Redstar Records, I say. – They're based in Camden.

– That'll be interesting, he says.

I know from college that Moses is not into rock music.

I doubt he's remotely into anyone on the Redstar Records roster, but he wears an expression of excitement on my behalf, and that's kind of him, I think.

I respond, – Well, it'll help me learn about which part of the industry I want to be in.

– And is it definitely that side of the industry you're after? Moses says.

– What's that supposed to mean?

– Oh. Just, like, I thought from the course that you wanted to produce, he says, watching me as he takes a sip of his pint.

– I can't afford a computer, and there's nowhere I've found that I can use music-production programmes. I've to pay my rent. If I can do that at a record label, then that's a win in my book.

– Okay, okay, he laughs, holding his hands up in surrender.

I take a mouthful of my pint and turn to Carlos beside me. – Carlos, did you know Neema is training to be a lawyer? This big fancy law firm is paying for her to go to college and giving her an allowance to live in London.

His doughy face lights up. – Wow, you must be very clever, he says to her.

– Not particularly, she answers, looking at me instead of him: a warning look, a don't-try-and-set-us-up look.

As the drinks flow and the voices around us become louder, I end up squeezed in beside Moses on the banquette. When he leans over the table, the jagged line of his spine pushes through his T-shirt. I have to stop myself from running my finger along the bone. Instead, I watch as Carlos tries to entertain Neema, doing an exaggerated impression of Ant and Dec in his broken English that Neema dutifully laughs at, but I can tell it's a fake laugh. He must have sunk six pints by this stage.

As I watch them, I realise Moses is watching me.

– So what's it like working here? he asks.

– It can get a bit dark at times. Like, a bit sad. Just the state of some of the old men who drink here. See that guy? I say, pointing to Eamonn in the corner. – He comes here every day of the week. A lot of the time he cries. Just sits there, weeping.

– Heavy, says Moses, looking over at Eamonn, and then back to me. – Are you enjoying London, though?

I nod. – It's deadly living with Neema, and it feels like I'm in the right place to do music at last.

He nods. – I can't wait to live here, he says. – Moving all my decks and vinyl is a pain in the arse, though. Hey, I meant to say, Carlos has a computer. I'm going to put FruityLoops on it.

– Do you think I could come and use it sometime? I ask.

– Well, we should make some music, you and me, he says.

I look at him for a second before I speak: – Really?

– Why not? I liked the tunes you made in college. – And you've got a good voice, he says, punching my shoulder lightly and shining his grin all over me.

86

I reach my arms around his neck and pull him to me in a tight squeeze.

– Woah, he says, laughing, but he squeezes back.

We get the lock-in. We move to the banquettes at the back of the pub and talk quietly as Pat shuts off the main lights and busies herself pulling down the blinds. There's about eight of us in all. Mayo Dave and Gerry sit on the banquette next to ours, Gerry's hand glued to his pint as if someone might swipe it away from him any second.

– Oh, I'm sorry, Gerry, I'll take my big-hun bum back to Dublin, will I? I say, when I have to brush past him to sit down. He's off, wheezing with laughter into his pint. I introduce them to everyone. Gerry does a good job of keeping a straight face when Moses leans over to shake his hand.

Moses and Carlos sit at the far end of the table. I go to help Pat pour the pints. When I come back with a tray of Guinness and a rum and Coke for Neema, she has shuffled over the seat to chat to Gerry. He's all charged up from her attention.

– Your parents came over from India? he's asking her.

– Yeah, they did. Well, my dad was here first and my mum came over to marry him.

– Was it that arranged business? says Gerry, taking great care around the word 'arranged'.

– Yeah, they only met once before they married, Neema says. On seeing his slow, disbelieving headshake, she adds,

– But they get on well, considering. When did you come here?

– When I was seventeen. Haven't been back since, says Gerry. His hair is thinning on his crown and sticking up vertically off his skull with static. He sits on the edge of his seat.

– Do you miss Ireland? Neema asks.

– Oh, I do. The landscape, you know, it was very beautiful. And I had a big family. I'm the eldest of twelve.

– Gerry Connolly, how did you never tell me that before? I say, gawping at him.

– You never asked, says he, before taking a sip of his fresh pint and smacking his lips.

– Surely they must come and visit? Neema says.

– My brothers have been visiting me here me whole life. Some of them stayed for years. He chuckles to himself. – Herself was driven demented.

– I'm staying with my brother right now, says Neema.

– Well you should be glad he doesn't have a wife to disapprove of you, Gerry says. Mayo Dave nods in agreement.

Neema nods along too, looks at me and back to Gerry and says, – I think *he's* very glad to not have a wife at the moment.

– I'd be very glad to not have a wife at any moment, to be honest, says Gerry, giggling, and Neema looks to me, all worried, as if all this wife talk is going to remind me of my parents' divorce and crack me open, right here on the barstool. But my mind is cool and blank. Dark as stout. I'm halfway through my pint, and I finish the other half in one

THE MESS WE'RE IN

go. When Carlos wobbles off to the toilet, I turn to Moses and slap my thighs to get his attention.

– Moses, how's your girlfriend?

His smile is slippery now he's drunk. – I don't have a girlfriend anymore.

– Oh right, I say, pretending I've only just learned this fact.

He says, – You knew that, I thought?

– Oh, I was just checking, I say, smiling at him as I lean my face in closer to his.

He picks up a beer mat and taps it on the table. – How about you? Met any nice London men?

– Nope. Still waiting for one to come along.

And I match his grin with one of my own as, underneath the table, I feel his fingers take hold of mine.

When it's time to go, Neema hugs Gerry and his cheeks grow even more pink. Pat shushes us as we fall out on to the High Road, and we do big, exaggerated whispers and waves goodbye, because we're not allowed make any noise.

– Come back to ours. The boys are away on tour, so we have the gaff to ourselves, I say to Moses and Carlos.

Moses takes my hand and we hang back as Carlos and Neema walk ahead of us. I try to enjoy the feeling of walking through the darkness with him, and to not worry about how big my hand must feel in his skinny one. I see Neema turn around and notice the handhold and look at me. I'm trying to keep from grinning like an eejit.

89

Moses is six feet tall, which means he has to bend down slightly when he goes to kiss me on the corner of our road, right on the site of the fruit stall. He holds my arms when he leans in, as if to keep himself steady. The kiss is wet and urgent, and not awful. And when we walk down Mill Road together, he takes my hand again, and this time I let myself grin, because he can't undo it now, that kiss. A kiss is a kiss. Putting your tongue in someone else's mouth is a commitment. I can see Neema further up the road, clearing a good distance between her and Carlos as he veers from one side of the path to the other, and then they both disappear as they get to the house.

Moses kisses me again outside the house. This time, I close my eyes and allow myself to enjoy all the nerve-tingling sensations of it. When he finishes kissing me, my eyes are still closed, and when I open them, I see his face illuminated under the streetlight. I can see how pleased with himself he looks, and that makes me laugh.

– What? he says.

– You had a plan tonight, I say. – This was your plan the whole time.

– If that's what you think, Orla, he says, following me up the steps.

CHAPTER 9

HASH PIPE

I'm in the back garden, sitting on an old pink armchair with a ripped cover, through which dirty yellow cushioning bulges out like the blisters on a cold sore. The grass is up to my knees out here. I'm holding a cigarette in the fingers of my right hand, smoke curling up into the warm air above me. In my left hand, I'm clutching the neck of Kesh's guitar.

– Hellooo! Anybody home?

– Out here, I yell, putting the guitar on the ground and pushing my cigarette into a cup with some cold coffee in it.

– Hey. Neema walks out the back door, dragging a chair under her arm. Her legs are bare under her pencil skirt, and she wears ballet pumps on her feet. She plonks the chair down beside mine, opens her spliff tin on her lap and pulls out a packet of rolling papers.

– Is that Kesh's guitar? she asks me.

– Yeah, I took it from his room. Do you think he'd mind?

She contemplates this question and says, – He'll either not give a shit or throw a total hissy fit.

– I'll ask him next time.

The door had been open, and the guitar was lying flat on his bed. In the soft light of the morning, the room had a low hum of unwashed clothes and stale tobacco, but the net curtains and the big window gave it an airy, breezy feel compared to our tiny cave in the roof. Next to the bay window was a poster of Prince, all haughty in a puff of smoke and purple frills. A black-and-white framed poster of Billy Corgan from Smashing Pumpkins looked down from above the bed. Underneath the portrait was what looked like his printed signature and the quote:

'I WANTED MORE THAN LIFE COULD EVER GIVE.'

Sounds like a cop-out to me. Billy's face was in profile, but his eyes seemed as if they were watching me, in a kind of knowing way, as if he had been waiting for me to creep in and take the guitar.

– Were you playing? Neema asks me now.

– Yeah. I wrote a song, I say.

– Oh, can I hear?

– I haven't played for years. It's probably shite.

– Maybe in a bit? she asks, and I nod. She relaxes back into her chair. – Any news from Moses?

Despite my best efforts to 'just jump on him' (Anna's advice) after the night at Fahy's, Moses had insisted that he and Carlos had to head back east after one drink at ours.

92

He left with promises of meeting up as soon as he could. I texted him the day after:

It was good to see you. x

It took him five days to reply to my text, but when he did, it was worth it. I'm smiling at Neema as I say, – He texted saying he's moving to London the weekend after next.

– Ooooh, you're going to have a boyfriend. Neema sings it like a nursery rhyme.

– It's about time, I say, and add, – I literally see his name in my head when I close my eyes at night. In big, lit-up letters, like on the front of a cinema or something.

– Wow, you're obsessed, she deadpans.

I lean in to her and say, – Neema. I haven't had sex in six months. What if my hoop is closed over?

– Orla! She laughs as she licks her Rizla and says, – Hey, Kesh texted me telling me to buy *NME* this week because there's a bit about 'Bricks' in it.

– No way!

– They say that the song sounds like a Smashing Pumpkins rip-off, but that's no bad thing.

– Well, he does love Smashing Pumpkins, I say.

– Mmm. They're back on Wednesday, you know, she says, smiling as she twists the end of the joint into a tight roll and burns it with the lighter. Before I can ask her why she's so happy about them coming back, she asks, – When do you start at Redstar again?

– Next week. Pat has let me do just late shifts for the weeks I'm there.

– Oh, that's good, she says.

We sit in silence as a train rumbles along the track that runs along the end of the garden, bringing people from Queen's Park to Kilburn and on to Euston. A shopping trolley lies upturned in the back right-hand corner of the garden. Frank told me he'd found a hedgehog and kept it there in the winter months. I can imagine the hedgehog would have preferred not to be imprisoned by Frank, but he seemed so proud of himself when he told me, I didn't want to upset him.

Neema stares at the train and I wait to speak until the noise of it has died away.

– How was your last day of temping?

She sighs and says, – Just depressing. All the management are older, white guys. Most of the women are receptionists. Including me, today.

– Well, soon you'll be in law school and you can be a boss lady.

– I hope so. I hope I like the real world of law. I mean, I like learning about it, but working in it might feel really different. She says this as if she's telling herself.

I watch her as she takes the first drag of her joint. She blows the smoke up to the sky and crosses one leg over the other in time with her exhalation. Blow it out, cross it over, shoulders sink and relax.

– Any news from home? she says.

94

I reach down to take a swig of coffee, remembering just in time that the cup is now an ashtray. I sit back in the armchair and shake my head at her.

She persists. – Are you angry with your dad?

– About the divorce? It's all . . . It's very out of character for him, to be so assertive. It'll be her pushing him to do it.

– I suppose from her perspective she's living with a married man, Neema says.

– Well, divorce only became legal in Ireland a few years ago. It's still weirdly taboo. Like, I don't know anyone's parents who are fully divorced, I say, as Neema passes me the joint. I take a long, deep drag. She watches me as I exhale, her eyes clouding over as if she's gone somewhere else in her head. She speaks eventually.

– I think it's healthy. People should be allowed to change their minds. Then she furrows her brow and shakes her head violently. – I mean, God, sorry. I know it's hard for you.

I nod and hand her back the joint.

She changes the subject. – Did Damian ever get back to you about your demo?

– No, the fucker.

– I'd call him and ask him if you can meet him for feedback.

– And humiliate myself even more? He would have called if he liked it.

– Well, either way, you need constructive feedback. He manages Shiva, so he has to help you out. Even if it's just to tell you how you can improve.

95

I make a face at her to show how much I don't want to have to ask him, and she says, – People are busy. He just needs reminding. Anyway, will you play me your song now?

– Really? I ask.

– Really.

– Maybe it'll sound better to you if you're stoned, I say, as I pass the joint back to her. I take up the guitar and fasten the capo in place, then pick up the plectrum from where it fell on the grass. The song came quickly. It's a hymn to the city, about how I like feeling small in a big place. I close my eyes for some of it, because it's easier to not have to think about Neema sitting there watching me. And when I'm finished and I open my eyes, she's looking at me all dreamy, her hand clutching the joint, suspended halfway to her mouth. She claps then, and I put the guitar on the ground and say, – Give us that, gesturing at the joint. I can't keep the grin off me as I go to smoke it.

I wake up to the sound of the door of Shiva's tour van sliding shut outside. *Ssshlump.* The clock beside my bed shows 2am.

– They're home. A small voice appears out of the darkness, and I turn in my bed to see Neema lying on her side, eyes shining straight at me. We lie facing each other, holding each other's gaze, listening to the boys talk quiet instructions to each other as they load in all their gear.

– Are you glad? I whisper to her, and she nods, a tiny, nearly imperceptible movement, and I feel a twinge of something, because I know that I am not glad. I've got used to the dynamic of Neema and me in Mill Road. Used to being able to play Kesh's guitar without disturbing anyone. Used to the sound of Neema's key in the door, and us snuggled up here in the loft, like nesting birds.

As the bedroom doors close one by one, Neema blinks at me, which means good night, and I blink back and turn over to face the wall.

In the afternoon, they start to appear around the house one by one, dazed and pale. It's as if they have been through something traumatic and need time to process it. I decide to make a big pot of coffee for everyone, and Richie joins me in the kitchen to make his breakfast.

– Alright, Orla.

– Richie, you're back, I say, but he doesn't respond. He bends down to rummage in his food cupboard next to the doorway. The kettle clicks and I pour the water into the cafetiere that Neema bought when the boys were away.

Then Richie makes a strange sound. – Eeeuugh! It's a sort of a bass-toned yelp. I can hear the fear in it, and as I turn around, I see that he is standing with his back flat against the kitchen wall, a box of cornflakes lying on the floor.

– Mice, he says, pointing at the box.

I walk over to the cupboard and bend over to look inside. Nothing there. I turn to pick up the box from the floor and peer into it. There are six baby mice curled up in the bottom of the cereal box. The flakes of corn are crushed and nibbled down to crumbs, and the mice are huddled together in a perfect circle in the middle, hairless, pink, squirming, their tiny tails wrapped around each other. I scream, and seconds later everyone is in the kitchen.

Frank holds the box and we take turns to peer inside.

– Fuck, he says. – I knew we had mice, but I didn't know it was this bad. Orla, have you seen them?

They all turn to me as if I had invited the baby mice in personally and prepared a three-course meal for them. I feel myself blushing as I say, – I mean, I've heard them scratching. Mostly in the gear room. I think they hide behind all the amps and stuff. We were going to tell you.

– Right, says Kesh, running his hands through his hair. There are new bags under his eyes. – I'll go and get some traps today.

Richie is still not speaking. As we all head back to the living room, he turns and walks up the stairs towards his bedroom.

The day is mild as I step out to walk to Fahy's for my shift. I'm getting used to the energy switch that happens when I turn on to the High Road; the smells and sounds hit me and I'm part of the current of pedestrians: no hesitating, forward motion only. I imagine Moses walking beside me now, taking my hand in his, leaning in to kiss me for no reason. I can conjure up his smile in an instant. He could come to Fahy's for last orders and walk me home. He could show me the good clubs in east London. We'll need to go looking for inspiration for our music.

An old man shuffles past, slight hunch on him, craggy-faced with a reddish tinge to his nose and cheeks. I can pick the Irish on the High Road now. The women, too, hardness etched on to their faces, always hurrying. I'm a different kind of Irish to them. I didn't come here when I was a teenager to send money home to my family like they did. I didn't lift bricks until my hands bled. People like Gerry never went back, but it's all they think about. I don't cling on to the idea of home like him. I've been away a whole year now, and I don't miss it at all.

Eamonn's mobility scooter sits by the door, and sure enough, he's in the shadowy corner next to the door for the toilets, his gut spilling out over his trousers, his betting slips on the table, his eyes fixed on the TV.

– God, it's so dark in here, I say, as I walk behind the bar, pulling my coat off and hanging it up on the hook.

– I thought you'd be used to it by now, Pat says, glancing over at me. She is in her usual attire of jumper over blouse, sensible black trousers, and those shoes with the comfy rubber soles that nurses wear. I suppose some of the qualities required of that job have similarities to her own: administering medicine to old-age pensioners and listening to their woes. Pat doesn't try to wear any sort of expression of patience, though. She looks irritated from the moment anyone opens their mouth.

– Dave, I say, in greeting to Mayo Dave, who graces the far end of the bar in his usual spot. He raises his face slowly from under the peak of his baseball cap and nods. His thick neck runs into his shoulders like that of a bull.

– Right, I'm off upstairs to check on himself, says Pat, walking to the hatch. – Phone up to me if you need me.

There's a group of old men I don't recognise in the corner. They all have the same worn-down look about them; the same big, battered hands wrapped around their pints.

One of the men looks up to the bar, and the other two follow his gaze. I nod at them as they size me up. It's taken a long time to get used to the stares of the patrons of Fahy's Bar. There's a stark contrast between the feeling of being invisible in the public spaces of the city, and being on display for eight hours a day behind the bar in this pub. There are times when I feel a sense of creeping discomfort being stuck in their gaze, stuck in their notions and presumptions of women – young women, young Irish women. But mostly, I am something for their eyes to follow when their thoughts are elsewhere, like the racehorses on the TV.

I scan the tables for empty glasses, then perch on the stool in the corner and wait to be called.

CHAPTER 10

THE NEXT EPISODE

The sky is overcast and spitting warm rain as I step out from Camden Road train station on to the busy crossroads of Camden Road and Royal College Street. I'm wearing my high-heeled ankle boots, and it's awkward to keep my balance on the uneven cobbles. I concentrate on my steps and try and take everything in.

It's a relief to have a reason to be out of Mill Road. The boys seem to be avoiding each other since they came back from tour. Frank has taken it upon himself to tackle the garden jungle with a pair of shears. He's been out there hacking at the grass for hours, sweating and sunburned, giving out about the state of the garden. He found a toad yesterday and christened it Bob. Kesh plays guitar and sings all day in his room. When he's not watching TV, Richie plays on his practice kit in his room. He could be up there for three or four hours straight. The thwacks are dull and muted. You get used to them after a while.

I turn on to the road that homes Redstar Records. When I see the red star of the logo hanging over the front door, I feel a little pulse of anxiety and try to swallow it down. I think of Neema, off to her first day of law school this morning, dressed formally in tailored trousers and a blouse, her hair tied tightly back from her face with a scrunchie, her face set in a frown. I showed her how I thought she should walk into class like she's in Destiny's Child, singing about throwing her hands up and swinging her hips like they do in their music video, and she allowed herself a little laugh then.

– But Neema, our destiny starts today!

– You're such a drama queen, Orla.

I take a deep breath and push the door. The reception area is dominated by one huge desk. The red star of the logo is repeated as a mural on the wall behind the desk, with the words REDSTAR RECORDS underneath. The receptionist directs me towards a glass door that leads to a long, open-plan room. There are stacks and stacks of CDs and vinyl on every surface, with pot plants and posters of bands and a huge Union Jack flag draped across the wall. I'm staring at it when a voice calls my name.

– Orla! Gwen is at the kitchenette in the far corner. – Come over here, she says. She's holding a cup under a drinks machine, and she lifts her arm for me to walk under it, then closes it around me and squeezes. She's wearing full make-up. I smell hairspray and perfume and fags.

– Welcome to Redstar, babe.

– Thanks, I say.

– You're going to work with me and Emma today. She gestures behind her, to a tall, broad-shouldered woman sitting at a desk, who raises her hand in greeting.

– Emma is my assistant, and together we do all the publicity and promotions for Redstar artists.

Emma looks at me and says, – Ready to work?

She beckons me over to her, then stands up and shakes my hand. I am encouraged by how plainly she dresses and the fact she wears no make-up.

– So, your job today is to put this pile of CDs – she picks up a long box of CDs from a pile on the floor and carries them to a desk – into envelopes and label them.

And this is my morning. I'm relieved by the simplicity of the work. It gives me time to watch and listen and record everything I see to tell Moses about at the weekend. Everyone here seems to use their desk as a kind of art installation. They listen to music on headphones that are plugged in to the front of the computers, brightly coloured iMacs with stereo speakers built in. Cut-outs of different singers and cultural figures have been Blu-Tacked around the edges of each computer screen.

Gwen's computer is all bands, but Emma's seems to be a shrine to women in rock. There's Björk, Justine Frischmann, Patti Smith, Kim Deal, Courtney Love. Andy is the press guy. He is from Leeds, and has a pointy face and a small mouth, which he uses to loudly take the piss out of everyone and everything. His computer features photos of Liam Gallagher and John Lydon, and a man with huge backcombed hair and sunglasses that I don't recognise. He catches me looking at the photo and says, in a dry voice, – He's a poet. His name is John Cooper Clarke.

– Oh.

I listen to Gwen on the phone.

– Yes, Sam, I mean there's just something about Kesh isn't there? she's saying. – Yep, his voice is unique, no one else is even close to it. But it's his stage presence, man . . . Yep, they're a three-piece . . . What do you mean you haven't seen them live?!

She is absentmindedly clicking on her mouse, and I can see that she has three different MSN messages on the go in the corner of her computer screen.

– Okay, next London show isn't until December, but I'm putting you down right now. LA2. Yep, it's a big one. They're growing fast, Sam. You need to be getting on these boys. We're posting the new Atlas EP today, but I'll post you some Shiva to listen to, too.

Gwen, Emma, Andy and I go out for lunch to a little Vietnamese place, where we are served steaming hot bowls of noodles, mushrooms, shrimp and chicken. As Emma painstakingly removes each piece of mushroom from her bowl with her fork, the others discuss what press they will aim to get for the new Shiva album.

– So we want features in *The Fly*, *Kerrang!* and *NME*, obviously, says Gwen to Andy, who is nodding into his broth.

– Is it worth taking to the *Guardian*? – says Emma.

– Definitely, says Andy, – and I'll send it to Mark at *The Face*. He'll want to be up on it, even if he doesn't print anything now.

Gwen turns to me and explains. – Orla, we want to get people invested in the album early and talking about it. It's all about word of mouth.

– What radio and TV will you try for with the album? I ask her, and she's straight in, conducting the flow of her sentence with the chopsticks in her right hand.

– It all depends on how it builds. Shiva stand out because of Kesh being Asian. There's interest there from a media perspective. We just need the songs to catch on.

Then Gwen asks me about Mill Road, and I tell them the story of Richie and the baby mice.

Andy shakes his head and says, – A mouse nest in his cornflakes. That's fucking legendary.

– And on a massive comedown after the tour as well, Gwen says, shaking her head.

– You should have heard the yelp out of him when he found them, I say.

Emma snorts with laughter then, but her mouth is full, she puts her hand over her mouth to hold in the noodles. Gwen and Andy are off then, and it's hard to resist the sound of their laughing. I tell them about Richie and the swans when we went on the pedalos on my birthday. – He doesn't have much luck with animals. As I laugh with them, I catch eyes with a woman walking past the window looking in. I wonder what our little gathering must look like from her perspective: a girl blushing with pleasure in the corner of a small, steamy restaurant, surrounded by laughing faces. I wonder if I look comfortable in my skin to her. Does she think I belong here?

– *Hello?*

– *Orley.*

– *Da, it's eight-thirty in the morning. On a Saturday.*

– *Yes, sorry about that, Orla, but I've been trying to reach you.*

Pause.

– *One sec . . . (Carol, I'm in here; I'm on to Orla. Yes please. I'll be in in a minute.) . . . Orley? Can you hear me?*

Pause.

– *Yes, Da, I can hear you.*

– *So, how are you getting on over there?*

– *I've just finished my first week working at a record label.*

– *Great. And what do you think?*

– *I'm learning a lot. And I had a meeting with Shiva's manager. He said he'd listen to my music.*

– *That's a good start. And have you been playing much?*

– *I sent him my songs from Cheltenham.*

– *Are you singing on them?*

– *A tiny bit. But I produced them all.*

Pause.

– *Right. And can you get a record contract off being a producer, Orla?*

Sigh.

– *My teacher in college told me, if I can't get a label to release them, to approach some TV-production companies to get them considered for soundtracks.*

– *Well, that would be a sensible move. Michael Whelan's brother works in RTÉ. I could ask him if he knows someone.*

– *Okay.*

– *Anyway, Orley, I've been trying to reach you, because I have some news for you.*

– *I know the news. Ma told me on my birthday. Great birthday present.*

– *Oh, about the divorce?*

– *Yeah.*

– *Ah, okay. Well, I tried to call you on your birthday, but you never rang me back.*

Pause.

– *This is different news. New news, heh heh . . . I hope you'll be happy. For me. For us.*

Pause.

– *Orla, Carol's pregnant.*

Pause.

– *Is that biologically possible?*

Sigh.

– *She's forty-two, Orla. Still very much of child-bearing age.*

– *And you're fifty-two, Da. Fifty-three next January.*

– *Which is when Carol is due.*

Pause.

– *I wanted to tell you first.*

– *Before Ma?*

– *Yes.*

– *Why? Why me first?*

– *I thought you would be happy about it.*

– *Well, Da. Let me make this very clear to you. And your Carol . . .*

– *Orley, I understand that it's strange. But I really think in time, you will see how happy we are. If you could come home and spend some time with us . . .*

– *That works both ways, Da. Don't put it all on me. This is . . . this is fucking insane.*

– *Orley, please.*

– *I have to go.*

CHAPTER 11

ROMEO

There's a song by The Strokes called 'Someday'. It starts with jaunty drums and a jangly electric guitar playing melodic chords. Up and down. After the first four bars, a rhythm guitar kicks in, thrashing and fuzzy-sounding, and even though the jaunty guitar and drums are still playing the same lines, this rhythm guitar makes the whole song sound chaotic, fraught, noisy and dense. The guitar and the drums are my life. The rhythm guitar is my brain.

– Hello?

– Moses? Moses, are you in London yet?

– Hey, Orla. What's up? I've got, like, six missed calls from you.

– Shit. Yeah. I wanted to see if you're in London yet. We're eh . . . we're going out tonight, and I thought you might want to come with us.

– I'm still at home. I'm coming up tomorrow with all my stuff.

– Okay. So, what are you doing tonight?

– Packing. Sorting all my shit out. Why?

– Maybe I could come down and see you.

– I thought you were going out?

My da's having a baby. My da's having a baby. My da's having a baby.

– I'm grand. Don't mind me. Let's hang out next week when you're all settled in.

– Okay, enjoy tonight.

– Yep. Bye.

The shame of it. And no mobile phone credit so on the phone in the hall for the whole house to hear. I look up as Frank thumps down the stairs, rubbing his eyes, his legs darkened with hair under his shorts. He sees me and nods as he turns to walk to the kitchen.

– Where are you playing again today? I say.

– Kent.

– A festival, though?

He nods and disappears into the gear room.

That's it. I run up the stairs two at a time. The attic room is empty.

– Neema?

– Yeah?

I hear her voice coming from the direction of the bath-room, so I run back down and knock on the door. – Neema, can I come in?

There is a soft click as she turns the key and opens the

111

door. She is brushing her teeth and looking at me suspiciously. She leans back to the sink and spits, and then says,
– What's up with you?

– Let's go to the festival with the boys.

– Mmm, she says, – aren't they bringing that journalist, though?

– Maybe we could be immortalised in print! I say, and stop as soon as I see her look of disapproval.

She says, – I'll ask. But Orla, we can't get in the way.

– Jesus, Neema, I'm not that bad.

Shane, the tour manager, arrives in the van just after midday. The boys are bleary-eyed and monosyllabic as they load their gear into the storage compartment. Afterwards, Kesh climbs into the front beside Shane; Neema and I choose seats together in the back with Frank and Richie. Neema wears green baggy combats that sit perfectly on her hips. Her hair is gathered up on her head, with wispy bits hanging down. The type of hair me and Ma have always dreamed of. Shiny and soft and luxe.

Ma. What will she say when she finds out? God. Oh, God almighty.

Frank is sitting in front of me.

– What time did you get in last night? I ask him as the van pulls away.

His curls are out and frizzing around his face. He's wearing his leather biker jacket today, with a patterned shirt underneath. He always looks as if he's dressing up as someone in a

112

rock band, as opposed to Richie, who is slumped against the window behind us, wearing sunglasses and a tie-dyed T-shirt, and looks like someone who was born to be in a rock band.

Frank half turns around so I can hear him. – Not until three. The Castle were having a party, so we got stuck in after rehearsal.

Kesh has turned around on his seat, too, and is frowning through the hole in his headrest. His hair is cut short now, and bleached white-blond.

– I feel rough, man. Has anyone come across this journalist before?

– Nah. Gwen said he's been around for a while though, says Richie.

– I hope he's actually a fan, says Kesh.

We go silent for a bit, looking at the suburbs of London whizzing by. After about half an hour, Kesh points out the window and says, – There they are.

Shane pulls the van up on to the kerb, and Richie leans over and slides open the door to reveal Gwen's red head, her pale face set into an expression of resolute boredom above the dark plumage of her fur coat. A bird of prey in Shepherd's Bush. Beside her is a pudgy blond guy with glasses, wearing a Radiohead T-shirt.

– You lot, this is Ben from *NME*, she says, by way of greeting as she clambers in and plonks herself on the seat beside Frank. Clinking noises come from the plastic bag she lays by her feet.

– Hi. Ben waves awkwardly at everyone as he clambers on to the bus and tries to close the door behind him. We all say hi back and he shakes everyone's hands. His hand is wet with sweat. Frank helps Ben with the door, and he sits down in the two seats across from Gwen and Frank. I hold out the palm of my hand to Neema and look horrified. She rummages in her handbag for a tissue, hands it to me and gives me a long, warning look. A look that says, *Don't stir any shite, Orla, this day is about them.* I give her a brief, reassuring look back as I wipe my hands, and then look away. Any more than that after the morning I've had is dangerous. Her eyes are like emotional quicksand for me; if I stay in them too long, I cry.

I lean forward to Ben and say, – Ben, Neema and I live with the band, so if you need an inside scoop on who spends the longest on the toilet, I've got you.

He laughs gratefully and leans towards me, saying, – So, where do you lot live?

And we're off into small talk as the van crawls through the thick traffic of Goldhawk Road. The boys are on their best behaviour with Ben, discussing different venues they've played at and asking him about journalists they know.

We are cruising along a dual carriageway in comfortable silence when Frank says, – This guy. He holds the copy of *NME* he's been reading up so we can all get a good look at the photo of Fran Healy from the band Travis. He's doing a strange pose, as if he's about to fall over. – What a pillock.

Frank shakes his head. – He's saying that bands exist purely to entertain the audience. Like they're there to make them happy and nothing else.

I see Ben pull a small machine from his shoulder bag and press a button on it.

Gwen says, in a playful tone, – You're on record, Frank. Careful what you say, or you'll end up in a fight with Fran Healy.

– Now, there's a fight I'd pay to watch, says Richie.

Kesh shouts over his shoulder from the front seat. – Yeah, but Travis's music is so surface-level; that's all they can do. Like Starsailor or something.

Richie speaks from behind us now. – What's wrong with entertaining your audience? Seriously, like? What's the point of being in a band if you don't want to end up singing 'Day-O' in Wembley fucking stadium?

We all laugh at Richie, who looks to Ben and says, – And you can quote me on that.

Kesh turns around and adds, – And therein lies the fundamental crack in the Shiva ideology. Richie wants us to be Queen. Frank wants us to be Mogwai . . .

– And who do you want the band to be, Kesh? Ben asks.

Kesh is straight back: – We're Shiva, man. That's enough for me.

Ben nods, a knowing expression on his face.

As the van pulls to a stop at a set of traffic lights, Frank turns the page of the *NME* and says quietly this time so only we can hear him, – Well, let's hope our fans aren't coming to leave happier. Seeing Kesh on stage will soon put a stop to that.

Gwen elbows him in the ribs and looks to Ben to see if he heard, but Ben has turned to look out the window. She turns back to Frank and makes a shushing gesture with her finger over her mouth.

An hour into our journey, Kesh passes a small bottle of whiskey around the bus. Ben and Neema refuse; Richie and Frank take some; Gwen abstains and passes it back to me. I have a small drink and then a big drink. It takes my breath away. When we stop at a shop, I buy my own bottle and a box of cigarettes. By the time we arrive at the festival, my bottle is a third gone.

The festival is on a farm in Kent, and is ingeniously titled Rock on the Farm. The first stop is the artist-liaison office, a Portakabin at the edge of the site, where Shane queues up to get our wristbands and lanyards. Then we drive slowly around the outside of the site to get to the tent the boys will play in. With the parking pass, the van drives right up behind the stage. We pile out, and the boys slowly stretch their arms up in the air and take it all in. Neema, Gwen and I go to queue at the lone Portaloo, which stands at a slight angle in the corner.

– Gwen, you got any . . .? I say, nodding at her intently.

– Jesus, you're keen, says Gwen, with an irritated expression on her face.

– I have money. Don't want to be scrounging all day.

– All day, yeah? – says Gwen, looking at me askance as a man rushes out of the Portaloo buttoning up his flies.

– Give me a second. She pinches her nose shut with her fingers and gingerly steps into the Portaloo.

On her way out, she hands me her wallet. I can tell by the way her eyes are flitting about the place that she's had a go herself.

– It's in the front pocket, she says.

With Ben in tow, we all form a rough circle outside another Portakabin, this one acting as Shiva's dressing room. The sounds of shouting and shrieks of laughter drift in from beyond the boundary; then a surge of cheering and applause as a band finish a song on another stage. Kesh and Shane head over to the stage, and I see Kesh shake hands with the sound guy and start to fire questions at him, pointing to the sound rig. Beside ours, there are another two Portakabins, outside which the members of various other bands mill about. Everyone seems to be looking and simultaneously pretending not to look at each other. Richie and Frank busy themselves rolling cigarettes.

– How long until you're on? asks Ben, and Richie and Frank look at their watches. They're nervous, I realise.

Richie says, – Long enough for a drink. Who wants one?

– Get one for me, Neema! I shout as Neema follows Frank and Richie into the Portakabin. Ben and I loiter outside. He's sweating again, I notice. Black jeans in the heat will do that to you. I'm itching to talk.

– Are you a fan of Shiva's music? I ask.

He glances at me briefly, then looks away. – It's not my job to be a fan. It's my job to be a critic, he says, all matter-of-fact.

– Well, who are you a fan of? I persist.

His face softens suddenly; he pushes his glasses up his nose and gives me real eye contact as he speaks. – At the moment, I would say that I am mostly a fan of PJ Harvey.

– Oh. Me too, I say, and buoyed by his thin smile, I carry on, – She's so little, but her voice is so powerful. It makes me feel angry and like I want to cry all at the same time, know what I mean?

He nods, knowingly. – She's a once-in-a-lifetime artist, he says, with real authority.

– Totally, I say, and in the gap that follows I add, – But God, isn't that depressing, thinking that no one as good as her will come around in our lifetimes?

– I'd be glad you got to hear her at all, he replies.

Neema brings me a beer and Ben a water, even though he didn't ask for one. He drinks from the bottle gratefully. Kesh is back in the Portakabin, pacing up and down past the window. Strange, guttural noises emerge from the thin walls; the sound of a throat clearing and the occasional grunt. We all turn and look towards the cabin.

– Wow, that's quite a show Kesh is putting on. I giggle.

– Vocal exercises, Neema says. – He's got some seriously high notes to reach.

Ben nods and blinks behind his glasses. A band on the main stage crashes to a finish. We hear the muffled 'thank you' from the singer and the ensuing applause. As the sound dies out there's a cheer from inside Shiva's tent. – Are there people inside already? I ask Ben.

He turns around, peers into the back of the tent and says, – yep. And they've shut the lights off. Looks like they're on soon.

Right on cue, Kesh walks past us and pauses at the bottom of the ramp. The others have come out of the Portakabin now, too, and there's a moment of stillness as we all look to Kesh. He stands with his back to us, right in the glare of the sun, and starts to breathe, deeply and dramatically, his shoulders moving up and down with each inhalation and exhalation. He is striking in the light, his peroxide hair highlighting the rich brown tone of his skin. I can see the contours of the biceps and triceps on his arms.

Frank, as if reading my thoughts, says, – You know he used to a be a gymnast as a kid?

And as I'm trying to process a picture of Kesh swinging himself over a bar, Shane charges down the ramp and nods at Kesh, who then turns and nods at Frank, who throws down his cigarette and shouts, – Richie. It's time.

Neema and Gwen grab me to go into the tent to watch them perform.

– What about Ben? I say.

– He's insisting that he wants to watch it by himself, Gwen says, as she takes my arm and starts to pull me through the crowd, with Neema holding on to me. The Bollywood intro fills the tent, the band walk on stage. Kesh picks up his guitar and strums the first chord. I notice that there is a stream of people filing into the tent. As Richie starts banging out a beat on the kick drum, bodies close in around me. I squeeze Neema's arm, but she is craning her neck to try and see the stage, where Kesh is leaning into the mic, his voice wound tight into a prolonged screech. I take my whiskey from my bag and take a swig; it burns my throat.

The band finish the first song and crash into the next one, Kesh clenching his teeth in concentration at the solo before he starts to sing again. The crowd are bumping into me, or am I bumping into them? I'm not sure, but I nearly fall over and Neema catches me.

My da's having a—

The crowd surges, and I cling on to Neema and she clings on to Gwen, who punches the air and sings along to the words. Richie's eyes are closed, his arms a blur of movement. Frank is moving more than last time I saw him on stage. He rocks the neck of his bass from side to side in time with the beat until he reaches the start of the chorus, when he doubles his body over the guitar completely and pulls it back up again in an exaggerated bow. And all the time, he looks deadly serious, eyes locked first on Richie and then Kesh, as he prowls from one side of the stage to the other.

At the beginning of the next song, Kesh jumps off the edge of the stage and pulls himself up the front of the railings that separate the stage from the crowd, pulling the microphone cord behind him. He stays there for 'Brick by Brick', singing out over our heads, and as I swig my whiskey, I'm reminded of the image of Jesus on the stained glass window in our church when I was a child, the way Kesh stands up against the railing like this, hands grabbing at his arms and chest, his expression melancholy as he sings. And I feel my own eyes stinging with tears, too.

When they reach the penultimate chorus, Kesh pulls himself up over the railing and hurls himself on top of the crowd. His legs kick up in the air as he is carried, his voice wavering on and off mic as his arms are pulled away from him. The whole crowd is centred on him now, but I look back at the band on stage, where Frank is still playing, but searching the crowd for Kesh, a worried look on his face. And then he is smiling, because Kesh is suddenly, somehow, back onstage, and Richie is standing up over the drums, face screwed up in concentration as he rolls and rolls, and Frank plays along with him, and it's chaos again, screeching feedback and thrashing bodies, and then it's over, and we are clapping and shouting with all these people; all these people who must be fans now, they must be totally won over.

Backstage, we all hug each other.

– I could cry, Gwen says to Kesh. – I could actually cry.

– They fucking knew every word, says Kesh. He is top-less, bouncing around the small space, clutching a bottle of water in his hand.

– That's got to be up there as one of our best gigs, says a pink-faced Frank, as he tries to dry the sweat out of his hair with a towel.

– Definitely. Damian walks into the dressing room and thumps Frank on the back with the flat of his palm. – Definitely the best one for the *NME* journalist to see.

Where did he come from?

He sees me and nods, and I nod back.

– It's time to celebrate, says Richie, rubbing his hands together.

– Allow me to do the honours, says Gwen, who has pulled a bottle of champagne from somewhere and is opening it. The cork pops, and everyone cheers, and in the same moment, Andy from the label steps inside and holds his fists up in the air as if he's won a victory of some sort.

He catches my eye.

– Neema, this is Andy from Redstar, I say, delighted to know someone in my own right. And Andy's straight in for the hug, and it's chaos then, people wandering in and out, smoking and back-slapping and toasting the success of Shiva. The whiskey and champagne disappear fast. Ben reappears, and sits stiffly on the sofa, sipping on a bottle of beer, as people take turns to talk to him.

122

As the light of the afternoon melts into dusk, Richie stands on the table in the Portakabin and shouts: – It has been decided that the party will continue at the main backstage area. Everybody grab your drinks and follow me.

Out in the festival, people are walking in all directions, giddy, drunk, and yelling through the dusk. Thick, greasy smells from food trucks mix in with wafts of weed. It's a cacophony of noise, layers and layers of it, with sound systems from the stages clashing with speakers from stalls and fairground rides. My head zings and rings with it all.

I feel a hand on my arm and look behind me to see Neema.

– Slow down, she says as she links her arm into mine. I grin at her, and she grins back. Her smile arrives more easily these days. She swings her hips as she walks, and I wonder if she always did that and I'm only noticing it now. I imitate her, but deliberately badly, clownish.

She laughs and says, – Fuck off, Orla.

I say, – Jesus, Neema, it's fun though, isn't it, going to festivals when you're with the band.

We show the security guard our wristbands and enter the backstage area. Picnic tables are scattered around the ground. Richie turns around to us as we follow him into a large tent that holds the bar, a look of joy on his face as he sings and air-guitars along to the Wheatus song coming through the speakers. Inside, Damian introduces Kesh to various industry people. Neema elbows me in the ribs.

– Ow! I say, what was that for?

– This is your chance, she says. – Go and ask him about the demo. She nods at Damian, who is now standing on his own as Kesh chats with a group of people a few metres away.

– Oh Jesus, I say, but I'm all loose and buoyed up from the bumps and the booze, so I walk right up to him. – Damian?

He is holding his phone in one hand, and composing a text with the forefinger of his other hand. – Oh, hi Orla.

– Sorry to disturb you. I just wanted to ask if you ever got a minute to listen to my demo tape?

– Ah yes, he says, narrowing his eyes at me as if he's trying to remember.

I decide to help him out. – I sent it with Kesh, about three weeks ago now.

He's nodding and squinting at me, the phone still in his hand.

– It was in a brown padded envelope with your name on it, I say, because I can't handle him flailing for an answer. I want to put him out of his misery.

He's still lost.

I laugh, a big, free, unloaded laugh, and nod the words out of me. – Right. It's clearly left a big impression on you.

He's pointing at me now, a flash of irritation on his face. – No, no, I do remember. I think we listened to it on the same day, which is why it's taken me a while. It was something to do with butterflies?

He's remembering now, and it's causing him to smile. He

quickly rearranges his expression to look serious again. He's trying not to laugh at me.

– Oh, right. You read the letter I put with it. I guess it's pretty naff. The concept—

He interrupts me. – I didn't hear much of your singing on it, if I recall correctly.

– No, there's only singing on one song. It's three productions in all. I made them all myself—

We're interrupted.

– Damian! A big bearded man is punching Damian on the arm and then enclosing him in a bear hug. He has a pint in each hand and he manages to hug him without spilling a drop.

– Jim! Damian laughs.

– I've got Dolly with me, and Leo over in the bar, look. Jim points in the direction of the bar.

Damian looks over. – No way, Leo. I haven't seen him in so long.

– Come and say hi.

Jim and Damian go to walk off, then Damian turns towards me. – Sorry, Orla, I've got to head. Stay in touch about it, okay? We can talk some more.

I stand and watch them walk away, all best pals, Damian and Jim, the man who stole my feedback from under my nose. As they walk, Damian says something to Jim and they both burst into laughter.

★   ★   ★

Outside the bar tent, drunken revellers shout and stumble through the darkness, charged up for the night ahead. I find Neema, Richie and Andy sitting on a picnic table at the edge of the guest area. Neema gives me the big eyes. I shrug. It means, *Nothing happened, and please don't talk about it.* She gives me a tiny little nod and then hooks her arm through mine and cuddles into me.

Andy takes out a little key and does a bump out of the vial of cocaine around his neck.

– Giz a go on that, mate, Richie says.

– As long as your *NME* guy doesn't see. I don't want to get in trouble, Andy says, looking around nervously.

– Kesh racked up in the dressing room, mate. It's already too late, Richie says, laughing. After Richie takes his bump, Andy has to offer it to us.

– Where are you staying? says I, after my bump, offering Andy a cigarette and lighting it for him.

– I'm camping on site with a group of mates. Got a tent to myself, he says, nodding, as if that's a confirmation of something.

– Do you, now? says Richie, laughing softly. – Watch out, ladies, Andy's on the prowl.

Andy smiles and exhales his smoke into the darkness.

At around 1am, when the bar is closing, Shane gathers us all back at the van. We bring Andy with us. Kesh has collected some stragglers on the way, who are told to wait outside as we pile into the Portakabin. Richie has his arm flung across Ben from *NME*'s shoulder, and is shouting in his ear. Kesh is drunk, pleading with Shane in a shouty voice. – Come on, Shane. Let's just stay over and go in the morning.

Shane shakes his head in exasperation, rolling his eyes and says, – But I didn't book us a hotel.

Then Gwen pipes up. – Shane, Andy is camping, so we can sleep with his gang or in the van, and you can sleep in the cabin so you get some peace.

– I love Gwen pretending she's going to sleep, says Frank as an aside to me, and I laugh loudly at that.

– Go on, Shane, says Richie. – You know you want to. And Ben, he says, pulling his arm tighter around Ben's neck. – You're up for it, aren't you?

Ben blinks furiously behind his glasses and looks to Gwen, who says, – I can get you a hotel room if you'd rather?

He shrugs and says, – It's okay, prompting Richie to exuberantly slap him on the back and shout, – That's what I'm talking about!

We all start to goad Shane then – Come on, Shane, it'll be fine, Shane – and even Kesh's fans are joining in from outside the door. As the volume gets louder, Kesh takes some poppers out of his pocket and unscrews the lid, hovering the bottle close to Shane's nose. Everyone starts to cheer as the poppers get closer and closer to Shane's nostrils, until Shane rolls his eyes and says, – You'll have to pay me for a double shift, before pressing his forefinger over his left nostril and breathing in sharply. We all erupt into triumphant cheering.

– YES, Shane! FUCKING LEGEND, Kesh shouts, and along with Frank, jumps on him to hug him. After they pull away, Shane stumbles and reaches out one hand to the wall to steady himself, his face the colour of cement.

The only music still playing is at the small dance tent on the other side of site. We head there together as a big raucous mob, and I lose count of the pieces of pills that are slipped into my mouth. Richie tries to give one to Ben, but he shakes his head violently. Neema puts her arm around him. – Ben, are you okay?

– I'm fine, he says, a little defensively, pushing his glasses up his nose.

When the music stops at the dance tent, we go to another party in a circle of tents in the campsite. Kesh hugs Neema saying to people, – This is my sister. Do you think we look alike? Who do you think is older?

Frank impresses a girl with blue hair enough that she lets him snog her. Richie holds court with another band on some camping stools, while I get chatting with some law students.

– You'll have to meet Neema, I say. – She's in law school. You guys should get together . . . Neema is pulling me away as I say, – No, seriously, you should ask her out. I can hear my own voice slurring, and Neema telling me to shut up.

Kesh is pulling a worried-looking Ben on to the ground

by the fire, talking incessantly in his ear. And now Andy's face is leaning into mine.

– Toilet, I say. – I need the toilet.

Neema is here again now. Her eyes are big moons, staring at me. – Are you okay, babe?

Andy is talking to her. – She needs to go to the toilet. I'll show her where they are.

I cling on to Andy's arm tightly as we walk. I keep tripping over tent ropes and giggling. There are cascades of lights on wires lining the path. When I try to focus on them, they turn fuzzy.

At the toilets, Andy says, – I'll wait for you outside.

I close the door behind me and the smells hit me, and I have to stand with a hand pressed flat against each wall to balance. I have to stay upright. I'm rushing, big surges of energy are moving through me, but it's not a nice feeling, because now the energy is nausea and the surges are heaves and I'm vomiting into the black hole of the toilet and the smells are attacking me, causing me to vomit more, and I can only hold on to the sides and keep myself upright in the black.

I'm trembling all over. I wipe the seat in the dark and try not to think of all the other people's excretions I'm wiping, too. I sit on the toilet and try to breathe through my nose, but the smells are too strong, so I breathe through my mouth instead. After I pee, I stand up and wipe my face with a tissue.

Andy is pacing outside. He looks at me from under his blunt fringe. – You okay?

129

– Yeah, I say, because compared to five minutes ago, I am okay. The heaves have turned back into rushes, the nausea has melted away.

– Do you want one? he asks, holding out a packet of chewing gum to me, and when I can't grip the stick with my shaky fingers, he takes two out, unwraps them for me and puts them in my hand. As we walk back along the path, I hook my arm in his and concentrate on the peppermint taste of the chewing gum, until he stops and says, – My tent's over there. Want to come and see it?

I murmur out the words. – Why not.

CHAPTER 12

IT WASN'T ME

The air in this tent is thick with the stench of alcohol and farts. There's no escape from the light. Andy is lying beside me. I know it's Andy because I can see the collar of the shirt he was wearing last night; it has a blue paisley pattern on it. He's so still he could be dead. I move my hand down my body. My underwear is on, my trousers are not. My bra is unhooked and sits around my neck like a necklace. My head feels as if someone's taken a hammer and chisel to my skull. I try to clear the debris in my head to find a formed memory, but there's nothing. Nothing. Rubble and dust.

I sit up to find my trousers and lie down again to pull them on. It takes ages to find my bag. I unzip the tent and crawl out into the grey, damp air of dawn.

The tent ropes are like tripwires set to catch me out. *Focus, Orla. You just have to find the others.* I reach for the bottle of whiskey in my bag, but it's empty. *Mind the ropes. Stay alert.*

I find them back at the circle of tents. There's a fire going, and everyone is slumped around it. Neema is asleep beside Richie, curled up with a coat over her. Kesh is holding on to his knees, staring at the fire as a guy pokes at the embers with a stick. There are other people there, people I don't know.

I stand where they can see me and raise my hand. The shame of it.

– Morning, says Kesh. His face looks as if someone's deflated it like a balloon. His chin is moving all over the place.

– I'm going back to the van for a lie down. Is anyone in it?

– Yeah, Shane's there, and Ben and Gwen. We'll come with you.

I wait while they all unfold themselves and stand. We don't speak as we walk back. Neema trudges along with Richie's coat over her shoulders, as if she's been pulled out of a fire. When we reach the van, Shane is asleep, sitting upright in the driver's seat, mouth hanging open. Gwen, Ben and Frank are curled up on the seats at the back. We knock on the window, and Shane wakes up. Gwen pulls herself up and opens the door from the inside.

As we clamber in, Shane grunts and starts the ignition.

The stop-starting of the van when it hits the London traffic nudges us awake. Kesh opens some beers and we all join in, one by one, except for Ben, who looks exhausted. The sky darkens as we crawl along with the traffic, spilling out heavy rain just as Shane pulls the van over for Ben to get out so he can jump on the Tube. He doesn't look any of us in the eye as he leaves.

Back at Mill Road, Kesh pulls out a crate of cut-price beer that the boys brought home from The Castle. Neema gets changed into her pyjamas, black fake silk, and watches us all from the corner of the sofa, her moon eyes orbited by dark circles of tiredness.

Gwen pours her cocaine on the table to join Kesh's. – Frank, tell us about your new girlfriend? she says.

Frank smirks under his curls. – Definitely not girlfriend material, he mumbles.

– Who is she, though? Gwen asks.

He shrugs. – I don't know. I didn't ask her many questions.

They all laugh at that. Gwen says, – Well, someone has to take over from Richie.

– Why, what did Richie do? Neema asks.

– He's always been the ladies' man, Gwen says.

– Well, do you blame them? Richie says, circling his face with his index finger. – Look at this perfection.

We all chuckle at that, apart from Neema, who is silent.

Cocaine and cans are consumed through lunchtime, through the *EastEnders* Omnibus, until there's life in us again and words arrive easily through ravaged throats. Sometime in the afternoon, Richie puts on Black Sabbath. He takes his top off and swings it round his head. We laugh until we don't know why we're laughing, and our words are sloppy and slurred.

When I crawl into my bed at teatime, my shoulders ache from the inside out, as if someone has put a match to the nerves there. My throat is raw. I have no awareness of falling asleep. But there's a knocking sound in my head, and it won't stop. It forces me out of the black and into a painful, breathless state of sobbing, and that's how I wake up. I am crying. Really crying: big, shuddering sobs. Crying out in distress. I don't know what's going on.

– Orla. Neema is holding me by the shoulders. – Orla, it's okay.

I can't stop crying; my whole body's shaking.

– I wanted to check on you, I'm so sorry, babe.

– Why did you knock? You never knock, I sob, and her moon eyes are full of tears now. She's been drinking all day, hot tea with rum in it.

She holds me and brushes the hair out of my eyes, and as my tears subside, she takes my hands, and says, – I'm so sorry. I should have just let you sleep.

I heave in a big mouthful of air and she continues. – Orla. What the fuck happened last night? Where did you go?

My mouth is dry. I lick my lips and whisper, – I woke up in Andy's tent. That's all I know.

– So, you can't remember?

I shake my head. My face feels swollen. A throbbing ache builds in the front of my head. I breathe in deeply and fumble on my bedside table for paracetamol. She helps me with the water. I start crying again because her kindness

134

is too much for me. I pull the duvet up over my head and lie back down.

She's talking now. – You had to go to the toilet. He said he'd take you, remember?

I don't move. – Was I really out of it? I ask from under the duvet.

– You were pretty out of it all day. I was worried about you. You tried to get me to snog this guy in the campsite.

– Oh God, I croak. – I'm sorry. Neema. My job . . . I've fucked it all up. My shoulders shake first before the tears come. She pulls the duvet down, and I see the look of concern on her face. I cry even harder, and I can't stop now, convulsions wracking my body.

– Orla, I'm sure it's not that bad . . .

– . . . And my da's having a baby. With Flatface.

And I see her face freeze and then collapse in dismay at this news, and she's hugging me then, rocking me back and forth like a baby, and I let her.

– Hello?

– Hiya, love, it's me.

– Hi Ma, I've been waiting for you to phone me.

– And why's that?

– Well. Have you spoken to Da?

– He rang me and told me his news on Sunday.

– And did you talk about it with him, Ma?

– Sure, what is there to talk about?

Sigh.

– Maybe the fact that you put his dinner in front of him every night for twenty-four years. You sacrificed your career to raise his two children. And now he's fucked off and started another family.

– Orla, what good is your carrying on like this to me?

– I'm just so fucking furious with him.

– Well, don't take your fury out on me.

Pause.

136

– *I'm sorry, Ma.*

Pause

– *Ma. Don't you think he'll be so shite, like, when the baby comes? Like, just flapping and getting in the way.*

Sigh.

– *He wasn't in the room for either of you, so he'll get the shock of his life if he watches this one come out.*

– *Seriously, though, Ma. Are you okay?*

– *It's more embarrassing than anything. Just the humiliation of it. I can't bear the whole estate talking about it.*

– *Fuck them all, Ma. You'll get through this.*

– *I rang to find out how you are, anyway.*

– *I'm grand, never worry about me.*

– *How's the work experience?*

– *It's . . . It's okay. I've a week left. Most of them are nice.*

– *Right. good.*

– *And I'm still at the pub.*

– *Mmm-hmm. Good. Right, well, I'd better go now. I'm going to try and get an early night.*

– *Ma. I'm sorry. About that.*

Click.

CHAPTER 13

THE MODERN AGE

It is two weeks into September and I'm watching the back of Moses as he DJs at his decks, his right shoulder jumping to the beat. The windows are propped open, the air still sticky with heat even though it's nearly midnight. Moses' building backs on to another, bigger block, causing his living room window to be filled entirely with the doors and balconies of other people's homes.

The news has been relentless. Rolling footage of the falling towers. The streaks of movement as the planes hit the buildings. The plumes of black smoke in the sky which seemed so impossibly blue. The visible ripples of energy moving up the glass of the Towers before their collapse. The firefighters who lost their lives. The looks on their faces. Frightened eyes pulled wide through the grime. And the ash. So much ash, huge clouds of it chasing people through the streets. It doesn't feel real.

Neema isn't sleeping. She can't hide the exhaustion in her face, no matter how expertly she applies her make-up in the mornings. A few nights ago, she and I sat in the living room with the boys watching the BBC News as Tony Blair pledged to stand 'shoulder to shoulder' with the US in their war against terror. I find it hard to take him seriously knowing that ludicrous smile is hiding in his face, waiting to flash all those obnoxious white teeth at me.

Kesh leaned forwards on his armchair, scowling towards the TV screen. – War against brown people, more like. Fuck this. It's so dangerous for us already. It's going to get even worse.

And Neema said quietly, – I swear people are looking at me more than usual on the Tube.

I never thought I'd live in a country that has launched a war on another one. I never thought I'd feel like I want to travel with Neema to law school in the morning, to protect her from the force of the glares of her fellow passengers. Maybe, when we're not around, Kesh displays some sense of protectiveness around his sister. I hope he does.

Moses swooped in as sweet distraction yesterday when he texted: *Come over and see where I live*, after I'd texted him to see if he had arrived in London okay. He wanted me here. I've never been so happy to have a purpose. I arrived with two bottles of wine and my black dress on. Nails painted blood red by Neema. I walked from Old Street Tube station as slowly as I could, but I was still half an hour early.

He's been up and down from the decks all evening. While we were drinking the first bottle of wine, he jumped up to change the records, but by the time we had finished the second, he was up there for good, shouting snippets of conversation back at me over his shoulder. He's naturally good at DJing, and this time he's kept the two garage records in beat for a minute or two. He leans over the mixer, tweaking the equalisers, his whole body coming into the movement now, thrusting forwards and backwards.

– Ooooh, that was smooth, I shout at him.

He turns round and takes his headphones off his ears. – What did you say?

– I said, nice mix, I say and give him the thumbs-up.

He leaves his headphones on the table and flops down on the sofa beside me, casually swinging his arm over the back behind me. His hair has grown out, and he's had it twisted into short, stumpy dreadlocks. His T-shirt is faded pink, with a Rawkus Records logo on it.

– So where were you? On Tuesday. When it happened, I ask.

– I was unpacking here. It was all so surreal, he says, shaking his head, and then asks, – What about you?

– I was at Redstar. The boss sent us home after the second tower fell. I walked all the way to Fahy's.

Pat had hugged me when I arrived. I think she surprised herself. I hugged her back until she pulled away. *We'll be busy tonight Orla*, she'd said, and we were. The bar was packed and silent, as if people needed the comfort of other people to watch the horror unfold.

Moses' eyes are on mine. – Do you reckon you'll get more work at Redstar?

– Don't think they need anyone. I'm going to stay in touch with them, though.

Gwen took me to Quinn's for lunch on the Monday. She was direct as usual. – I should have warned you that he'd probably try it on. He's got a reputation.

– A reputation? I said. For what?

She looked at me, bemused, from under her pink fringe and said, – A reputation for shagging.

I tried to feel something about this revelation, but it was as if someone had pulled the plug on all my feelings. My head was an empty sink. I said, – I don't even know if I shagged him. I just woke up in his tent.

Gwen drank half her pint in one go, lit a cigarette for her and me and said, – This is none of my business, so tell me to fuck off if you like, but are you on the pill?

I nodded and she sucked on her cigarette, surveying me through narrowed eyes.

– Well, if I were you, I'd just forget it. Everyone else will in a day or two.

She was right. When we came back to work on Wednesday, all anyone was talking about was the attack on the Twin Towers. Andy walked round with a smirk on his face all week, but never caught my eye, not once. I wanted to squish his little rodent face under my foot. Last week, I had a plan to ask the boss, Alistair, for coffee, to see if he would listen to my demos. Then I saw Andy in his office with him on Friday morning. Not now. No way.

Moses' hand is tapping the back of the sofa to the beat. His eyes are planted on me. – Were you into the job? he asks.

I wonder if Alistair will tell Damian about me and Andy, over a pint. Will they be laughing at the Irish girl, sending out demos and putting herself about?

– It's fun to have to listen to music all day for a job. Like, I could get used to that.

He nods.

– But I'd rather be the one making it, I say. I quickly follow up my answer with a question of my own. – Hey, have you set up FruityLoops yet?

He looks out the window now as he talks.

– Nah, not yet. But me and Carlos have got a DJ gig together in a bar in Shoreditch. You should come.

– Yeah, I'll come to that.

I love Moses' flatmate for not being here tonight. *Thank you, Carlos.* I move closer to Moses on the sofa.

– So, I say. – I was thinking we could make a four-four beat, but, like, skippy and steppy, like two-step, and I could write to it. Kind of like Moloko, but more dancefloor.

He grins and says, – I have that first Moloko album on vinyl next door. Come.

He stands up and pulls me up by the hand, leading me

out the door and across the corridor into his bedroom. He switches on a light switch inside the door, and the room is flooded in soft red light. *Jesus Christ. Anna would have a field day.*

– Moses, do you live in a brothel? I say, laughing.

– Carlos only had red light bulbs for some reason, so I just borrowed one – thought it was better than nothing. I kinda like it now though.

In the crimson light of his room, we lock eyes. *My heart.* He goes to a stack of records in the corner and starts to sort through them. I walk around the room, brushing my fingers over the posters and club flyers tacked to the walls. Over the head of his bed is a poster of Nina Simone, eyes closed in anguish as she sings at a piano. Another one, of Biggie and his cane, is opposite her, Fabio and Grooverider beside him. Moses' trainer collection is piled up in a wall of shoe boxes at the end of his bed.

He pulls out the Moloko album.

– My twelves are out there, and my albums are in here, he says as he slides the vinyl out of the sleeve and places it on his turntable beside the records. Róisín Murphy's voice purrs from the speaker, all playful and suggestive, *la la la la . . .*

Moses stands up and walks over to me, rubbing his eye so I can't see his face. I step towards him, so that when he stops rubbing and opens his eyes, I'm right there.

– Hello, I hear him say before putting his lips on mine. I kiss him back, afraid to pull away as he slowly introduces his tongue to mine and I worry how my mouth must taste, but I bat that anxiety away as this is going well, really well now.

His hands are on my face, and I pull him towards me by the belt loops of his jeans so our hips are touching. I slide my hands up the back of his T-shirt, and slowly and gently push him backwards in the direction of his bed until he is sitting on the side of it. I stand over him and I reach down to pull his T-shirt up over his head. It's like his skin is clingfilm over his skeleton. There's not an ounce of flesh. You could drink out of the trough between his collarbone and his neck.

Róisín tells us about her dreams over a squelching bassline as Moses pulls me down on to the bed. He is all ribs and elbows, jutting bones. He kisses me like he is trying to gobble me up, trying to consume me. I try to find some rhythm in it, but I can't, so I pull away and nuzzle his neck. His hands squeeze my breasts roughly, to the point that it's painful, so I move my hands down his body to between his legs, then shift my hips and try to coax him inside of me. A new song sounds from the record player, Róisín singing soft staccato words about day and night. As he moves on top of me, I squeeze my eyes shut.

Afterwards, he falls asleep fast. I can feel the beginnings of an ache creeping into the front of my head. I want to brush my teeth. I want to close the curtains to block out the lights from the flats across the way. But I lie still, under the dead weight of his arm across my stomach, until sleep swallows me up.

In the morning, when he starts to stir, I turn over in the bed so he has time to remember I'm there. He gets out of bed quickly, picks up some clothes from the floor and leaves the room. I hear the toilet flush and then the slow, gathering surge of the kettle from the kitchen. The slam of a cupboard door jolts me into movement. When I walk into the kitchen, he is standing over the sink, wearing tracksuit bottoms and a vest, looking out the window.

– Morning, I say and he turns, eyebrows raised, awkward smile, taking me in. I'm wearing his T-shirt from last night. I don't like how his smile makes me feel, so I walk towards the bony plate of his chest and I hug him, resting my head on his shoulder. He smells of dried sweat and smoke.

– Want a cup of coffee? he says.

I nod into his chest, waiting for him to put his arms around me.

– How are you feeling? he asks, at the same time as he tries to manoeuvre himself towards the kettle, but I don't loosen my grip.

– Hungover, I say into his neck. I walk towards the bony plate of his chest and I hug him, resting my head on his shoulder.

He has stopped trying to move, but I can sense the tension in his body. I pull away and he's off immediately, opening cupboards.

– I've got to go and see a promoter this morning. About a potential DJ gig, he says.

– Do you need some company?

– Nah, I'm good thanks. You've probably got shit to do.

When Moses goes off for his shower, I climb back into his bed to drink my coffee, and I'm still there when he comes into the room with a towel round his waist. He dresses in a hurry.

– Shall we meet soon? I suggest, pulling myself up to sit cross-legged on the mattress with my back against the wall.

– Sure, yeah. I'll let you know about the gig, he says, but he's pulling his hoodie over his head when he says it, so I can't get a sense of any enthusiasm. He grabs a canvas bag from the floor and pulls it over his shoulder, turning to me just before he leaves the room.

– Laters.

– Okay. Bye, I reply.

I let myself out.

CHAPTER 14

I DO NOT WANT WHAT I HAVEN'T GOT

It's quiet in the bar this morning. Gerry was first in, muttering as he climbed up on to his stool. – Don't know why I come back here.

– You say that every time, Gerry, I told him.

Now, Mayo Dave is here beside him, red raised-up skin on his face, eyes in shadow under his baseball cap. Pat has been hovering about the place, muttering to herself, writing lists, disappearing upstairs. Now she is taking out all the glasses and wiping the shelves with Dettol.

I go to the CD stack and put a Sinéad O'Connor album on the stereo.

I flick it on to track two. Sinéad sings over a crisp, slow breakbeat, a bass groove underneath driving the song along. The music reflects the passion in her voice, all dark and urgent and raw. The overall sound is undeniably Irish, but modern, outward looking.

– Orla, what are you after putting on? Gerry asks.

– It's Sinéad O'Connor, Gerry.

He's shaking his head in exasperation, looking beside him at Mayo Dave for back-up. Dave dutifully shakes his head in disapproval.

– It's Irish music, lads. Just not *your* type of Irish music

The horses are back on the television, and it's a relief. For a few days after the planes hit the Twin Towers, the BBC showed rolling news coverage. I still see parts of it in my head; the tsunami of smoke and ash, the way it moved and mutated, spitting out debris, like some malevolent force from a blockbuster movie. One man in particular is branded onto my brain. He was short and round, stumbling down the road afterwards, wearing a shirt and tie and a pair of glasses, and he was completely white, as if someone had rolled him around in powder paint.

There's a bucket on the bar, a photo taped to it, showing a smiling man in his firefighting uniform, helmet under his arm. Underneath, in Pat's careful handwriting, a note is asking for coins to help support the bereaved family of this man in New York, her first cousin whom she'd never met.

I perch back on my stool, where my notebook sits open on the counter, half a song written and scribbled out already. Moses said he'd let me know where he's DJing this weekend, but he hasn't been in touch yet. Neema scolded me last night. *You have to keep your cool*, she'd said, before turning to face the wall, and I lay there wide awake for hours, thinking of all the ways in which I didn't want to keep my cool. Neema goes to bed earlier and earlier these days, but she still can't sleep properly. When I'm not working, I go to bed at the same time as her, for moral support.

– I'll have another one there, Orla.

I pour Gerry his third of the day. A tall, thin man comes in, holding a funny-looking guitar case.

– Pint of Guinness, he says, nodding at the Guinness tap, and then over to Gerry. They know each other.

– Well, Ciarán, are you playing tonight? asks Gerry.

Ciarán nods. – Later on.

– What is it you play? I say, squinting at the instrument case.

– Banjo, Gerry pipes up, before the man can open his mouth.

– Up and down the pubs of the High Road, he tells me.

– Very good. Did you teach yourself? I ask, taking his money. I think of my da's arms around me from behind, his right hand on top of mine as I tried to strum the guitar in rhythm.

Ciarán says, – I'd an uncle who used to play in the bars here.

– You grew up here?

He licks the Guinness top off his lips, nods and adds, – Kilburn born and bred.

– I don't think I've met anyone born in Kilburn, I say, looking at Gerry.

– Most of us are blow-ins, he says.

– You've spent your whole life here? I say, looking back at Ciarán, who shrugs, picks up his case, and speaks as he turns away.

– Somebody has to live here.

– I'll drink to that, Gerry says, tipping his pint in Ciarán's direction as he heads back to his seat.

Now I'm laughing. Behind me, Pat pulls herself up to standing.

Did you hear that, Pat? I say to her. – 'Somebody has to live here,' he said. What a sell.

Just then, the door to the upstairs flat opens and a large hand clutches on to the edge of it, followed by a big thick arm wrapped in a fisherman's jumper. Pat's other half, James, uses the door for heft as he manoeuvres himself into the space. I haven't seen him in a while. He stops and looks around the room, breathing heavily and blinking. He looks confused. He stares at Pat, mouth gaping open, as she walks around the bar, lifts up the hatch, scurries over to him and ushers him out the door.

I've never heard James say a word. Not even once. Do they talk up there, I wonder, or does it all just come from Pat?

Ciarán folds his coat and places it on the seat, gently leaning his banjo case against it before sitting down. The clock tick-tocks above our heads. Gerry has the paper open at the sports section. Mayo Dave rolls a cigarette. I perch on the stool as Sinéad O'Connor sings over an acoustic guitar about Margaret Thatcher on TV.

150

THE MESS WE'RE IN

Somebody has to live here.

When Pat comes back in under the hatch, the glasswasher beeps as if to greet her. She opens it and allows the steam to gush out.

– Is James alright? I ask.

She answers quickly, – He's the same as he ever is.

– And what exactly is it with him? You know, that has him needing your help?

She says it like I should know it. – He's got dementia.

– That must be hard.

– It's life.

I persist. – Pat, can you manage it? I mean, I know he's your husband, but at some point, might you have to . . .

– My *husband?* Pat is laughing now. She's closed her eyes and put her hands flat on the counter on either side of her, to steady herself. Her laugh is like her voice, staccato, sharp. When she's finished she looks back up at me and says, – James is my brother, Orla. She chuckles to herself.

– So, you're not married?

– Never married, she says, her face shining. Gleeful. That's what she is. She looks younger when she smiles. I pour a pint and a glass of wine for a worried-looking man, who brings the glasses back to a girl in the corner.

– Looks like a break-up to me, Pat says, glancing over at the couple.

– Is there a reason you never married? I ask her.

She's looking at me in that intense way she has, as if she's trying to figure me out. – I wanted to live a free woman, Orla.

– Free from what?

Now she's shaking her head at me. – Free from being used like a cow, to churn out babies. Free from the fear of God. The moral suffocation. Getting married in Ireland is a trap. Or it was when I lived there.

I blink at her as she talks, trying to imagine a young Pat on the boat to England, all steely and determined, sailing into her freedom.

– But couldn't you get married in England? I ask. It's not like that here.

– Twenty-seven years I've been running this pub, and I never needed a husband to help me.

– I know you didn't *need* to get married, but didn't you want to?

– Never met the right person.

She looks over my shoulder towards the windows at the back of the bar for a second, and then she's moving again, around the bar, towards the hatch, as she talks. – My brother looked after me when I got here, and I'll look after him until I'm not able to anymore. And I'm still able, thank you very much.

– You're a good woman, Pat, Gerry says, and Dave nods in acquiescence, clamping his roll-up between his lips, holding a flame to it and sucking, then exhaling a thick plume of smoke above our heads.

CHAPTER 15

DON'T PANIC

The first thing I see when I open my eyes is Neema kneeling on the floor. I watch her in silence as she applies layer after layer of make-up and slowly brushes through her lashes with mascara. In the small, oval-shaped mirror she has propped against the back of the chair, her mouth is downturned, her eyes heavy.

– How did you sleep? I mumble, and her forehead crumples.

– Another bad one.

– Are you going to be okay for law school today?

– I'm going to have to be, she says grimly.

– Any tests? I say, propping myself up on my elbows.

– No. But it's commercial law. My least favourite. She speaks into the mirror before spraying her neck with perfume, pulling herself up to standing, sighing and saying, – Orla. The room. Please can you tidy it? It's actually unhygienic now.

– Yeah, I'll do it today, I promise. I sit upright in my bed, rubbing my eyes and then looking up at her. She's wearing the most exhausted and pissed-off expression.

– Jesus, it's not that bad, Neema, I say to her.

She's straight back. – It is to me, especially when you're just sitting around the house all day, and you can't even take ten minutes to do it.

– Wow, Neema, do you want to sound any more like my ma? It'll be done by the time you get home.

– Good, Neema snaps and walks out, the bedroom door banging behind her. I try and go back to sleep after she leaves, but I can't. Instead, I take a long shower, get dressed, stomp downstairs, pour myself a bowl of cereal and go to the living room, where Kesh is sprawled across an armchair, shirtless, with a cup of coffee on the carpet next to him and a notebook in his hand. As I enter, he hurriedly scribbles some words down in his pad.

– Lyrics? I say, as I flop down on the sofa, my weight expelling an earthy whiff of hash from the cushions.

– No, a letter for the fans, he says, brow furrowed over his notebook. – A response to *that*, he adds, gesturing towards the table, where a copy of *NME* sits open.

– Oh, shit! When did this come out? I say.

– This morning.

He must have gone to the shop first thing. He still hasn't looked at me. I pick up the magazine.

Shiva's photo takes up the top half of the page, blurred

brickwork in the background. Kesh in the foreground, sombre and staring into the lens, then Richie half-tucked behind him, and Frank furthest away, staring at the pavement. The article is underneath.

Shiva me timbers!
Ben Asher-Smith voyages to Rock on the Farm to go hunting for songs with the aspiring Manc-rockers.

'We're going to smash up the scene,' froths Shiva lead singer Kesh Tiwari. 'There needs to be an explosion every now and again. A Big Bang. That's where we come in.'

Given that the band are named after the Hindu God that destroys the universe in order to recreate it, Tiwari's manifesto is at least consistent. But, as he practically trips over his own self-belief to convince NME of Shiva's cataclysmic import, are they actually the band to ignite this explosion?

I put down the bowl of cereal, feeling the dread rise in me as I read on.

Shiva take themselves seriously. Very bloody seriously. And as the sun begins to set at Rock on the Farm, the band get ready to unleash their furrow-browed detonation on an unsuspecting public. The conditions are perfect. Booze and festival sweeties are almost certainly kicking in; the crowd are ready. As Kesh reveals his possessed, twitchy, Thom-Yorke-impersonating stage presence, the crowd – and there is a small and determined hardcore following here – wait for any semblance of a song. And they continue to wait. Instead, they are assaulted by Kesh's live singing voice; a glass-shattering, fox-mating, Jeff-Buckley-piss-taking falsetto, that obliterates any chance of a song showing itself, even if there was one. But there are no real hooks, no big choruses to swing off . . . nothing.

Earlier in the day, in their dilapidated van, bassist Frank Harewood hoists a pudgy finger to a picture of Fran Healy, face beaming out from the cover of our very recent, very 'umble NME interview. 'All he wants to do is make his fans happy? What a fucking pillock.'

Drummer Richie Havers, sensing one of the day's few semi-exciting exchanges, chimes in bluntly, 'What's the point in being in a band if you don't want to be singing "Day-o" in Wembley Stadium?'

Perhaps they should both have a word with their singer. No stranger to the uptight and self-conscious, with a very healthy side order of self-importance, could Shiva's frontman ever connect in the way Mercury, or even Healy, has?

To smash up a scene, you need songs. There's only so long a band can trade on arrogance alone.

– Oh, my God, I say quietly. I daren't look at Kesh. But I sense the rage steaming off him on the armchair. Frank walks in with a cup of coffee in his hand. He sees the look on my face and the *NME* in my hand, and widens his eyes with a grimace.

– Oh, you've seen it. Ben was a Judas, he says.

– I just can't believe someone can be that . . . cruel, I say and flop back on the sofa, remembering Ben pushing his glasses up his nose. – He seemed so harmless.

I steal a glance at Kesh, who is gripping his pen tightly as he scrawls on the page.

Richie walks in, scratching his belly. Seeing the look on my face, he asks, – What's happened?

– They shafted us, Frank replies, pointing to the magazine in my hand.

– What the fuck? Richie says, and I hand it over. I try not to watch him as he reads it, but I can't keep my eyes off his face. His forehead crumples as his mouth murmurs the words. A shake of his head, disbelieving. When he finishes the article, he throws the magazine on the table, then walks out. We sit in silence, listening to thump of his feet on the stairs and the slam of his bedroom door.

Kesh closes his eyes and rests his head on the back of the chair. His jaw twitches.

Frank speaks into the silence. – What are you telling them? The fans?

Kesh talks to the ceiling. – I'm telling them that this prick has got it in for me. And that we've made our best-ever album, and we're proud of it. Gwen will get it posted out to the whole fanbase today. We're going to be fine.

Then he swings his legs on to the floor, squashes the butt of his joint into an overflowing ashtray on the coffee table and adds, – We have to go. We're already late.

He stands up and walks out of the room. Frank stays put, slouched into the sofa. We sit in silence for a second, and then we hear a dull, thumping sound coming from the gear room. We cock our heads at each other and try and decipher what it is.

– I think Kesh is kicking the wall, Frank says, and then he sighs. – Today's going to be fun.

– What are you doing?

– Promo. We're going to XFM and to Redstar to do interviews.

– Say hello to them for me, will you? Gwen and Emma?

He nods and then says, – I wouldn't want to be this Ben guy when Gwen gets to him.

– Are you okay? I ask.

He looks at the floor, nods and then mumbles, – Just don't want my mum and dad to see it.

I nod. I've never met Frank's mum and dad, but they call every Sunday at six. I hear Frank being passed from one to the other, telling them dutifully about the band's movements and Damian's plans for them. Assuring his mum that he has food and his dad that he has enough money.

As he stands up, I put my cereal bowl down and stand up too. I have an impulse to give him a hug. I rush over to him and wrap my arms around his shoulders. His hair smells of weed.

– Don't be sad, Frank. It's just one dickhead's opinion, I say down into his hair, and I wait until he nods before I pull away. He walks out the door.

They leave around eleven, all three of them grumbling and grunting at each other, with Kesh slamming the door so hard the whole house shakes. I spend ten minutes clearing the floor of my side of the bedroom, pushing my books and CDs under my bed. I even try and make my duvet like Neema's, all smooth and flat.

Sitting around all day and you can't even tidy your bedroom. She let it all out this morning, alright. She'll be livid at this review. Incensed. Her logical mind won't be able to compute that someone can do that. She'll be looking to find a way to sue *NME* – her and her new friend at law school. Amanda. Amanda with the French plait. I met her last week for dinner, at Neema's request, took the Tube all the way down to London Bridge, and we walked along the river for a bit before going to get pizza.

– So, what do you do, Orla? Amanda had asked.

– I work in a pub, I'd said, then concentrated on feeding them questions about their lecturers and the other people on the course. Amanda and Neema had lots to talk about.

How they've both got a training contract for the same firm. How Amanda's dad is an architect.

– I'm that person that geeked out about town planning in school, she tittered and flashed her eyes at me knowingly through the thick lenses of her glasses.

– Why do you dress like you're going to the office when you're just going to lectures? I asked.

Amanda went very serious. – You have to channel your professionalism. Everyone wears smart clothes.

Amanda wants to be a partner in a law firm. She said it was ludicrous how few females are actually partners. How *amazing* it was that she and Neema would be working at the same firm.

– Neema and I are going to change the game, she said, nudging Neema while looking at me, all smug.

Amanda. Imagine being called Amanda. Imagine doing your hair in a French plait every morning before you leave the house.

I try and slam the door as hard as Kesh did on my way out. At the post office, I choose three padded brown envelopes and write the addresses on them that I have saved from my visit to the library a few days ago. Three different record labels. Three cassette-tape copies of my demo. A note going in each one:

For the attention of A&R. My name is Orla Quinn. I am 22 years old and from Dublin. I'm a songwriter, a singer and a music producer. Here is my demo. I sang and produced all of it. I love your label and would love the opportunity to meet someone to talk about my music.

I walk for a while, up past Queens Park and through the long residential streets until I see a bus approaching. I jump on it and let it carry me in a horizontal line, past Kensal Green Cemetery and the wide beginnings of Ladbroke Grove, over the canal to Paddington station, where I jump on another bus to Hampstead. I sit at the front deliberately so I have full views of the approaching roads and I can cross-reference them with my *London A–Z* map book.

At the top of Parliament Hill I plonk myself down on an empty bench, unzip my coat and let my heart slow down after the uphill march. I keep going back to the hills. Sitting here, looking out, London seems endless, edgeless. There's something about being able to take London in visually that grounds me. From this vantage point, I can see myself in it. The sky is vast, electric blue, brushed with thin lines of clouds that fit together like vertebrae. The city glistens underneath it. I hold up my hand to shade my eyes and squint out at the sprawl. I can see the rickety BT Tower, the NatWest Tower, the shining glass of the buildings further in the distance, in the City. I can't see the river from here, but I love looking at it on the map, with its *Looney Tunes* curves, as if a child has scribbled it into existence.

I take out my notebook. I've written a new song. I start to sing the words softly to myself. My voice has got a huskiness to it. When I sing louder, it smooths itself out, but today on this bench, it's a weak, broken sort of huskiness.

My phone rings then, and I hurry to pull it out of my bag. – Hello?

– Hellooo, Orla!

– Gwen!

– How's it going, doll?

– Going good, thanks Gwen. Just in Hampstead Heath, actually—

– Listen, she says, bulldozing through my answer. I realise I wasn't supposed to elaborate. – I can't talk long, because I have your boys and they're just finishing up lunch. I was at The Castle studios in Angel this morning. I know their receptionist, Sofia, and she was saying she has to leave to go back to Spain, and they don't have someone to replace her. I just rang Biff, the guy who runs the studio, and offered you for the position.

– You did?

– I did, she says. – He wants to speak to you. Tomorrow, if possible.

– Wow. Okay. I went to The Castle after Shiva's gig in Camden.

– Perfect, so you know where it is. I'm going to text you Biff's number now. Call him. He's a bit of a perv, so just give him a wide berth, but he's harmless really.

– Okay. Gwen, thanks. That was so nice of you.

– I got your back, girl.

I hear shouting in the background, a roar, as if the football is on and someone has scored a goal.

– Gwen, I saw the—

– Texting you his number now, byeeeeeee.

I stare at the phone in my hand. *A job in a studio. A proper paid job in a place where you make music.* I go to my contacts, and Da is the first one. I hover my finger over the button. Then I press 'M' and try to call Moses instead. It rings out. I don't leave a message.

A bird calls out from a copse of trees nearby, its tone sharp and high-pitched, like the creak of a door. The trees are in full autumn performance, gleaming red, amber, gold, leaves shaking and shuffling in the breeze, catching the light as they fall to settle on the grass below. I scan the branches for the bird. It's hidden by leaves at first, but then it squawks again and I spy it as it hops out on to a bare branch. It's a bright green thing, tropical-looking.

I wonder what kind of song Moses and I could make at The Castle studios featuring the strange, abrasive call of this green bird. My da used to sing 'Blackbird' in the car. I loved that song, the lightness of it, and how the bird noises appeared through the music towards the end. I can still see the view of his head and shoulders from the back seat when we used to drive to Granny May's. I can see it as clearly as if I was there now, Anna beside me and Ma in the passenger seat, all of us quiet and him humming the melody as he leaned forward over the steering wheel. Always leading the charge with a song, like music was the default place he would go. He always surprised me with the tenderness of his voice.

CHAPTER 16

WHERE'S YOUR HEAD AT?

Saturday night in Shoreditch. I am standing in the shadows at the Electric Bar, watching Moses and his friend Carlos as they DJ to a half-full dancefloor. They are deep in concentration, leaning over each other to fiddle with the equalisers, stealing glances at the floor to sense-check the crowd's reactions.

When I arrived, Moses said, – Oh. I thought you'd bring Neema.

– She's busy, I lied.

I didn't ask her because I thought he wanted me here by myself. I imagined that he would come and talk to me now and again during his set, and let Carlos take over, but half an hour has gone by, and he hasn't left the booth. I see him turn to kneel down and flick through his vinyl, so I lean my head in and shout, – How are you doing?

When he looks up I see the tightness of his expression.

– Good, yeah, just got to hold the floor. Think it's filling up though, isn't it?

I look out over the crowd. – Well, it's definitely not getting any emptier, I say. When I look back at him, he's back flicking through his vinyl again, head bowed over the box.

I text Neema: *Moses is DJing. For three hours. I'm stood here on my own like a mug. I wish you were here.*

I could be . . . she texts back, and I start to type a reply as another message beeps through: *But I just smoked a big one and I can't move xx*

I picture her curled up on the sofa with her spliff tin on her lap, staring at the TV. We've been watching the news a lot. George Bush promised a 'sustained and relentless' campaign of airstrikes against the Taliban in Afghanistan. I imagine cruise missiles and B-52 bombers, hundreds of them, flying over the Atlantic like migrating birds. Neema's sleeping is still bad. I see the effects of it seeping into her face in the evenings. It doesn't help that ever since the *NME* review, Kesh has been doing loads of gear and sitting up all night playing guitar. Last night, Neema ran downstairs to ask him to stop playing. I don't know what was said, but she ended up screaming at him and he slammed the door in her face.

At the bar, I unwrap the half tablet of E I stashed in my wallet for emergencies and wash it down with my vodka and Diet Coke. The music is really good, I'll give them that. House and garage and broken beat: 'that London sound', Moses calls it, so casually unifying all the patterns and codes

165

of music that encompass an entire city and its residents, diaspora from all over the world, the sum of all their parts. As if I should know. Surely it is impossible to put a full stop on 'that London sound'. Maybe it becomes apparent when you've lived here long enough.

I float about the crowd, enjoying the sensation of being led by Moses' music choices, always within eyeline of the booth so that Moses can see me. At 1am, when the bar shuts, Moses and Carlos finish their set with Outkast's 'Ms Jackson', and the whole room shouts the words of the chorus together in drunken dissonance. I'm drunk too, from the four – or was it five? – vodka and Diet Cokes I drank during the set, and I am smiling, grinning from ear to ear. I catch eyes with Moses, who is grinning back at me, and I forgive him then.

The security guard starts shooing us in the direction of the door, and I walk over to the booth. Moses and Carlos fist-bump each other and I say, – Well done, you two.

– Thanks Orla, they both say in unison, and I can see they really mean it.

I wait while they carefully pack up their vinyl and have their words with the bar manager, who slaps an envelope into Moses' hand as he shakes it.

– Coming back to ours? says Carlos, beaming.

– Sure, yeah, why not? I say.

We squeeze on to a night bus to travel the two miles down Kingsland Road, and we laugh at the loud, drunken singing coming from the girls at the front. Just as an argument starts between another woman and one of the singing girls, Moses and Carlos's block looms out of the darkness ahead and we stumble off the bus.

In their flat, I light a cigarette while Carlos puts a record on.

Outkast – *Stankonia.*

Moses kicks back on the sofa and rolls a joint.

– Come and dance with me, Orla, says Carlos, so I do. Carlos has the broad-shoulders of a security guard and the loose hips of a salsa dancer. We dance in our socks on the carpet, his hips wiggling seductively, and I'm laughing now, which makes him wiggle even more.

– What, Orla? You no like my dancing?

– I *love* your dancing, Carlos. I wish I could move my hips like you.

– Try. Just do this. He puts his hands softly on his hips and rotates them gently one way and then the other.

I try to do the same, but I'm stiff and shy in front of Moses. I laugh. – I can't do it. I was brought up on Irish dancing, where you have to be stiff as an ironing board.

Moses' eyes are on us, but he's distant.

– Come and dance, Moses, I say. I walk over to him and grab his hands to pull him up, but he pulls them away.

– Nah. I'm good here, he says.

– Well, give us a puff of that at least, I say, and he hands me his joint. I plonk down beside him and beam at him. – Are you happy with how it went?

– Yeah, I'm chuffed. Thanks for coming, he says.

– Oh, here, look what I've done, I say, and rummage in my handbag for my notebook. I open it and hand it to him.

– What's this?

– It's a list of songs to use as references for when we start to make our music. Just stuff I'm inspired by, you know: a bassline here, a hi-hat there, the FX on her voice on that one, I say pointing to a song on the list.

I watch him as his eyes flit over my writing.

– What do you think? I ask.

– Nice, he says and rewards me with a brief blast of eye contact, but no teeth.

I smoke the joint and Carlos salsas in circles with his back to us, rapping along to Outkast. Moses stands, dusts the loose tobacco off his T-shirt, stretches his arms up over his head, and yawns loudly. – I'm knackered. He stands up and walks to the sink, pouring himself a glass of water. – Think I'm going to hit the sack.

I watch him from the sofa, waiting for the glance, the sign, the gesture that says, *Come with me*, but now he is walking to the door, raising his glass in the air and saying, – Night, you nutters.

And now the door is closed.

I wait the length of time it takes for Carlos to talk me through the origins of Italo-disco and for us to drink a whole bottle of warm red wine. Then I visit the bathroom, and afterwards

I stop outside Moses' bedroom, press my head against the door, but there's nothing, no sound. I go back to the living room to a red-eyed Carlos sprawled on the sofa. I curl up in the armchair and pretend to fall asleep, and at around four in the morning, Carlos drops off, his T-shirt riding up to expose a hairy belly, his nose expelling long, violent snores.

I stand up, tiptoe out the door and slowly, as quietly as I can, push open the door of Moses' bedroom.

He's drawn the blind. As my eyes adjust to the darkness, the faces of his musical heroes emerge from the walls, ready to watch the action. I take care not to trip up on any records or shoes on the ground. He's curled up in the foetal position, the duvet rising and falling with his breathing. I pull off my trainers and socks and hesitate a second before pulling off my jeans as well. I take my bra off from under my top, and then quickly climb into bed beside him. If he notices I'm there, he doesn't show it. Apart from a slight disturbance in the rhythm of his breathing, he stays stock still. After a while, I fall into a fitful sleep.

I wake to movement from behind me in the bed. I'm lying on my side, facing the door, and Moses is turning around behind me and pushing himself up against me, his hands creeping up underneath my top. I turn around to try and kiss him. He briefly kisses me back and buries his face in my neck. We have sex that way, with him behind me and me reaching back for him with my hands and my legs and my face. Afterwards, he groans and scratches his chest.

– Just going to the toilet, I say. I pull up my underwear and run out the door to the bathroom. I can taste the red wine in my mouth still. No wonder he didn't want to kiss me. I wash my mouth out and then pick the less gross-looking toothbrush and brush my teeth with it. Then I run some toilet roll under the tap and rub it around my eyes. I pull my hair off my face, and then let it loose again. I pull the skin of my cheeks tightly back with the palms of my hands.

Stop it, Orla.

When I get back to his room, he's pulling on his jeans. I jump back into his bed and say, – Where are you going?

– I'm up now, he says. – I'm not a lie-in type of person.

– Does that mean I have to get up too? I joke.

– You can do what you like. He laughs, but then his face goes serious and he looks at me expectantly. – But I do have shit to do this morning, so . . .

– *Sister Orla!*

– *Hi.*

– *Oh, you sound miserable.*

– *I am.*

– *Has something worse happened than your own father starting a family with someone else?*

– *Moses slept with me and now he's stopped calling me.*

– *Jeeeeeesus, men. Well, I hope you've drowned yourself in drink and wallowed in the misery of it all.*

– *Been doing my best.*

– *Is Neema looking after you?*

– *She's busy with law school. But she's still around, yes.*

– *Any luck with the music stuff?*

– *Oh, yeah, I got a job. As a receptionist in a music studio.*

– *Good to see you're following in your mother's footsteps.*

– *Fuck off, Anna. It's an in.*

– *An in?*

– *Yes, like a way in. You have to have a way in.*

– *And does it pay well?*

– *No, it pays shite, but don't tell Mam. I'll stay working at Fahy's.*

– *And have you spoken to Johnny about this new job?*

– *Johnny?*

– *Our Father, who art in Stillorgan.*

– *Since when do you call him Johnny?*

– *Since he put his seed in Flatface's cervix.*

– *Jesus, Anna.*

– *Well, have you?*

– *No I haven't spoken to him since he told me his news, and I don't intend to either. I know what he'd say, anyway.*

– *What?*

– *He'd say, 'Give yourself a deadline. At the job. Give it six months or a year to get the leg-up you need.'*

– *He would, of course. And what did Mam say?*

– *She was on her exercise bike. She said something like, 'Live your life, Orla. You only get one.'*

– *Jesus, she's fucking addicted to that bike.*

– *It's better than being hammered all the time, no?*

– *Yeah, and the house is fucking chaos with the painters in. Listen. Orla. It's a sign. New job. New era. New man!*

– *I'm sick to death of men. I have to go, Anna.*

– *Carpe Diem. That's all I'm saying. It means . . .*

– *I know what it means. Goodbye.*

CHAPTER 17

LET ME BLOW YA MIND

Of all the places in London, I have chosen to work in caves: places where natural light is an inconvenience, places that do everything they can to block out the outside world. First it was Fahy's, now it's The Castle Recording Studio Complex. The Castle is dusty. It smells of disinfectant and cigarettes. The windows are all at the front, which means the communal areas have minimal light. It's dark all day long. It suits my mood.

This first week, I've been working alongside Sofia, the receptionist who is leaving. She chews gum relentlessly and rolls her eyes like it's a sport. She has crooked teeth and the dirtiest cackle of a laugh. The reception desk is on the first-floor landing. My job is to receive the visitors and show them to their studios, to oversee the bookings schedule, take new bookings and send out charge sheets to make sure we're paid. I am also in charge of the cleaner's schedule, making sure the studios are all cleaned between reservations, and that the tea area, the toilets and the drinks machines are stocked up.

– Don't feel like you have to stick around if someone is staying late, Sofia tells me. – But if you do leave, you have to make sure that someone else is here to lock up, or you have to ask Biff, who is normally hanging around and can nip in and kick people out. Everyone listens to him.

I feel anxious about the responsibility of this place. Of all these rooms with all this equipment. And even more anxious at the idea of having to call Biff late at night.

– Olive. You made it, he said as he arrived at the reception desk on my first day. Sofia and I stared at each other, neither of us knowing what to say.

– What's the problem? Biff said then, and I had to come out and say it.

– It's Orla. Nice to meet you in person.

I stuck out my hand to his, and my cheeks burned as the realisation dawned that he wasn't going to shake it. He just stood there and smirked at me.

– Orla, he said. First thing you need to learn is that a Kiwi never admits he's wrong, okay?

– Okay, I said, with what I hoped looked like a good-natured smile.

– You said you were Irish, right? he said then, looking me up and down.

– Yes. I'm from Dublin.

– Well, Sofia, whatever you do, don't give her the key to

the bar. He showed us his laugh then, a strange ascending bark of a thing that ended abruptly as he turned away. He carried on talking with his back to us as he walked up the stairs to his office. – You girls gonna sort the full clean for Sunday lunchtime, right?

– Yes, Biff, I'm on it, chewed Sofia beside me.

– And don't forget we've got that guy coming to fix the computer in Studio Two today.

– Yep.

And that is Biff. His beard is more dirty white than grey. Black two-pence-piece sized circles sit in his ear lobes, pushing the skin around them into a thin stretch. He works from a room at the top of the building.

All day long, musicians traipse up and down the stairs, and they're all men. I study them as they appear mid-morning, rumpled and tired-looking, tattooed and smelling of unwashed bedsheets and roll-ups. Mostly we ask them what band they're in, and then point them in the direction of the studio they need. Sometimes, I show them where the toilets and the kitchen are, as if I'm an air hostess. And all day long, I hear short bursts of music escaping from the heavy soundproofed doors when they're opened, before they *thlump* shut again.

This morning, I met Max properly. Max is the main in-house engineer. He's a short, mousey guy from Essex with full lips and an enthusiastic, big-eyed way of talking that makes me feel like he's genuinely interested. He knows Shiva, having engineered part of their album.

– Great guys, he said. I love Frank.

And I agreed with him.

– You'll be seeing a lot of me, he said.

Sofia elbowed me as he left and said, – He's a sweetheart.

– Do you ever go into the studios? I asked.

Sofia shook her head. – If you start ringing and asking if they want drinks, they'll take the piss. We're not waitresses, we're receptionists.

She said this with real authority, and I nodded gravely in response, hoping it was enough.

– So, do call in, but only if you're bored – and always let them know that it's only because you're not busy.

I'm not busy this afternoon, so Sofia gives me permission to call up to Studio One and ask about refreshments. I hesitate in the antechamber and catch a glimpse of Max through the window of the inside door, leaning over a huge desk covered in knobs and faders, talking into a microphone at someone through the glass. My heart is thumping in my chest. *Don't fuck up Orla. This could lead to something.* I knock and Max turns and beckons me in.

– Hi. I wondered if anyone might want a cup of tea? We're, we're not busy so . . .

Sure thing, I do, says Max. – Milk and two sugars please. Orla, isn't it?

– It is.

– Si? he says to a guy sitting on the sofa right behind the door.

– That would be great, he says from under a beanie hat. – Just milk for me.

Max talks through the microphone at what I can now see is a huge set of drums with a man behind them, then turns back to me. – And a coffee for Daniel.

– Coming up, I say, and ten minutes later I am back, carrying the drinks on a tray. Daniel is drumming and the sound is huge in the soundproofed room. Max is pressing buttons and pushing a fader up and down. There is a computer to the right of him with a sound wave forming as the drums crash through the speakers. When the drumming stops, I realise I am standing, staring, holding the tray.

Max turns around and looks at me. – Thanks, Orla! he says.

– Oh. Yes. No trouble at all, I say, and nod at Si on my way out.

Back downstairs, I ask Sofia, – What programme does Max use, do you know? Like, for recording?

– Fucked if I know, babe. Ask him yourself.

Sofia declares the day is done at 7pm. Max and the boys are still in the studio. Sofia allows me to come with her to visit Studio One again.

– Guys, we're outta here. Max, you okay to lock up again?

– Yep. We're only going to be another hour or so, he says.

I'm squinting at his computer screen, trying to see what programme he's using, when he says, – It's called Pro Tools.

I retreat towards the door, mortified.

– Sit in if you want to watch, Max says. – That's cool isn't it, Si?

Si looks at me with heavy-lidded eyes. – Oh. Okay. Yeah. Cool.

Sofia heads off and as the soundproofed door closes, I sit down at the other end of the sofa from Si.

– Okay, says Max. – Let's work on that fill a few times. I'm running.

As Daniel starts to drum, Si moves up on the sofa and hands me a huge spliff. I don't want to smoke it, because I need to be able to focus on Max, but I take two short tokes and hand it back to him. It doesn't take long for the weed to infiltrate my head – I'm light-headed anyway, from having had no food since lunchtime. Daniel is doing retake after retake of the fill. I can't hear the song he's playing over, just the click-clock-click-clock of the click track that's there to keep all of the instruments in sync.

After three takes in a row, I see Daniel shake his head in frustration.

– Don't worry, man, we're going to get there, says Max, and I wonder if he feels as calm on the inside as he sounds on the outside.

Si hands me the spliff again, and I take one drag this time. As I hand it back, I feel very, very self-conscious, and I'm wondering if Daniel fucking up is something to do with me and my presence in the room. Have I put him off course? I turn to Si to seek reassurance. He has hung his head back on the sofa and his eyes are closed. I start to wonder if he has fallen asleep, but then his hand lifts the spliff toward his mouth.

Relax, Orla. Chill.

I sit back and take in the space. The room feels incredibly small, and the sound being so loud and compacted makes me feel as if I'm not really here, *maybe I'm in a dream*, so I try to stay in the room and I focus on Max's hands as they move around the desk, trying to figure out the puzzle of what he's doing. Daniel keeps stopping halfway through the recordings. He's getting tetchy in there. I see him leaning over to his talk-back.

– Why the fuck can't I do it today?

– Let's go on to something else and come back to it, Max says soothingly.

I turn to look at Si again and his eyes are open, staring at the ceiling now. I look up too, and as I do so, I have the sensation that the room is shrinking around us. I can feel the walls closing in. I open my eyes as widely as I can; I feel movement. Is it me? Am I moving? I force myself to look down at my hands, and realise that the movement is coming from the vibration of my phone in my bag. I feel around in my bag for what feels like an embarrassingly long time, and eventually pull out my phone to see a missed call from Da. I take a slow breath. A fog of nausea is creeping into the front of my head. I'm going to leave the room now. I just need to figure out what to say.

I wait for Daniel to start drumming again, and then I stand up and say under my breath, – Back in a minute.

I know Si won't have heard me, but he will have seen me telling him something, and that's enough. The door is heavy as a horse; it takes all my strength to push it open. In the antechamber, I hold myself steady against the cloth wall and force myself to open the next door. The stairs are hard. The nausea is overpowering now; I run down the last few steps into the bathroom and cup my hands under the cold tap, splashing my face over and over again, heaving in big lungfuls of air, but it doesn't work, and I reach the toilet just in time to vomit up the four cups of tea I've had since lunch, and then the lunch too. After I flush, the grated carrot from my falafel wrap remains floating on the oily surface of the water.

It's hard to hold my head upright, so I rest it sideways on the toilet seat. I wanted to tell Moses all about this. I wanted to tell him about Pro Tools. To tell him all about Biff and Sofia and Max and the boys in the band. He would have laughed at me having a whitey. I see his smile again, those impossibly straight teeth. His voice all buttery bass. I wanted to draw a line from his heart to mine, like PJ Harvey said. Keep us bound together, safe. *We should make music*, my arse.

The fucking prick.

My tears roll over the side of my nose and splash into the toilet below.

When I'm strong enough to pick myself off the floor, I

drag myself back to the sink and splash my face with cold water again. I blink at my reflection for a moment. My face is pale, almost translucent. I curl my fist into a ball and hold it up to the glass, then push it until the skin around my knuckles flowers white. Then I go back to my desk and scrawl a note on a piece of paper: *Max! Had to run, sorry.*

I'm glad of the dark outside. I'm glad of the new chill in the air, the fumes and the sirens and the taillights of the cars as they whizz by me on my way to the Tube. I take out my phone and hold my finger down on the number one to listen to the voicemail my da left. It's all false cheer and *Call when you're free*, as if it hasn't been six weeks since we last spoke. I press 'end' and speed up my pace, jogging the last stretch to Angel Tube station, and then it's down, down, down, my hair dancing in the headwind that blows out of the depths of the underground – down, down, deeper below ground.

CHAPTER 18

RIDE ON

The sun was setting as I walked from the station this evening to Fahy's, streaks of orangey pink lighting up the clouds from behind so that they glowed like molten lava. The extravagance of it hanging over the High Road felt nearly garish, like a pantomime backdrop. I didn't see one person look up.

– Orla, you're far away tonight, says Gerry, eyeing me up.

Mayo Dave holds up his glass in front of his face to show me it's empty and that he wants a new pint. Fahy's is quiet tonight, both in the quantity of walk-ins and the volume of conversation. Christy Moore sings live from The Point Depot on the CD player.

I hop off my stool and say, – Well excuse me, Gerry.

– Is it that Moses fella? Gerry asks.

– Him? No, he's just a friend, I lie, as I put Dave's pint of Harp down on the counter in front of him.

Gerry's at me again. – So, what's up with ye?

– Jesus, Gerry, am I not allowed to be quiet once in a while? I snap.

– Alright, no need to get tetchy. Just trying to make conversation.

I take Dave's money, check for any other people at the bar, and then plonk back down on my stool facing them. – My career prospects are depressing, I say, looking down at my feet.

After a brief silence, in which Christy stops singing and The Point Depot crowd bursts into applause, Gerry giggles. – 'Career prospects'. Would you listen to her.

– What's funny about that? I say.

– You're lucky to *have* career prospects.

– Oh, here we go, I say, rolling my eyes.

– When I came here, my career prospects were to make enough money to send home and still have enough for a jar at the end of the day, Gerry says. He talks like a tin whistle: big gusts of melodious words with the odd heave-in of breath, and then he's off again. – You had to cash your cheques in the bar, too. Feckers had you over the barrel with that. So, you'd drink your fill and pick up your cash at the end of the night, and by the time that was put in a postal order, you had fuck all left.

A slow blink of confirmation from Mayo Dave. Gerry's little hand is wrapped around his pint. His shoulders slump under his V-neck jumper.

– Were you a hard worker, Gerry? I ask.

He's deep in his memories now, staring into the middle distance. – I was good enough at the bricklaying.

– So, what happened when you got too old to do it? I say.

– Depending on who was in charge, a lot of the boys would just work until they dropped, he says.

Eamonn sticks his hand up from his perch under the telly. He's stopped coming up to the bar now he's realised I'll bring his pint to him. Pat doesn't approve, but I don't mind. I pour his Guinness and leave it to settle.

Gerry's still going. – 'Career prospects' he scoffs, before draining the remaining half of his pint and gesturing across at Mayo Dave with his head. – The best jobs were the wagon drivers, Gerry says.

Mayo Dave nods in agreement, looking right through me into his wagon-driving past. I swear you can feel like a ghost in this pub. A long silence follows. I bring some extra napkins to Eamonn, along with the pint of Guinness. He's been crying again.

When I'm back on my stool, I try out what I've been wanting to say, to see how it feels. – My da's having a baby with another woman.

The two of them stare at me, blinking. It's satisfying to render Gerry speechless, even for a second. He crosses one leg over the other and says, – Well, Dave's your expert there.

I look to Mayo Dave, who has raised his enormous white eyebrows half a centimetre, which means he's engaged in the conversation.

Gerry continues. – He has children to two different women. In the ensuing silence, he adds, – I wish I'd tried a few more.

– And what sort of relationship do you have with your ex? I ask Dave.

– Which one? says Mayo Dave as he shifts his hulking weight on his stool.

– The first one?

– She's dead, he says.

– Oh, Jesus, I'm sorry about that, I say to Dave, and look at Gerry as if to say, *Why did you lead me down this road?*

Gerry looks between us, his face all wound up with excitement.

– What about the second ex? I ask Dave.

– I wouldn't mind if she was dead, he says, and his shoulders move before his mouth, a slow chug, picking up speed, until they're pumping up and down, and now Gerry's are pumping too, in tandem with Dave's, Little and Large, in perfect harmony.

I watch them in silence as they wind down. Eventually, Gerry sighs and says, – Herself'll nag me all the way to hell, I tell you. I'll be dead, but at my wake, she'll still be in my ear, nagging me. I can't do anything right.

Mayo Dave takes an inch of his pint, smacks his lips and says, – You gave her four children.

– Oh, no. Even that's not right, because, apparently, some of them are like me, God help them.

Mayo Dave chuckles, and Gerry taps the nail of his forefinger against his empty glass to say he wants another one.

At the end of the night, Pat stands at the open drawer of the till, her mouth whispering numbered incantations as her hands sort through the day's takings. I've already mopped the toilets; now I'm sloshing soapy water on the brown tiles by the front door, while Christy Moore sings mournfully through the stereo speakers behind the bar.

– Come on now, Orla, time to go home, Pat says. When everyone's gone from the pub, Pat lets her tiredness take her over, her mouth sagging downwards into an upside-down U.

I nod and pull the mop bucket back to the cleaning cupboard.

Back at the bar, Pat peers over her glasses at the shift schedule. – Right, so, I'll need you back on Thursday night. And then Friday and Saturday.

– Okay, I say resignedly.

Pat looks up at me. – Is that a problem?

– No, Pat! I say, a little more irately than I mean to.

– Good. Is it that Moses fella that's bothering you?

– I *wish* he was bothering me. He's gone AWOL.

– Sounds like a piece of work to me, she says.

– I liked him, I say and blink quickly as the back of my eyes start to tickle.

– Look, if a man isn't treating you with respect, he's not

worth your time. He should be at your door, asking for the privilege of your company, Pat says.

I laugh at that.

– I mean it. Get home now, and get a good rest.

– I will, I say but I don't move. Instead, I watch her as she puts away her notebook with the shift schedule into the box under the till. – Pat, how do you stand it? I say then. – Being around this lot, I mean. I point at the barstools. – How do you do it, day in, day out?

She stares at me in that intense way she has, and then towards the front windows, and sighs before she speaks. – You know, when I came here first, I wanted to move out of the digs I was sharing with my brother, so I went hunting for digs of my own. Everywhere I saw was disgusting. She looks back at me and stresses, – *Filthy.* Eventually, after looking for weeks, I found a place on Walm Lane. The owner was an Indian fella. As soon as he heard my accent, he said, 'No way.' He didn't take Irish people as tenants. So, I asked him why. He was a nice enough man. A gentle man. He brought me in to a room in the house where there was a big hole in the wall at head height. His last tenant was Irish, he told me, and had punched right through the plaster.

– So Irish people had a reputation? I ask, not sure what she is getting at.

She frowns, and picks up the trays that were drying in the sink. Slotting them back into their place underneath the taps, she continues. – They came here as boys, Gerry and Dave, and the others like them, leaving all their families behind. It was a hard life. A lonely life.

– So, you feel sorry for them?

She shrugs. – I understand why they are the way they are, I suppose.

– Do you ever meet their families?

– Not unless they die.

I balk at that. – Do they die often?

– Oh, God, yes, she says, as she picks my coat off the hanger. – We've had a lot of wakes in this pub. That's normally when you meet the wives.

– Oh, well, it's good to have something to look forward to, I suppose, I joke, as she holds out my coat for me.

She follows me to the door. – Walk fast now. Be alert, she says as I step out into the darkness.

– Night, Pat.

She closes the door behind me, and then, click. Click. Click. Three consecutive closures. I feel her satisfaction in those actions, the relief in them. I wonder when Fahy's will get too much for her. When she will have to sell up and move on.

The coldness of the air feels hostile. I push my keys between my fingers and set off walking down Kilburn High Road, looking in every direction, keeping a constant eye out for stumbling drunks or fast-walking men. I pass The Eagle, which is shut up now too, just a dim light coming from the back, and then the market, everything covered and closed. The lights are green but there are no cars, so I run over the bottom of Brondesbury Road and start to relax as I turn the corner on to Mill Road. The moon is full, looming over the end of the street, as if to light my way home.

CHAPTER 19

GET YOUR FREAK ON

I am coming up on an MDMA bomb that Frank put in my hand an hour ago.

Shiva's album came out on Thursday, but they wanted to save the big house party for Friday so that all the people with normal jobs would be able to get really stuck in. The whole living room of 74 Mill Road is full of people. It's me DJing, and I'm delighted about it because Andy from Redstar is in the corner, and I'm safe avoiding him here behind the turntables. Anyway, he's taking a hash cookie from a tray that Richie is handing around, so it won't be long until he's tripping his balls off; then he won't be able to have a conversation even if he tried.

I invited Moses. He graced me with a reply: *Thanks for the invite, Orla, but I'm already out that night. Link up soon!*

It's been three weeks since I've seen him. Three weeks of him haunting my thoughts at every hour of the day. I'm glad of the distraction of tonight. I've never known 74 Mill Road to mobilise like we did preparing for this album launch party. Kesh and Richie were in the kitchen for hours, Kesh chopping up fruit to make rum punch, Richie chopping up a coal-sized lump of hash for hash cookies. Neema and I opened all the windows and vacuumed, and then draped fairy lights around the doorframes. Frank even bought a little strobe light to plug in at the decks.

I press play on AC/DC's 'Back In Black', and as the first chunky chords crunch through the speakers, every member of Shiva, all the Redstar Records lot and all of their friends stop talking, turn to look at me, and then simultaneously roar with approval.

Gwen has brought two girlfriends, Sal and another pretty, oval-faced girl with a brown bob who is mooning all over Kesh already. There's no sign of Amanda with the French plait. Frank is over in the corner, swigging from his beer bottle, chatting with one of the guys from Redstar.

– I'm here for all your DJing and drinking needs, Emma from Redstar said when she sidled up and pushed her coat under the trestle table an hour ago, and she's been here ever since, pouring me vodka Cokes and helping me DJ, but not in an annoying way, more just enthusing about the same things I do. Turning to me to sing *'Bombs over Baghdaaaad'* in between André 3000 and Big Boi's verses, and to mouth the words of PJ Harvey's 'Good Fortune' along with me. Those important things that need to be done.

– Neema! Emma shouts as Neema comes rushing into the room.

– Hi giiiiirls, Neema says, and I can see the MDMA is kicking in; she's blinking like mad. She always blinks on MDMA. I think it's because it makes her eyes open wider, so they get dry quicker. She leans in to talk so we can hear. – Someone's already been sick in the garden. Are you both okay?

I nod at her and smile. Emma looks out into the throng of people in the room and declares, – I think I fancy Sal.

Neema rubs her hand up and down Emma's back as she asks – Which one's Sal? Emma points at the black-haired girl standing with Gwen, wearing heavy eye make-up and a severely low-cut top.

– Well, get over there and talk to her then, Neema says, and gently pushes her in the girl's direction. Emma turns around with a nervous expression on her face, and I give her a motivational double thumbs-up, so she turns back and does a very goofy dance-walk over to Gwen and Sal that sends Neema and me into laughter.

– Oh, my God, she's such a dork, Neema says.

– Do you think she's in with a chance? I ask.

– Anything is possible, says Neema.

– No Amanda tonight?

– I think we can safely say that Amanda would hate tonight, Neema says.

– Ah, I dunno; I would have liked to see her after a few of

192

Richie's hash cookies, I say, and make a face like I'm wasted. While Neema's laughing, I flick through my CDs and pull out 'Teenage Dirtbag' and point at it. She nods excitedly.

As the first notes of Wheatus's song occupy the room, Richie shouts, – Yes, Orla! He jumps up on the arm of the sofa in the corner, leading the men of Redstar Records through the verses and right up to the chorus, loudly yelling along with the words.

– Talking about dorks. Neema smiles, her eyes on Richie.

Just then, Kesh walks through the door of the living room with a crazed look in his eyes. He is dragging a girl by the hand; it's Gwen's other pretty friend, she has a triumphant expression on her face. Neema and I turn to exchange a knowing look, and I keep my eyes on her and sing the chorus of 'Teenage Dirtbag' right up to her face until she shoos me off.

As the MDMA kicks in, I'm not very good at sitting still. I have to bounce around the room and chat to everyone I see. – Hello, I'm Orla, the Irish house guest. Yes, Neema's friend.

I hug everyone I know.

– There's my little Irish cutie, says Gwen. She gets me in a headlock-hug situation where I can't move for her squeezing, until I manage to wriggle out of it. I keep moving, into the kitchen, where Kesh and Frank are doing enormous slugs of cocaine over the worktop, and I say, – Stop! You need to be hugged!

Each one stops and turns around to let me hug them,

193

Frank picking me up and squeezing me so hard that my ribs hurt. – Have a line, Orla.

– Wow, you did well picking me up there, Frank, I say, taking the note Kesh is holding and hoovering up the drugs.

Frank is shouting my name as I leave the room.

– I can't stop moving, I shout back at him as I walk through to the hall. I notice the open back door and I step out into the garden jungle, and the air is like a cool embrace. I breathe deeply and feel a slow swell of pleasure move through me. Then I realise I am being watched, and there is Shane and another man whom I haven't met before.

– Orla, says Shane. – What the hell are you doing?

– I am breathing, Shane, I say. – It's necessary to survive, and when you're coming up, it's actually really fucking nice.

Shane laughs his croaky laugh at me, and I see his yellow teeth and the blurred letters of a badly applied tattoo on his neck. – Have you met Vinnie? he asks, using his cigarette to point at the other man, and now Vinnie is sticking his arm out and I put my hand in his and it's very big and soft and warm and I let him squeeze it as I look at his face. He has big brown doe eyes, a dimple and a gold tooth.

– Hello, Vinnie, I say. – My name's Orla, I'm the Irish house guest.

– And how on earth do you manage to live with this lot? Vinnie asks.

– I manage because they are away most of the time, I reply.

Vinnie's laugh is low and throaty.

– And where do you live, Vinnie? I ask.

– I live in Leyton. A really long way away from here. I also live with a band. Half a band. But I'm part of the band, so I'm part of the problem.

There is a pause then I say, – I recognise you. I think I've seen you before. I say it partly to cover up the fact that I'm staring at him and I can't seem to stop.

– Oh well, we're signed to Redstar, so you might have. There's a smile in his eyes.

– You're from Plane Trees, I say. – I've seen pictures of you about in the office. And I've read an interview with you lot, too.

– Well, here I am in real life, he says, and we are staring at each other, and I feel like he's telling me something entirely different with his eyes than with his mouth.

– I have to go back. I say, I'm supposed to be DJing.

– We'll come with you, says Vinnie.

As I float back into the hall, Gwen is closing the front door. She turns and sees me, gives me a big exaggerated wink and says, – That's Andy gone.

– What happened to him? I say.

– He had a whitey in the toilet. God help that taxi driver.

The living room is full of people, shouting over the music. Shane goes to join Richie, who is stationed behind the decks, punching the air and singing along to Nine Inch Nails. I deliberately walk to the far side of the room, to see if Vinnie will follow. When I turn, he's right beside me. His face is cartoonish in its animation: big toothy grin, eyes boring into me

– What do you do in the band? I say, moving close to him because Shane has turned it up.

Vinnie puts his arm on the small of my back as he says, – I play bass.

I nod and smile again, and at some point the music is too loud, so we move away and hover at the door of the living room so we can hear each other. Vinnie pulls something out of his pocket, a little see-through baggie filled with pills, and offers me one. As I place it on my tongue, he talks to me, his hot breath in my ear.

– I've never met anyone called Orla before. It sounds like Oral.

– You wish, I say.

And he laughs then.

Suddenly, it's 6am. The darkness outside has diluted into the cold insipid grey of a new day. Emma has fallen asleep face-down on the carpet, underneath the decks. We throw popcorn at her head, but she will not be stirred. Shane fiddles behind the decks, carefully putting all my CDs and vinyl into their correct casing. Gwen, Kesh, Richie, Frank, Neema, Vinnie and I sit around on the sofas. Kesh's new girl, Sharon, is asleep in a slump on the armchair.

From behind us, Shane says, – Is there somewhere I can lie down until I'm able to face the world?

– Take my bed, mate, Frank says. – I'll wake you when I need it back.

And Shane waves goodnight to us all, his face looking the same washed-out white as the crescent moon hanging outside the window.

I make a big pot of tea and pour it into freshly washed mugs on the coffee table.

– Right, let's see what we've got left, says Kesh, and stands up, searching his pockets. His jaw is still moving left and right, rather than up and down. We all empty our pockets until there is a small mountain of loose pills, wraps and bags on the table.

Gwen does the audit. – I reckon we've got enough to get us to The Eagle.

We have to wait until 10am and opening time to set off. Neema drops out first, then Sharon is transferred to Kesh's bed. Richie says he wants to sleep so he can watch the Liverpool match later, which leaves Kesh, Frank, Gwen, Vinnie and me walking up to the High Road.

It's already chilly and overcast. No one is speaking much. I wonder if they are trying to hold it down like I am, trying to not let the world see how mangled they feel. I wave at Mustafa who mans the fruit stall, and Kesh buys a bag of oranges off him. He peels them as he walks, handing out quarters to each of us. The orange is fresh and juicy on my tongue and somehow symbolises the newness of the day and all the possibilities it may bring. It's the only thing I could have eaten now and I'm glad of it.

We cross Brondesbury Road and walk past the market, which is already up and running. Right in front of the entrance to the pub, on the pavement, there is a man talking into a microphone, looking all around him. He wears a smart two-piece grey suit, as if he is dressed up for Sunday service.

– I want you to hear the message, he says, as we move to walk around him. – I want you to hear the gospel of Jesus Christ, who sacrificed his life for the people of the human race. I don't want you to go to hell, my friend. He addresses Kesh directly as he walks past, and we all snigger. – God will take your sin and cast it as far as the east is the west. The good news is Jesus Christ paid the penalty for your sin. And if you accept him, he will save your soul and give you strength in times of need. He will give you hope when you have none. He will help you to walk in a way that pleases him . . .

– Yes, but will he get us in the top twenty? says Frank, and we all laugh some more, big bravado laughing to show each other that we're not freaked out, but we quicken our pace as we walk away from the Kilburn preacher man who doesn't want us to go to hell.

We slouch in the corner of The Eagle and take turns to play pool and put money in the jukebox and visit the stinking bathrooms to suck up more drugs. Somewhere between twelve and one, I lose my voice, so I stop any attempts to speak altogether and smoke more cigarettes instead. The pub fills up with people, a smoky haze beginning to form over our heads, and across the room the TV shows the horses, rippling muscles catching the light as they are led to the track. Kesh and Frank are playing what seems like their twentieth game of pool.

Vinnie is beside me, talking. There is white congealed spittle in the corners of his lips.

– We went on this tour around North America, and it was fucking brutal because we were in a splitter van doing ten-, twelve-hour journeys at a time. We got all our gear stolen in Pennsylvania and had to do the gig that night with all borrowed gear . . .

As he talks, I stare at the wood-panelled ceiling. I squeeze my eyes shut and open them again. As the words spill out of him and the horses race around the track on the TV, this wire hanging down, and the dusty white lampshade that hangs from it, this whole light, is moving, slowly, across the width of the ceiling, one way and then back the other way.

– Orla? Vinnie has finished talking and he's looking at me. So is Gwen.

– I think I should maybe go home, I croak.

– I'm going home now, I'll take you, says Frank, who is walking around the table from behind, pulling on his coat. He stops and looks at me. I look to Gwen. She's looking at Vinnie, who is frowning at Frank, but Frank is holding his arm out to me now, like an old-fashioned gentleman, and I'm glad to take it. Gwen helps me put my coat on and hugs me. Vinnie kisses me on the cheek and talks into my ear.

– Goodbye, Oral. Don't be a stranger.

And then we're outside. It's a sensory onslaught. Frank and I walk slowly down the High Road, through the throngs of Saturday shoppers, the road all clogged up with cars and buses, and I blink and blink again. We don't say much, because my voice is entirely gone.

– Look up. Frank points to the façade of an old cinema building. – It's beautiful. Original art deco, that.

And I nod dutifully towards the building and smile, for it's nice to be led, to be shown London and a different side of this street. When we get close to Fahy's, I speed up, and Frank speeds up with me in silent understanding. Further down towards Mill Road, I wait outside the newsagents while Frank goes to buy tobacco, and I shake my head when he offers me a roll-up. When we get home, I'm so relieved to be there that when he mimics the gesture of a drink to me, I shrug and nod.

He plonks himself down beside me on the sofa and hands me a can of warm beer. We sit side by side, looking out into the mess of the room. I open my can and tap it against his and take a drink. I feel heavy, as if, if I tried to stand up, I wouldn't be able to carry my own weight. I want to look up to the light bulb to see if it's moving, but I don't let myself.

– How are you feeling? Frank asks.

I try to talk, to say 'Okay,' but it comes out in a comical croak and I give up. He laughs, his heavy eyelids pushing down over his eyes.

– Your eyebrows, I croak.

– What? he says, smiling.

– Your eyebrows. I lean into him and pull his hair away from his face to look. – They look like big brown caterpillars, I croak, and I'm laughing now, at Frank's enormous eyebrows, and as I'm laughing, he's laughing, too.

– Jesus, Orla. Leave my eyebrows alone, he's saying, but he's grabbed my wrists now and he doesn't let them go. Instead, he pulls me towards him and tilts his face into mine. Both his arms are around me now and we're kissing, just like that. His mouth tastes like beer and smoke. I don't like the feeling of his kiss; it's a big, wet smothering, with no definite stops and starts, but I kiss him back, and we manoeuvre round so that I'm leaning back against the sofa. He leans in over me now to kiss me, and as he does his curls brush against my face. Something about the feel of them on my skin jolts me. I push his shoulders back and take a breath and laugh a little bit, which turns into a painful cough, and he sits back down and laughs too, still with his eyes on me. He's holding my hand, and he hasn't let go.

I look at him and shake my head as I try to form the words. – I . . . I . . . Frank . . . I pull my hand out of his and he immediately tucks his curls behind his ear. He looks back

201

at me then, and I can't handle it, the look in his eyes. I shake my head. – I'm wasted.

Disappointment clouds his face as he turns towards the table to roll a cigarette. He doesn't look up when I get up to leave.

I wake in darkness and blink myself into the room. Neema is not in her bed. I can hear music coming from downstairs. An image of Frank's face on mine flashes up in my head at the same time as a sickly tasting swell of sour alcohol in my throat. I sit up, switch on my lamp and swig down some water from the glass by my bed. Neema's footsteps are light on the stairs before she sticks her head around the door.

– Heeey. We're getting pizza. You want some?

I try out my voice. – Frank kissed me.

– What? She hurries into the room, closes the door behind her and sits on the edge of her bed, staring at me expectantly. – Did you kiss him back?

– Yeah. For a little bit. Then I freaked out and came upstairs.

– Why did you freak out?

I cough. After swallowing painfully, and taking another sip of water, I say, – Because . . . it grossed me out. I don't like him that way.

She looks at me hard, and then at her feet. After a brief moment, she stands up, – I'll get you a small margherita. And Orla. Look in the mirror before you come downstairs.

I do as I'm told, and it's a shock. There are red-wine stains like scabs around the outside of my mouth, and black smudges of mascara set into the bags underneath my eyes as if to strengthen the darkness of them. In the bathroom, I wash my face with steaming hot water until it looks like a boiled ham, and all the while my head rings and thumps, rings and thumps.

As I walk back upstairs, Frank's door opens and he walks out on to the landing, in a T-shirt and boxers. He keeps his head down as he moves past me, his hair curtaining his face, so I can't see his eyes.

– Frank, I croak.

He keeps walking, but he slows down.

– I . . .

– Forget about it, he says and closes the bathroom door behind him.

CHAPTER 20

TRUE LOVE KNOWS NO SEASON

The relentless darkness that November brings makes Fahy's feel even more cave-like. Smoke and shadows. Dingy light. I take off my coat and settle behind the bar. There's an album on the stereo.

Planxty – The Woman I Loved So Well.

The music is picked acoustic guitars, fiddles, pipes, mandolin: the good auld music of home and the Kilburn High Road.

Pat is stooped over a sink full of suds, staring blankly towards the coloured glass of the front façade.

– Pat, what is the point of having a glasswasher when you're still going to wash the glasses?

– These ones went through the feckin' thing and they're still covered in streaks, look! And she's holding up a pint glass in front of me to examine it.

I don't see the streaks, but I nod and say, – Fair enough.

Afterwards, she dries her hands on a tea towel and says, – I'm off upstairs to make his dinner. I'll be down later.

The door pulls open and Gerry walks in. His hair is blown sideways, his cheeks are lobster pink. I watch his frown fall away as the spread of the bar fills his vision.

– Here he is. How are you, Gerry? I say as he plants himself on his stool. I pull the pint for him.

He takes out his little leather purse, tips coins into his hand and picks out the precise amount, handing them over. – Still above ground. Busy enough today.

I nod and place his pint on a clean beer mat in front of him.

He takes a long, slow gulp of his beer, smacks his lips and says, – And how's yourself?

– Well, I've never lived in a country at war before, Gerry, not this type of war anyway.

– It's a disgrace, he says. – And Tony Blair trying to lick up to Bush like one of your little teachers' pets in school. He's out of his depth. That's it now. It'll be World War Three.

– It's World War Three in my house already, I say, thinking of the last few days. Cocaine crumbs on the kitchen counter. Richie pouring buckets of boiling water on to the front step to dislodge the dried vomit. Neema banging on Kesh's door and shouting at him to do his bit to clean up, and Kesh slamming the door in her face. And all the while Frank has been stomping about the house behind his wall of curls, no eye contact, no words exchanged.

It felt like a relief when they went on their album tour

yesterday morning, a twenty-date headline tour of venues across the British Isles, ending with their big show at the LA2. They were bumbling around the house at 8am, piling up bags and equipment, and I came down and made them coffees, just the way they like them. Shane was outside revving the engine, and Kesh was pissed off with Richie for not being up and ready in time, and Frank wouldn't even look at me. When they left, I waved them off like I was their mam or something. – Look after yourselves, I shouted from the porch.

Richie was the only one who waved back.

Now, it's just me and Neema until the end of November. She seems angry with me since I told her I kissed Frank. Her face is all tight. I hate when her face is tight. This morning, in my half-sleep, I caught her whispering to herself as she pushed my clothes out of the way so she could kneel in front of the mirror. *It's a fucking shithole in here.*

It's probably a good thing that she's going home for a few days at the weekend for Diwali. Kesh said I can borrow his guitar while he's away. I've to get some music around my new song.

I pour four pints for a gang in the corner and come back to Gerry.

– How's Herself? I say.

His face slackens at the mention of his wife. – Had a row with the youngest, Liam. Threw a glass at him.

– Jesus. Did she hit him?

– No, it hit the wall. Liam got a fright, though.

– Where are the rest of them? I ask. Gerry has four sons in all.

– They're all out. Liam's the only one still young enough to have to deal with her.

– And is he okay now?

– He's in his room now, so he'll be in there all the night.

– And her?

– What about her? He looks at me sharply.

– Is she alright?

– She's never alright. And his nose is in his pint again.

From the stereo speakers, Christy Moore sings us stories about wanted men and days of sorrow long years ago. His voice reminds me of my da's.

– How did you meet her again? I ask Gerry as Mayo Dave arrives, patting his friend on the back and nodding at me. I go to pour his pint as Gerry replies. – We met at the National, the Irish dancehall up the road.

– And how long did you go out with her before you got married?

– She got pregnant after a few months of us courting, and we got married then.

There's a pause. Gerry looks deep in thought. The door bangs shut as a man walks in, blowing his hands warm from the cold.

I say, – It's a wonder you didn't use contraception, Gerry, after moving to England and having it readily available.

Gerry laughs bitterly as I take Mayo Dave's money in

exchange for his pint. – It's a wonder indeed. Mind you, it didn't make much difference for you either, Dave, Gerry says.

As I suspected, the joke doesn't land with Mayo Dave. He's not drunk enough yet. Sometimes, it only takes the first sip of his drink to see his shoulders relax. Sometimes there are no words exchanged beyond the order of a drink until it is quietly and conscientiously gulped to the last drop. Then there's a transference of sorts, his eyes soften, and he's able to smile. But he shakes his head slowly now, in disapproval, and Gerry turns pensive again before saying, – You mightn't have been able to get a condom for love nor money in my town, but I'll tell you something, it was still a better life than London.

I laugh at that, and say, – Good auld Ireland. Always better than anywhere else in the world. And I sit back down on my stool and rest my eyes on the stained-glass windows as the men drink beside me.

Pat comes back about half an hour before closing time and goes to the glasswasher.

– It's empty, I say. – Everything's done.

She looks irritated with me for leaving her with nothing to do. She folds the tea towel, then goes to the till and opens the drawer. Then looks at the clock and closes the till drawer again with a bang.

– Pat, I say. – Do you ever sit down?

She turns her head but not her eyes. – Excuse me, miss lady of leisure here, but some people don't like taking breaks.

I feel the attention of the drinkers at the bar now. Gerry, Mayo Dave and the straggly-haired man to the right of him.

– Alright. I shrug. But it might be good for you to take the occasional rest.

– I've been doing this for twenty-seven years, Orla. If I sit down, I'll never get back up.

Mayo Dave's shoulders jump gently with laughter.

– Well, have you thought about what you'll do with the pub when . . .

– When what? Pat interrupts, with her hand on her hip now, her head cocked at a slant. There's merriment in her eyes. She's waiting to pounce, I know it.

– When . . . You're gone, like. I look to our audience for support. – We're all going to die. Right, lads?

Gerry is piping up now. – Pat, she's after the pub. You'd better lock up your will.

– You'll have to find another time to talk about my impending death, Orla, Pat says in her teacher tone, and I nod and take the next order from the guy who has been watching us with an air of impatience. I know when people need a drink now, before any words are spoken. It's the twitchiness. Little scratches and movements, shifts of weight, beer mats lifted and tapped against the bar.

– What'll you have?

– Guinness, he says, looking at the tap as he says it. I pour his pint and leave it to set.

He's watching Pat as she stoops down to pull some new

glasses out of a box. – Don't you want to go back to your country before you go? he says, in thick London speak.

We all turn to look at him then.

– Back home to Ireland, he says, as if to assure us that he knows where we're all from.

– And why would I want to do that? says Pat, rising up to face him.

– To end your life where you started it. He shrugs, his eyes flitting to the pint settling by the side of the tap and then back to the bar top.

– I'm not sure you've ever been to County Clare . . . I say, and immediately Gerry is wheezing giggles, and even Pat turns to me with a half-smile and raises her hands in a helpless gesture as if to say, *What can I do?* I top the pint and place it down in front of the man. He pushes his hair behind his ear and shakes his head resignedly.

– Where did you start your life, then? I ask.

– Born and raised in London. I'll be here till the day I die, he says. All proud of himself.

– Well, isn't that great for you, I say and Pat shoots me a warning look.

He says, – You belong where you're born. That's all I'm saying.

And I'm off. – Says the man drinking his nice pint of Guinness in this nice Irish pub surrounded by Irish people. If we all belonged where we were born, you'd be drinking in The Royal George down the road.

Gerry says, – She's on fire tonight.

I look at Pat. She turns back to the man and says stiffly, – Enjoy your drink.

He raises his eyebrows in response, glass tipped up to his mouth, his face disappearing behind his pint. Mayo Dave pulls out his liquorice tobacco, his cap hiding his eyes, his lower lip hanging wet over his chin. Gerry blinks, looking at his pint, and says, – We don't all get the luxury of belonging where we're born.

And in the speakers, there's a pipe of some sort meandering its way around a melody, up and down and around and back on itself until it breaks down into one long single note, expanding into a chord. And then it's over, just like that: a line drawn.

CHAPTER 21

BOOTYLICIOUS

Vinnie is sitting at the bar grinning at me when I arrive, his gold tooth glinting against the last of the daylight. He passed through The Castle earlier, calling in to see Biff, he said. On his way out, he turned just before going down the stairs and said, – Come and meet me later. I'll be at The Oxford Arms. Around eight?

– Alright, I said. I didn't want to sit in the house on my own, anyway. It's scary with no one in it. Last night, I sat in the loft and played Kesh's old guitar and sang until my throat hurt and the tips of my fingers throbbed from the strings. I woke up at 3am, my stomach groaning, and realised I'd forgotten to eat dinner.

I wish I had a better outfit on. *It's just a drink. Not a date.*

It's quite apparent that Vinnie is already oiled up from booze. When I sit down on the stool opposite him, he pulls it closer, so that my thighs are wedged between his open legs. We drink with our eyes on one another. It's only been ten days since I saw him, but he's different than I remember. There's a slight overbite to his mouth, and his teeth are large and yellowing. His eyes are the same dark pools of brown, though, and they are boring into me.

– What's been happening? I say, trying to hide my blush.

– Did some shows in Europe, he says.

– How did it go? I ask.

– Not great. Hard to play to an empty room. Not as hard for us as it is for Finn, though.

– Finn is your singer, right?

– Yes, and he just gets more and more pissed off until he's fucking seething. Then afterwards he likes to break things.

– Like what? I gawp.

– Oh, you know, furniture, pint glasses, the wall, if he can punch it hard enough . . . it's really relaxing. He smiles wryly, then takes a drink.

– You guys need to go on a support tour rather than have to sell out venues yourselves.

– Yeah, it might be sensible, he says, looking over my shoulder around the room. I wonder who he's looking for.

– And did you have fun at the party? I say.

– Yeah, it was a laugh. You were out of it in that pub, though. On the word 'you', he sticks his finger in my chest. It hurts.

– I started tripping, Vinnie. The light bulb was fucking moving.

213

But his eyes are fixed on something behind me. I turn to see what he's looking at.

– Oi oi, he says, his face breaking out into a grin as two men walk towards us. Vinnie fist-bumps them.

– Alright, says the first one, nodding at me and looking shiftily around the bar.

Vinnie hops off his stool. – Orla, I'll be back in a minute. Get us another pint, will you? He chucks a fiver on the bar and walks out with the two guys. His pint is only half full. When he comes back, I am still waiting to get served. He looks slightly flustered.

– What was that all about? I say.

– Oh, they were just looking to buy some stuff.

– What kind of stuff?

He looks at me with a surprised expression, as if I should know. – I move stuff, just to make some cash on the side. Just recreational shit. Nothing heavy.

I blink at him, trying to take this in. He leans in close to my face and says – Guess what, Oral? Being in a band does not make you a living. And with that, he downs his half pint and smacks his lips. – Cheers. He clinks my glass with his empty one.

– Cheers, I say. So, what have you got in your pocket now?

– Ha! Are you looking for a livener?

– Maybe I am, I say.

*   *   *

Two hours later, the pub is heaving, and Vinnie and I are being knocked and pushed, but we remain steadfast on our stools by the bar. He shouts something at me and I lean in and say, – What? He shouts again, and I cup my hands over my mouth and go right up close to his ear and shout, – I can't hear you!

And he laughs and takes my head in his hands and kisses me. And there we are in a packed bar, that couple who are kissing with no embarrassment, just stacked up with that sense of entitlement that cocaine affords. Stripped of all inhibitions.

He pulls me off the stool and we hail a taxi, and he kisses me all the way home, pushing me backwards into the seat with the force of his tongue, and his hands are in between my thighs, and he only has a fiver for the cab so I pay the rest, and as I hand over the money, I can't bear to look the driver in the eye.

Vinnie leads me up the steps of a terraced Georgian house, into a hall and up three flights of stairs to his flat, then into a bedroom. He closes the door behind us and pins me up against it. I am out of breath from the stairs, but it feels right to be breathless in this moment. It feels right to be already panting as he grips my wrists in one hand and holds them up against the wall over my head. As he pushes his tongue between my teeth, he fumbles at my shirt, trying to pull it up over my breasts, but it's too tight, so he uses both of his hands to rip it open and then pushes my vest top and bra down. My nipples are in his mouth and my hands are on his head; I can feel the soft stubble of his blade one as he unbuttons my trousers and probes with his finger between my legs.

He lifts me up and plonks me down on his bed, pulls off my trousers and then his own. It takes no time at all for him to climax. Afterwards, his face drops in relief and he sighs loudly as he rolls onto his back beside me. I turn to him and nuzzle his neck and his ears. He gives me a quick, perfunctory kiss on the mouth, then sits up on the bed and leans over to the windowsill to take a small tin box and roll a joint.

He doesn't speak as he rolls. My heart is clapping inside my chest. *Encore, Encore.* I sit up beside him and look around the room. There is no furniture in it apart from the bed and an upturned box for a bedside table. A suitcase sits on the floor in the corner, opened, with clothes spilling out of it. Flyers are thumbtacked to the wall by the door. He sparks up the joint and hands it to me, and I take it, because I'd like to sleep tonight through all this cocaine zinging around my head. We smoke it in silence, passing it back and forth a few times, and when he stubs it out, he turns his body around to mine and says, – Now, it's your turn.

He starts kissing me again slowly, and then a little harder, and I feel a swell of pleasure moving through my nerve fibres, building and building, until there is nothing but the taste and feel of his tongue. My mind flits to Moses and his wet, awkward kisses. *This is what kissing is supposed to be, this is grown-up kissing.* Vinnie bites my bottom lip gently, and it feels like he has set off a flare in my mouth that drips light and electricity all the way down my body to my groin. He kisses me on the neck and chest and moves his head down to between my legs. I try to relax, to not think about what my body must look like from where he is. And then I'm not thinking about anything at all.

Afterwards he says, – There's your oral, Oral, as he flops back on the bed beside me.

I laugh at that.

In the space of a few minutes, Vinnie is snoring loudly. I want to sleep, too, but there is a thin line of sound in my head that won't leave. A ringing. I try to zone out of it and tune my ears into something else. My heart is thumping in my chest. Ferocious thumping. There's not enough space between the beats. I look out Vinnie's window for a long time, long enough for the sky to blend from indigo to black. Long enough to try and count the stars creeping out of the darkness, their light flickering as if their batteries are running out. I think of PJ Harvey, on the cover of the album I love so much, *Stories from the City, Stories from the Sea.* She is in clear focus, crossing a road in New York City, shades on, handbag over her shoulder, cars and people and lights blurred all around her. She is so small and slight, with this big, careering voice, as if she could carry the city on her back, drive it forwards. When I listened to her sing, I hoped London would make my heart beat faster. I hoped that my life here would click into an intense new rhythm of sex and thrills. This is me, now, alone in the city, in the middle of it all, and I'm numb. I want to pull my heart out of my chest, hold it in my hands as it pulses, and gently squeeze the feelings out of it. I want to feel something.

– Hello?

– Hi, Ma.

– Hiya, Orla.

– I won't keep you long. I'm just ringing to let you know that I got cheap flights for Christmas, so I'll be home the week before.

– Christ. Christmas. I was trying not to think about it.

– We'll have fun, Ma. Maybe we'll do it differently this year.

– Mmm-hmm.

– Ma, are you watching the telly?

– The sound's down.

– So you are watching the telly.

– I'm looking at the pictures, Orla.

Pause.

– Is Anna okay?

– She's been out every night. You'd want to see the state of the kitchen in the mornings after she's got in, pissed. It's enough to make me want to throttle her.

– How's your work, Ma?

– I'm leaving.

– What?!

– Yes, I'm leaving. I don't want to do the job anymore, Orla. I'm only fifty-two. I want to do different things.

– What different things?

– Eileen's brother's wife, Maeve, has a boutique out in Glasthule, really nice clothes. She's looking for someone to work there with her. And I've offered my services.

– Ma! This is amazing. You get to try on clothes all day.

– I get to persuade other people to try on clothes.

– But you're made for that job. I've worn out that leopard-print jumpsuit you persuaded me to buy in Topshop last year.

– Well. We'll see. I handed in my notice yesterday. I've to work out two months.

– Did Chris take it well?

– No, he didn't. But only because it's an inconvenience to him.

– Well, fuck him, Ma. You've been amazing for him. You'll be missed.

Pause.

– Have you spoken to Da?

– No. It's all just letters from his solicitor to mine. Anna tells me his news.

– Does she talk to him much?

– You'd have to ask her.

Pause.

– *Well, I'll leave you to* EastEnders *anyway.*

– *Lovely. Before I go, how's your job in that recording studio, anyway?*

– *I've got the hang of it now. My boss is a dickhead, though.*

– *Jesus, I don't know why all bosses are dickheads. There must be some unwritten rule. I'll be dancing out of this office when I'm done.*

– *We'll celebrate at Christmas, Ma.*

CHAPTER 22

MURDER ON THE DANCE FLOOR

I wait for the end of the day, then I walk up to Studio One. Max is in there, head bent over the computer.

– You on your own? I ask.

– Yeah, he says, turning around to me. His hair is standing on end, as if he's been running his hands through it. – They say they're coming back but they've gone to the pub, so God knows how long they'll be.

– Can't you just call it a day?

– Nah, we've got to get it to mastering tomorrow. It's gonna be a long night, Orla. And with that, he lifts his arms and stretches, squeezing his eyes shut. He looks like a little pug.

– Well, do you mind if I head on? I ask.

– Go, go, go. I'll lock up.

– Okay, thanks . . . Um . . . Max? I was wondering if some-time, when you're not, like, mad busy, I could watch you work Pro Tools? I studied music production, you see, and I know FruityLoops and stuff, but it would be cool to know how you do stuff on Pro Tools.

His face transforms again, from squished-up pug to smiley bear. – Why didn't you say? I use FruityLoops as well, you know. Of course, I'll let you know when I'm on my own next and you can sit in.

– That's so nice of you, thanks. I will buy you many pints.

– And I shall drink those pints, he says gravely, and swings back around on his chair again.

I run down the stairs, grab my coat and push through the heavy metal door. Maybe I'll show him my demo, if I'm feeling brave enough.

Outside, the Christmas lights are up. They make the darkness in London feel denser somehow, more claustrophobic. I walk up to Upper Street and join the rush, chin tucked into my neck, eyes watering from the cold.

I'm to meet Neema. She's just back from Bolton. We haven't talked for a week. She left her bed neatly made, the shiny ivory quilt tucked under the mattress just so. A few days ago, I decided it was good for me that she had gone; it would be sensible to know how to live in London without Neema. I've been playing Kesh's guitar to fill the emptiness in the house, writing a new song about how I hold my breath when I go up the escalators at Angel Tube station. My head fills with pressure, and there's no room for anything else. I can forget who I am in the time it takes to breathe again.

I got two verses and a chorus, but I still need a bridge. I'm going to call it 'Lunglocking'.

I jump on a bus down the hill to Old Street roundabout and cross over to City Road, heading towards The Dragon Bar. Neema's waiting outside. She's wearing a beret and a scarf up over her chin and nose, so only her eyes are visible.

– Hey, I say, giving her a hug and holding open the door for her. The bar is busy already. I push a path for us through the after-work drinkers, and we find a clearing at the end of the bar. There is one stool free.

– You take it, I say, and she doesn't argue. We pile our coats and bags at the bottom of her stool, and I order the drinks. She is jumpy. Avoiding my eye.

– How was home? I ask.

– Same old shit.

When I look at her with a questioning expression, she sighs and leans in to my ear. – I'm basically a spokesperson for Kesh. I have to cover for him being monumentally shit. Lie on his behalf. It's great, she says flatly, and then leans back, picks up her drink and says, – How was here?

– I was at Fahy's mostly. And I wrote a new song, and . . . I went on a date.

– A date? With who?

– Vinnie from Plane Trees.

– Oh shit! she says, lighting up a cigarette and blowing the smoke out of the side of her mouth in the direction of the bar. – And? Did you have sex with him?

– Sure did. Neema, he's *so* good in bed, I say, widening my eyes for emphasis.

She looks at me, not in the excited way I'd hoped, but more amused, as if I'm entertaining to her. Then she sucks up her vodka and Coke through her straw and looks around the bar.

– Those guys are looking at us, she says, her eyes flitting to the other side of the room and back to me. – Don't look.

I turn to look. – Who?

– They're over there. In suits.

And I catch eyes with one of them. He's handsome in a scruffy way; unshaven, and with his shirt collar loosened. His friend is smarter looking, shaven-headed, sallow-skinned. I grin and nod over at them.

– Orla, Neema says, through gritted teeth.

I laugh. – Fuck it. What have we got to lose? Come on, they're telling us to come over.

– What if they're dickheads?

– Then we leave.

They're not entirely dickheads, but they definitely do have some dickheadishness in them. They work in the City. In funds. Ed, the scruffy one, says, – We like coming over to Shoreditch; the music's much better here.

Neema and the other guy, Rob, are quiet, looking in every direction except at each other.

– You heard of Shiva? I say to Ed, and Neema looks at me with an enigmatic expression.

225

– Shiva. That rings a bell, you know. I might have read about them in a music mag, could that be right?

– Yeah, they've been reviewed a few times.

– What about them?

– Oh, we live with them. Over in Kilburn.

And I see Ed's eyes re-evaluating us.

– What's it like living with a band? Rob asks.

I turn to Neema, but she is silent, so I speak for both of us. – It's cool, actually. They're away on tour at the moment. So, it's not too intense.

The bar is getting louder now. When Neema and Rob strike up a conversation, I allow Ed to tell me about his flat and his flatmate and his job, and yes, we'll have more drinks please, and why not bring a shot. I know Ed has got stuff on him as soon as he comes back from the toilet; his eyes dilated and pulled that little bit wider, the sniff and the wipe of his nose with the back of his arm. I ask him straight out and he is delighted to provide. I pull Neema with me to the bathroom to do our share.

– What's Rob like? I say, locking the door of the cubicle behind us.

– He's really trying it. Fishing for boyfriend info.

– You should get with him, I say, wiping the back of the toilet cistern and pouring out the powder.

– Why? she says from behind me.

I look at her briefly as I slice the powder into lines. – Um, because it's fun? You might end up fancying him?

She laughs a little and says, – Isn't it better to fancy people *before* you decide to get with them?

– Alright, well, shall we lie and say we have boyfriends? I say, rolling up a five-pound note.

– *Do* we have boyfriends? she asks.

I turn around to find her glaring at me. – Fuck off out of it, Neema; it was only one date. I snort my line and hand her my rolled-up note.

– I don't want it. I have a library day tomorrow. I need to be able to concentrate.

I stare at her, and then back at the line. – Fuck it, I say, and hoover it up.

At 1am, we are still in The Dragon Bar, but we are standing up now around a table, dancing to the music, which has been turned up so that we have to really shout to be heard. Neema downs shots and dances. Rob and Ed have their arms around each other's shoulders, mouthing along to the words of Kylie Minogue's 'Can't Get You Out Of My Head'. I tap Rob and ask if we can have some more coke, and he shrugs, a big, drunken exaggerated shrug, and he asks Ed, and Ed hands it to me really unsubtly around the back of Rob's waist. I take it and give Neema the big eye, but she shakes her head at me, so I go to the toilet by myself and hoover some more up.

When I arrive back at the table, I give the wrap to Ed and say, – Thanks so much. Let me get the next round.

He puts on an expression of exaggerated concern and says, – No way, you're not getting the drinks. That's our job.

So, he stumbles off to the bar, and I let him. Rob goes to the toilet with the wrap, so it's Neema and me. So Solid Crew's '21 Seconds' comes on, and she's moving again, and as I'm grinning at her I ask, – Have you heard from any of the band?

– No. You? And then again, for extra emphasis, – Have you heard from them?

– No. They're in Tunbridge Wells tonight. At the Forum. I've been following the dates. I feel her eyes drilling into me, and I meet the force of her gaze. – Neema, what's your problem?

She's straight back at me. – Why did you kiss Frank if you don't like him?

– I didn't kiss Frank. He kissed me.

She rolls her eyes and shakes her head, as if I've just dropped the punchline of a hilarious joke.

– Neema, I was fucking wasted. He tried it on with me after an all-nighter. I was tripping, for fuck's sake! And I stopped it.

– Not before it happened though, Neema insists.

– What?

– You have no idea, do you? says Neema. You know he properly likes you?

– No, he doesn't. Says who?

– Richie. He's liked you this whole time.

228

– Well, I didn't notice that.

– There's a lot of things you don't notice, she says before looking away, mouth to her straw.

I move so that I'm right in front of her, and lean into her face and shout, – Well, why didn't you fucking tell me, if it's so obvious to you?

I can smell the sweet, fruity scent of her perfume. Pearl-drop earrings trembling from her earlobes. She blinks slowly.

I add, – And did you tell Richie I snogged Frank?

She says nothing here, so I seize the moment, pull my head back and throw up my arms in despair. – Oh, great. So, everyone's bitching about me behind my back, going on like I'm some evil fucking temptress who's deliberately fucked Frank over.

She looks at me with an incredulous expression on her face, and then she's shouting back. – You *did* deliberately fuck Frank over. You snogged him and then changed your mind, and now you're shagging someone else.

The boys are back now, worried looks on their faces. Ed puts the drinks down. – Woah, girls, what did we miss?

– Nothing, Neema says, and all of the noise of this place, all of the chaos and the shouting and snorting and flirting, all of the big, booming bass line of Daft Punk, shrinks down to nothing. It's just her, glaring at me, waiting for a reaction.

– Wow, I say, blinking and trying not to look away. Her eyes are wide on mine, eyebrows raised in high arcs above them. I hold, hold, hold her stare, and even with the hostility in her eyes, there is something in me that is enjoying being right in the centre of her attention. As soon as I allow this thought to flower in my head, as if she senses it, as if she feels it too, she breaks away. She turns to Rob, picks up her fresh drink and says, – Cheers.

I hear the noise of the bar again, the music, the shouting. It's all heavier sounding now. I stay watching her as she carries on drinking, cupping her hand over her ear for Rob to shout into it, laughing loudly at his words and dancing in that way she does, moving the heel of her left foot from side to side.

Ed puts his arm around me with his right hand and passes me the drink with his left, and he keeps his arm right there, as if I belong to him now. – Are you okay? he shouts overly loudly in my ear.

I nod and I drink more and watch as Neema deftly avoids Rob's clumsy attempts at hand-holding. I ask Ed questions so he will answer them and fill the gaps, and all the time I am aware of the fluttering feeling in my heart, as if it has broken away from its ropes, and is floating precariously inside me, bouncing off things. I watch her and she doesn't look at me. Not even once. And after the final gulp of my drink, I say to Ed, – I have to go now, and I grab my handbag. I shake my head when he says, – Let me come with you.

– Well, at least let me take your number, he says agitatedly, so I give him my number, and I notice Neema seeing me do that, and I hope she sees my coat over my arm and my bag over my shoulder, too. I pat Rob on the shoulder and say goodbye, and walk away without a second look. *Fuck her.* I push my way through the throng to the door. People gather outside in clusters, smoking, snogging, hailing taxis. I tuck myself into a doorway a few buildings down from the bar, and shiver as I light a cigarette. One fat drop of rain splats on the pavement in front of my feet, then two, then four. I watch until the whole slab is dark and my cigarette is soggy in my hand.

– Oh, you're still here. Neema is suddenly in front of me, pulling on her coat, slightly out of breath.

– What happened? I ask her.

– They went to do the last of the coke, and I ran away, she says with the tiniest hint of a smile. I feel my mouth move to smile too, but I stop it. Instead, I pull the last drag out of my cigarette, then throw it on the ground and step on it. I push my hands into my pockets. The rain is coming down hard.

– Shall we split a taxi? she says, holding her handbag over her head with one hand and waving her other at the oncoming traffic to hail a cab. I don't object.

After we settle into the warmth of the taxi, our breath fogging up the windows, I speak into the silence between us. – What the fuck was that? I look over at her face in profile and the hardness returns.

She speaks to the frayed leather of the back of the passenger seat in front. – Orla, I get that you're high and you want to talk, but I don't.

– Why are you so angry at me? I persist.

She sighs an enormous sigh, as if this whole journey is an ordeal to be endured. When she looks at me, her eyes are bloodshot. – I said, I don't want to talk about it.

I lean my forehead against the window and watch the streets slide past in a blur through the rain-splattered glass. We don't speak all the way home.

– What's up, Sister Orla?

– Are you hungover, Anna?

Pause.

– Yes. How did you guess?

– It's not hard. Who are you shagging these days?

– Can't talk about that now.

– Right, so, clearly that's someone in work, then. Have you seen Da at all?

– Yup. He wants me to come and meet Flatface properly.

– And will you?

– I'm doing my damnedest to avoid the situation, if I'm honest, Orla.

– I don't blame you.

– How's Neema?

– She's pissed off with me.

– What happened?

– Frank kissed me.

– You shagged Frank?

– Did I say I did that? Did I?

– No, but hang on, why does she have a problem with that?

– She said that he likes me and I led him on.

– And did you?

– Not knowingly. I genuinely didn't know he fancied me.

– And couldn't you just fancy him back? For the sake of convenience?

– No, Anna. Anyway, I've met someone else.

– Ooooh, who's the man? Let me guess . . . Jamiroquai.

– Jesus Christ.

– He's split up with Denise van Outen! Do you think he takes the hat off in bed?

– Anna, I've truly never thought about it.

– Okay, what about Jamie Theakston? Nice and lanky for you.

– It's a guy called Vinnie. He's in a band called Plane Trees.

– And?

– He's very good in bed.

– Jammy bitch.

– Hey, I'm coming home at Christmas. Got cheap flights. I'll be there for a whole week.

– Well, whoop dee doo.

– Listen. Just hold off seeing Da until I'm there and we'll go together.

– Why don't you call him and tell him that?

Pause.

– *Can't you do it, Anna?*

– *Orla, answer me this. When's the last time you spoke to him?*

– *Who, Da?*

– *No, David fucking Beckham. Yes, Da.*

– *I haven't spoken to him since he told me.*

– *Okay, so that was at the start of September. That's two and a half months ago.*

– *Fuck's sake. Do you really want me to call him?*

– *YES.*

Sigh.

– *Okay. I'll call him.*

– *Great. I can't wait to meet our new pregnant stepmother . . . Byeeeeeee.*

CHAPTER 23

GOTTA GET THRU THIS

The escalators at Angel Tube station go on forever. Caverns of time pass as I'm carried upwards to ground level. I can start at the bottom of that escalator miserable, be absolutely delighted by the middle, and then be miserable again by the time I'm at the top. I conjure up scenarios in my head: one where Vinnie cooks me dinner and carries me upstairs to his bed, which is made up with fresh sheets, and there's a bowl of pre-rolled joints waiting, and we don't leave it all weekend. Or, there's a regular scenario where Damian calls me to say he's sent my demo to an A&R, who wants to sign me on the spot for a three-album deal.

Kesh and Richie came back from tour the day before yesterday. They have a few days' rest before their big London show at the LA2. When they said that Frank went to spend a few days at home in Devon, Neema gave me a look that said, *Because of you*. It's a relief to have other people there to defuse the tension between Neema and I, even if they are mostly stoned and silent. I've been reliving the argument at The Dragon Bar in my head, changing the words, giving myself more spunk and wit in my dealings with her, and taking away that hatefulness she had on her. Turning it into playfulness.

This morning on the escalator, because I'm trying, really trying, not to torture myself with thoughts of Neema, I hold my breath. As the pressure balloons in my chest, my thoughts dissolve into nothing. I concentrate on staying calm. I stare at the hand of the person in front of me on the black moving handrail until my throat burns and I allow myself to inhale, feeling a pleasurable light-headedness as the air courses through my lungs again. I'm getting better at it. I get two thirds of the way up this time.

At the studio, I've only had time to put on the radio and take off my coat when two girls walk up the front stairs and stop in front of my desk.

– Hiya, says one of them as she walks towards me. She wears a loose leather jacket covered in patches and bright red lipstick. The other girl follows. She wears huge hoop earrings, dungarees and a bright yellow puffy jacket. I feel self-conscious all of a sudden.

– Hiya, I say in return.

– We're here to see Max?

– Okay, one second, I say, as I pull up the studio schedule on my computer. There is a booking for three days in Studio One made by Warner Records.

– Are you Postergirls? Warner Records?

– We sure are, says red-lipstick girl.

– Okay. Welcome. You're right at the top. Third floor. Studio One. Kitchen is here, toilets are through there.

– Cool! says red-lipstick girl. – Thanks a lot.

I watch them walk up the stairs. They must be a new signing, or I'd have heard of them. They'll love Max. He'll love them. I think of my empty email inbox. It's the last Thursday of November, and neither Damian nor any of the labels I posted my demos to have got in touch. I asked Kesh to nudge Damian, but I don't know if he did or not, and I can't make myself ask him again.

Kesh had to go to Redstar yesterday to meet their new A&R guy. When I got home from work, he was slumped on the armchair, his eyes half-closed from weed. I asked him how it went.

– He's a total fucking wanker. I played him the new songs I've written. He played me the Ash album. The one that came out this year. Said he wanted us to use it as a reference.

– But you don't sound anything like Ash, I said. Is it because you're a three-piece?

Kesh made a face. – It's because they sell records and we don't. He said something about how there's 'one girl and one brown person in every music scene'. We're *unique*. Which is good, apparently. He held his fingers up in quotation marks and mimicked the A&R guy. – We just need to 'work on our songs'.

Now, I stand up to go to the kitchen to make myself a coffee, but I stop before I leave my desk, because the word 'Beatles' grabs my attention from the radio. The DJ's tone has moved from chirpy to grave; there is news being announced. He's declaring a death. George Harrison. Lung cancer. Ashes to be scattered in the Ganges. He plays 'Here Comes the Sun', and I feel as if I've been hit by a train. I stand up quickly and run to the bathroom. At the sink, I splash water on my face. In any other fucking world, I would pick up the phone and ring my da. But not in this world. I lean over the sink and lift my head to look in the mirror. I have the same colour eyes as my da. That light, watery blue.

George was his favourite one. The quiet one, the clever one, the spiritual one. He's the one that held them all together, my da said. The one who didn't carry ego like the rest of them. In the neat library of Beatles vinyl, pawed at and played over and over on our hi-fi in the corner of the living room, George stood out to me as the most handsome: the sideways glance on *Rubber Soul*, the double denim on *Abbey Road*. Da's eulogising helped, of course. I know he related to George because Da was always the quiet one in his family, who went off to university when none of his siblings did. He was the 'clever clogs' as my uncle Barry calls him, never hiding the sneery tone in the way he says it.

His dad, my Grandad Jim, owned a construction company, and it was expected, assumed, that he would follow in his brother's footsteps to work in it, but he went a different way.

I remember the photos of him as a student in Dublin, all long bushy beard and denim flares and suede brown boots. Those round glasses that Lennon had immortalised. Those faded photos were like looking at a different person to the full-colour Da that I lived with: clipped beard, shirt and tie, shoes shined, giving out about the traffic. The only thing that bridged the man in those photos with the one I knew was the guitar. When he played and sang, he became someone full of mystery and feeling. I didn't fully understand as a kid, but I knew it was important. I knew that when he sang to me, we were sharing something special, something that allowed him to be all of himself. And something that allowed me to glimpse him as more than just my dad. 'Here Comes the Sun' was one of the songs he played on high rotation.

At 6pm, Biff walks past and slams an open bottle of beer on my desk. – Come on, we're going to have some drinks in the basement.

There is no choice here, but it's good timing, because I need a breather from the George Harrison and Beatles songs on the radio. I allow a few more heads to go downstairs, and when Max walks down to my level and raises his eyebrows at me, I scrape back my chair and join him.

Drinks in the basement is basically a one-man show, as people sit around getting told to fuck off in different ways by Biff. He communicates solely in the language of put-downs. – You're a pillock, he says now, as he clinks his bottle with that of the drummer of a band called Radius.

– Mate, you need to get in the bin, he shouts to a producer who tries to argue that Paul McCartney was a better songwriter than John Lennon. – Come out when you can admit you're wrong.

More big swigs, big smacks of lips. And he's into a story about a man who gets a butt plug stuck up him on a tour bus.

I've had two beers in quick succession, and I feel a little looser. Maybe I should just get on with it. – Back in a min, I whisper to Max, and I sidle out of the room past Biff, then run upstairs and sit at the desk. I pull out my phone and type Da's number into the desk phone. The thought of seeing Da and Flatface together makes me feel sick. And Anna has been dealing with this horror show on her own. I've never felt the need to protect Anna, mainly due to her absolute conviction that she's 'grand' in the face of all adversity, but I have to be the big sister here.

At the first sound of a ring, I slam the phone down.

Fuck. Just do it.

No, fuck him. Fuck him.

He hasn't tried to call me that much. He could have come and seen me here if he really wanted to make it right. I'm only doing this for Anna. I'll text him.

Hi, I type. *Anna will come and visit with me at Christmas. Home on the 20th.*

I put an X. Then I delete the X. I press 'send', and before I can do anything else, I jump out of my seat and run back downstairs. They're on to George now. Typical.

– I don't want any of that hippie-trippy sitar shite, says Biff, who is looking a little red in the face now.

Max is laughing at him, shaking his head. – Biff, he is saying, you're telling me that you'd rather Sergeant Pepper didn't exist? Because it wouldn't exist in that form if it wasn't for George.

Seeing that he isn't going to win this argument, Biff says, – Anyway, who's got the nose up?

– Aha, excellent timing, says a voice behind us, and Vinnie and another guy saunter in, big grins on them both. They get slapped on the back and man-hugged. Vinnie punches me softly on the arm and pulls a chair over to me and Max, and immediately starts to build a joint.

– Hello sailor, Vinnie says to me.

– What are you doing here?– I say.

– Rude. He pretends to look offended.

I laugh.

– Called in to see Biff about something, Vinnie explains.

– Fuck it, let's have a night of it, Biff says. – Who's in?

It's dark now. I'm lying on the roof of The Castle and there's people up here with me, spreadeagled around, despite the cold. I can't see the people, but I feel their presence. I feel the throbs of energy coming from them. Breath, blood pumping, hair pushing through skin. My teeth are chattering; the noise is like a train chugging over tracks in my head, and I'm grateful for it because it reminds me that

I'm actually in my body, and all the colours and swirling shapes in the sky are just the acid tab that was put on my tongue a few hours ago.

– Look at them, though, I say to no one in particular.

A voice beside me says, – They're not real. It's Max.

– But you can see them? I say.

– See what?

– Snakes. They're black and green. Look! There. I point into the clouds. The snakes seem very low in the sky, as if I could reach up and touch them.

– I can see snakes, too, says Max. – But mine are kind of cartoony. Like the one in *The Jungle Book*.

– I feel like Mowgli, I say. – When the snake makes his eyes go round and round. I feel possessed.

– Just go with it. It's not a bad vibe, is it? Max says.

The snakes are twisting over each other, in violent, thrashing movements, eyes flashing yellow. – No, I don't think it's a bad vibe.

– Well, there you go. Just enjoy the lovely snakes, sliding around the sky. And he says this in a sweet sing-song voice, and it makes me giggle, and then he giggles and I giggle even more and he's laughing and laughing and I'm laughing at him more than the snakes now, because it's funny to see Max so wild and unreserved. He's pissing himself. It's nearly maniacal – high-pitched, raspy yelps.

Another voice from the darkness. – You okay there, Max?

I try to blink away the snakes and focus on Max. I force

myself up on to my elbows and reach out to the dark shape beside me, putting my hand where I think his shoulder should be. He's not expecting to be touched, and he jumps.

– It's just me. It's just me, I say.

He is still laughing, face creased and eyes wet from it, but something is missing from his face. The fun. It's like he's having a fit now, as if he's been possessed by the laughter, as if it's taken control of him.

– I can't remember what's funny, Max, I say, desperate to be back on his level, but instead I am seeing Max like the anatomical drawing of the human body I had in my biology book in school. His face is gone. No skin, no hair, just shining pink muscles, stringy pink cartilage pulling his limbs together. I can see the white of his skeleton poking out from between the muscles of his cheeks. His neck is a thick pink rope and, as he laughs, it's all moving.

I try to look away in the hope that Max will come back, but when I look at the sky, the snakes are writhing all over each other, so many of them, in this huge, wet tangle, and now they are dropping from the clouds, beady heads, writhing lower and lower.

– Max, the snakes, I whisper, but the snakes won't stop, and they're so close now I can feel the flick of a dry tongue on my face, and then another, biting jolts of electric shock and I scream. At least, I think I scream. There are hands on me now, lifting me down from the roof, supporting me on each side, bringing me into the blinding light of the stairwell. I try to focus on my feet, but now they are turning into muscles like Max's, so I blink and look away, blink and look away.

Don't close my eyes, don't look at anything too closely – blink and look away.

Travelling down the stairs. I hear words stretched as if in slow motion, long, drawn-out guttural utterances layered over each other, hands on me again, pulling me down – *blink and look away, blink and look away.*

There's a face leaning into mine, a man's face, hovering, as if suspended completely from his body, frenzied eyes, flitting, Vinnie's eyes, and a huge, freakishly long nose, hanging out of his face. I back away and stand against the wall to feel something solid. *Okay, okay, okay, blink and look away.*

blink and look away.

blink and look away.

blink.

blink.

A phlegmy, snorting sound punctures the silence. I move my eyes across The Castle basement to see Biff snorting cocaine off a key around his neck. He jerks his head to flick his hair back from his face, his turkey jowls trembling under his beard, the skin on his arms yellow-grey and dimpled in the dim light. He is muttering something to one of the guys from Radius, who slouches in a chair beside him, eyes glazed over, mouth in a flat line. *Blink and look away.*

Vinnie is splayed across the sofa against the far wall, head dangling off the edge, mouth open wide as if to catch something in flight. I think he might have made a show of looking after me, ordering the lads around, covering me with a blanket and telling them to leave me to sleep. But I haven't slept, I'm sure of it. Traces of colour linger wherever I move my eyes, like a chemtrail following my line of sight. It's disorientating, but I can manage it. I want to be out of here.

Outside, the last of the darkness is fading into morning. I walk quickly to the Tube, where early morning commuters take their seats beside me, grim-faced and silent. I change at Baker Street where the platform is full and once on the Tube again, I stand with my hood up to hide my face, and grip a pole tightly with both hands. The batteries of my Discman have run out, and the noise of the engine feels like an attack on my ears. I keep my focus on the Tube map on the wall opposite so as not to accidentally catch someone's eye. Mike Skinner raps about his underground train on 'Has It Come To This': *'from Mile End to Ealing and from Brixton to Bounds Green'*. As if the Central and the Victoria lines are his trains, his lines. Maybe that's how you make a city a home, by claiming things for yourself.

My line is brown, from Harrow and Wealdstone to Elephant and Castle. My line cuts the London Tube map in half. It runs right down the centre, from north-west to south.

As I cling to the pole and stare at the map, a picture emerges from it, like an optical illusion. The London Underground map is in the shape of a bottle lying on its side. It's clear as day. I don't know how I never noticed it before. This city is a broken bottle, spilling drink.

Somebody has to live here.

When I arrive back at the house, Kesh and Richie and Neema are in the living room watching television. The room smells of weed and coffee. Neema is in her law school clothes, nibbling on toast from a plate on her lap. Kesh has brought his duvet from his bed on to the sofa and is curled up underneath it, smoking a joint. His eye sockets are dark pits in his face.

– Hi guys, I half-whisper.

– Oooh, someone's been out all night, says Kesh.

Richie laughs and adds, – Looks like you had a big one

Neema is looking me up and down, not even remotely trying to hide the disdain on her face.

– I took acid, I say.

– Oh, shit. You just need to sleep it off. Take some pain-killers as well, Kesh says.

– Do you have to work tonight? Richie says, and I shake my head.

Neema says, – Who was out?

I look away as I answer. – All the lot from The Castle. And Vinnie from Plane Trees. When I look back at her, she's nodding and staring at the television.

When I open the bedroom door, it takes a second to realise why the loft feels strange. Then I see that Neema has pushed all my belongings over to my side of the room, so that her side looks really clean – I think she even vacuumed it – and my side looks like a bomb hit it. I sit on the edge of my bed, staring at the neat order of her side; the three different make-up bags zipped shut on the floor beside the chair, arranged in order of size, the shoes lined up in pairs, the duvet cover pulled smooth, and Durga watching over it all from the poster on the wall. I stare and stare, until spots of colour flash in the edges of my vision. When I blink they disappear.

In bed, I curl myself into the foetal position and nestle my head into the pillow. I'm scared of what I'll see if I close my eyes. *What kind of scene did I cause there last night?* I hear the dull, muted thumps of my heartbeat in my ear. They sound like someone coming up the carpeted stairs beneath me, *thump, thump, thump.* I imagine that it's Neema, with chai and soft, comforting words. I wonder if the old Neema is ever coming back. *Thump, thump, thump.* I imagine my ma popping her head around the door, seeing me and sighing in disapproval, but coming to me on the bed and sitting on the edge of it to stroke my hair like she did when I was a child.

Thump, thump. Then I imagine my da coming into the room with his guitar, and me sitting cross-legged on the carpet between his legs, my back against the base of the armchair, feeling the vibrations of the guitar as he played.

The thrum would travel through me; a warm, fuzzy sensation that moved up my back and lingered around my neck. Gentle prickles on my skin.

I pull myself up and throw off my blanket, then manoeuvre myself to sit on the floor, back against the side of my bed. 'Ride On'. 'Blackbird'. 'Vincent'. 'You've Got a Friend'. 'Michelle'. 'Here Comes the Sun'. All the sounds of the house eclipsed by his voice, a voice made for singing. It was always me and him. Always that feeling of safety. Of belonging to him. I try to sing, 'Here Comes the Sun', my hand on my chest, feeling out the thump of my heart to use as a beat. I can't get it to work. The sound from my mouth, this pathetic humming, is cracked and frail.

I twist around to the precarious tower of CDs by the side of my bed and run my finger down the pile until I find *Abbey Road*. I push the CD into my stereo and skip the tracks to track seven, and sit with my back propped against the wall. He used to swish my hair with his hand before he moved it back to his guitar. As the first strums of the song arrive, I feel my body sag, as if all the air has been violently hissed out of me through a valve.

– Sister Orla. God be with you.

– Oh, hi Anna.

– Jesus. What's your problem?

– Anna, I'm not in the mood.

– Clearly. What did our Father Johnny say?

– It took him two days to reply.

– And?

– He said something like, 'This is great news, Orla. Can't wait to see my girls.' And he put three kisses at the end.

– Okaaaaay. I sense that you have a problem with Johnny's reply.

– Is he not going to acknowledge that we haven't spoken for three months?? Or has he just forgotten I exist? I could be fucking whoring myself around London and addicted to heroin for all he cares.

– I'd like to see his face with that revelation. Sorry, Johnny, I'm

no longer going to make it in the music biz: I've decided the sex industry is much more suited to me. No, not-so-great prospects, but fast cash, Johnny! Fast cash!

Pause.

– You know what he's like, Orla. He's always been shit at correspondence. Anyway, you said you weren't speaking to him either.

– Well, I'm back in two weeks, so I'm going to have to.

– Can you maybe have it out with him before we have to go and meet him with Flatface?

– I can't guarantee that.

Sigh.

– Well, us and Ma will have fun. Three fucking musketeers. All for one and one for all. How's it going in London, anyway? Has Neema forgiven you?

– No.

– If it's any consolation, me and Ma are fucking furious with each other about ninety-nine per cent of the time.

– Oh, no, Anna.

– Yeah, she's just nagging at me nonstop. It's doing me fuckin head in.

– Are you cleaning up after yourself?

– For fuck's sake, Orla, don't you start. I would clean up if she gave me time to! She's become obsessed with the house being clean since we did it up. Just because I don't fucking wash a dish the second after I've used it, suddenly I'm a fucking pariah. I honestly think she'd be delighted if I fucked off.

– Please don't. Don't fuck off yet.

– *That's alright for you to say, Missus Yoko Ono, hanging with the band over there in London.*

– *I know. I'll be back soon and you can take it all out on me, okay? You can shout at me nonstop for a whole day if you like.*

– *Alright, you're on. I'm going to tie you to one of the new kitchen stools so you can't escape.*

CHAPTER 24

BUILDING UP AND
TEARING ENGLAND DOWN

– Stick on a bit of Ronnie Drew, will you, Orla? says Gerry from his perch.

I swallow down the last of the cheese sandwiches I had for dinner and go to the CDs.

The Dubliners – Prodigal Sons.

I sit down on my stool again as Ronnie Drew's voice rings around the bar. I do three or four shifts a week at Fahy's now on top of The Castle. I would like to start saving money. Money means choices. December is the busiest I've seen the bar since I've started here. Pat has dealt with it by putting on the radiators full blast, draping some fairy lights round the windows and squeezing a fake plastic Christmas tree into the space in the corner beside the toilets. Eamonn is wedged into his seat next to the tree now, the big lump of him, staring up at the telly with wet eyes.

Gerry's in high spirits today. Or consuming them, anyway. Whiskey chasers with his pints. He's an even louder presence than normal, cheeks in a permanent blush, mouth motoring away.

– Orla, what are you at? he says suddenly, looking at me. Mayo Dave is staring too.

– Nothing, I say, but I was at something. I was looking at the Christmas lights, turning my head fast, flicking it to the left and right, testing my vision for traces of my bad trip. Biff has taken great pleasure in teasing me about 'the snakes' at every available opportunity. I've started telling him to fuck off. I don't even care anymore.

– I like this line, Gerry says, tapping his fingers on the bar and doing a jaunty little move with his head. He speaks louder over the music so we can hear him. – He's saying, we'll never get the OBE or the knighthood for our services to the hod.

– What's the hod? I say.

– It's the box for carrying bricks. You'd fit ten bricks over one shoulder. It'd leave you black and blue. He winces and rubs his left shoulder as he's talking, and then stops suddenly, blinking at the bar counter, his hand still holding his shoulder. – I had two little brothers born and die when I was working the building sites.

I look to Mayo Dave, who pulls his lips together in a grimace, before standing up off his stool and walking slowly to the toilet. Pat is nowhere to be seen. I speak as the song ends. – Gerry, how did your mother cope?

He shrugs.

I do a sweep of the bar and put the glasses in the washer. When I come back to Gerry I ask, – How's Herself?

He takes a big slurp of his pint and puffs up his chest to speak, all indignant. – Herself has left.

– What do you mean, she's left? I say, leaning over the bar to give him my full attention.

– She's after leaving me.

The chasers make sense now. – What happened?

– *Nothing* happened, he exclaims. The toilet door bangs shut and Mayo Dave lumbers towards us, zipping up his flies. His cheeks are in flames from the heat of the place.

– Herself has left, I say to him as he sits back down, and then I swing back to Gerry and say, – Where'd she go?

– Her sister's in Finchley.

– Does she work?

– She does accounts for Francis's hairdressers and a few other places. Bookkeeping.

– You never told us that, I say, seeing Herself in a new light now. Of course, she must earn money, because Gerry doesn't seem to have a regular income. He does 'jobs' for people.

– What about your boys? I say, – What about Liam?

– He's the only one still at home,' he says. The anger's gone from his face now, leaving a questioning expression; his brows raised over glassy eyes.

255

A while later the phone rings from behind the bar. I jump up and answer it. A boy's voice, in a London accent, asks, – Is Gerry Connolly there?

– Sure, I'll put you on to him, I say, and stretch the phone on its flex across the bar to Gerry.

He holds it up to his ear with the tips of his fingers as if it might burn him. – Hello.

. . .

– Go to the chipper.

. . .

– There's money under the sink.

. . .

– I'll be home by eleven. You'll be grand.

He hands me the receiver and says, without looking at me, – I'll have another.

And I serve it to him, wordlessly, taking the coins from the little pile he has fashioned on the bar in front of him.

The night creeps in and the smoke cloud lowers from the ceiling as the bar fills up and empties out again, the door bringing in a stream of icy air every time it opens. Eamonn starts crying at around 10pm, tears streaming down his swollen cheeks as he stares into the black of his stout. I bring him a fresh one with a clean beer mat and sweep the bar for empty glasses again.

An hour later, Gerry's money pile has disappeared, and his words with it. His cheeks are crimson from the heat and the whiskey. Mayo Dave buys him another pint and a short. I keep making a show of looking at the clock, in the hope that he'll see that it's past eleven. When he's finished his drinks, I speak to him gently. – Gerry, you said to Liam you'd be home half an hour ago. I look to Mayo Dave for back-up, but he's inscrutable under his cap.

Gerry nods at the bar and hoists himself down off the stool. His head bobs on his neck like a buoy on water. He takes a second to find his balance, gripping the stool with a trembling hand, then launches himself towards the door.

After closing, I'm wiping tables while Pat empties the slops behind the bar.

– Has that ever happened before? I ask. Gerry's son calling the pub?

– His wife used to ring, but not anymore. That's the first time his son has rung.

– Everyone's lost it, Pat.

– It's December, she says, shaking her head. – All this forced Christmas cheer. Doesn't help if you're on your own. Just makes it worse.

I walk around to the back of the bar to spray and wipe the tables there. – I'm dreading Christmas, I say.

She turns off the tap and looks at me, surprised. – Why?

– Because my family do my head in. And . . . nothing's the same as it was.

– Well, are you the same as you were? Since you were last home?

257

I stop wiping and think. – I guess I feel more grown up, more moved on from them.

– And are *they* not allowed to move on?

– Alright, Pat, alright, I say, pretending to be exasperated. I look over to see her laughing quietly to herself behind the bar.

CHAPTER 25

THE ROCK SHOW

Gwen's hands are wholly unremarkable but for the one long nail attached to the pinkie finger on her left hand. It is yellow-tinged and filed into a lethal point: a neat and dependable receptacle for the exact amount of cocaine needed for a bump.

We are huddled in a toilet cubicle backstage at the LA2 after Shiva's big show. Gwen's eyes are pulled wide in concentration as she scoops up a nail's worth of cocaine from a paper wrap and holds her finger up to my nostril. I hoover it up, tilt my head back and sniff a few times to make sure it's definitely up there.

– Got it? she says, and I nod. – Hey, how's Castle? she asks.

I sniff again. – It's good to have regular work. Max, the engineer, is sound. It's not as fun as Redstar, though.

Gwen nods as she helps herself to one nostril-ful, and then scoops another one up her other nostril. Double the measure for herself. – I heard you had a big one with some acid, she says.

I groan, – Oh, for fuck's sake. I'm mortified.

– It is what it is. Just be careful, babe.

Before I can process what she's getting at, she's asking, – Have you made up with Frank?

– How did you know about that?

– Richie told me.

– Well, we haven't talked about it. He only got back from Devon a few days ago, but he's not ignoring me anymore, which is good.

– He'll be fine.

– Mmm. So, what happened with the gig tonight? I ask.

Gwen rolls her eyes, sighs and says, – It was a slog to be honest. She pinches the base of her nose and continues, – They put the show on sale back at the end of the summer after the big festival gigs, and it felt right, but since the single didn't really pick up as much radio play as we thought, the tickets just didn't sell. She carefully refolds the wrap and slips it into a zipped-up compartment of her wallet as she talks. – We'd spent our whole marketing budget by the end of September, and then we had to spend so much more just to get it this full. But Orla . . . She holds her forefinger up to her mouth and widens her eyes, and I nod.

I know the code of conduct. There will be no talk of the empty space when we see them now, just of the adoring crowd. She unlocks the door and we slip out as another two girls slip in behind us. I copy Gwen and tilt my face back to check for any residue around my nose, and then we go back out to the backstage bar.

As soon as I arrived with Neema earlier, though, we knew. The centre of the floor was full enough, but there were whole swathes of space around the edges of the room that were empty. If you were standing in the middle of the floor, looking forwards at the stage, then Shiva had a full house and this was a band in their prime, on the cusp of big things. From our vantage point at the edge, it felt like they were the support band to a headline show. I wondered, as I watched Kesh closely during the gig, what it looked like from the stage. He sang with his head back, his eyes half-closed, as if he was trying to blur the crowd out of focus. He wore a white T-shirt with the word 'Slut' scrawled across it, which was ironic, Gwen said, since he doesn't seem to have sex with anyone, ever.

He was wild on stage, prowling around the huge space as the lights flashed on and off him, leaning up into Frank's face and shrieking lyrics into his ears. They played 'Holding' second last and finished with the current single, 'You Never Said', stumbling off stage in a blur of feedback and stumbling back on just a short while later, too scared that the crowd might leave before the encore, I presumed. They played out with 'Brick By Brick'.

The Redstar lot are in the bar. I see Alistair, grave-faced, talking with a blonde woman in the corner. No Andy, thank God. Frank is leaning against the far wall, laughing loudly at something Steve, the A&R man, is saying. Richie and Neema are talking to Kesh, who looks like he's spent some time in a cubicle himself recently. He's changed into a dark navy T-shirt and washed his face, but his eye make-up is still smudged around his eyes. He is talking incessantly, and Neema and Richie are listening intently, the same slightly concerned expression on their faces. Gwen and I make a beeline for them, but Gwen is intercepted by a loud woman at the bar, so I carry on. Kesh is still talking as I arrive.

– It's just not okay, like, it's just not acceptable. It totally fucking compromised my performance.

– What did? I say, and I feel Neema's eyes on my face. She'll know where I've been.

She replies on behalf of Kesh. – Shane fucked up tuning his guitars.

– And did you tell him during the gig? I ask.

Kesh's eyes are bulging, as if something is behind them trying to push them out of their sockets. – Course I fucking told him. I ran out to him three times between songs, and he just said the stage was too hot and gave me that fucking gormless expression of his and shrugged as if it was out of his hands, rather than his sole fucking purpose.

– Well, he has other jobs, too, mutters Neema, looking at the floor.

– What did you say to him just now? says Richie.

– I told him he doesn't work for us anymore. To pack down our shit and find a new job.

– You did *what?* Richie is staring at Kesh now, unblinking.

Kesh pushes his shoulders back and shifts his weight on his feet. – He's fired, Richie. I've had enough of making excuses for him. He's done. Kesh holds his forearm up to his nose and wipes the full length of it along his nostrils before catching eyes with Gwen and walking away from us.

– I presume you lot didn't get to be part of that discussion, I say to Richie, before slurping up a big, cool mouthful of vodka tonic through my straw.

– You presume correctly, he says, and walks off in Frank's direction. Neema is looking at me.

– What? I say.

– You're shit-stirring, she says. – Where'd you get the coke?

– Where do you think? I reply, glancing in the direction of Gwen. – There's going to be a shit storm tonight.

– Maybe, she says, pensively. – Maybe not.

We go back to the K West hotel because Finn, the singer from Plane Trees, is staying there and having a bit of a party. We lounge around in the foyer drinking, pretending to have room keys, until a room number is texted around. Then we divide into splinter groups and, one by one, each group sidles off to the lift.

It's a suite, and it's full of people. I search for Vinnie, but he's not here. Kesh is in deep conversation with Finn on the bed in the corner, as he racks out lines on the bedside table. Finn is a tall, wiry-looking fella with long brown hair and a long nose. His fingers and arms are adorned with letters and numbers and symbols crudely tattooed on, as if someone took a Sharpie to him. When he laughs, it's so loud it silences the room. Richie and another guy start trying to figure out the stereo, and I stand with Neema and Gwen in front of the wardrobe.

– Where's Frank? Neema asks.

– Think he went off to score.

On cue, he bursts into the room. – Well, this is cosy, he says as he looks around the room, and on seeing Richie, adds, – Shane's fucked off already.

– Who've we got here, anyway? Finn is standing in front of us. I hadn't realised the height of him until now. He must be as tall as the top of the wardrobe.

– Hello darling, Gwen says, and reaches up to hug him. She gets a half-hearted hug back. Neema doesn't go that far. She speaks for both of us.

– I'm Neema and this is Orla, she says politely.

Finn sizes us up. There's something menacing about his energy, something hostile.

– That's my sister, comes a voice from behind us. Kesh's head is turned sideways, hovering inches from the bedside table, a cut-up straw held to his nose.

– Okay. I see the likeness now, actually, Finn says, before turning to me. – And you? Orla, is it?

I raise my eyebrows at him. – Yeah, I'm Neema's friend, I offer, in the hope that it might prove interesting to Finn. – I live with them all.

– Where are you from? he queries with a half-smile.

– Dublin, I say, and then add, – In Ireland.

– We just came from there, he says, not taking his eyes off me. – You guys have got crazy accents. 'Hellaw, my nim is Arla, wud ye like a wee Guinness?' His eyes bore into me, looking for a reaction.

I blink slowly. I would like him to stop looking at me so intensely.

– Well, you managed to cover every corner of Ireland with that accent, says Gwen.

And my mouth moves into a relieved smile, but Finn still hasn't laughed. His mouth is moving again now. – What did you think, Orla?

– It was okay, I lie. – Did you like Dublin?

He sighs theatrically and slowly starts to lean towards me. – It was all, he says, leaning further into my face, – a bit . . .

Another pause, where he leans closer.

– . . . of a blur.

His face is so close to mine now, so I can see the lightning-bolt lines of his blood vessels zig-zagging around his pupils. A large lump of cocaine is wedged between the nose hairs in his left nostril. I'm holding my breath.

– Okay, you're weird! says Neema, taking my arm in hers.

She pulls me towards her. Her tone is bright, matter-of-fact. Fearless. She smiles at him, waiting for him to smile too.

– What's going on over here, Finn? Richie is with us now. He stands beside Neema, slightly in front of her, and looks at Finn, whose mouth has twisted into a smile. Even Richie is dwarfed by him.

– This young lady just called me weird. That's what's going on. Are you trying to be the knight in shining armour, Richie?

– Just a concerned friend, Finn, says Richie, with a fake smile.

– Well, I take offence at the idea that these girls need to be rescued. We were having a nice chat.

I hear a snort and look around to see Kesh sitting on the bed, holding his nose, looking in our direction. The room seems very small all of a sudden. Finn, looking down at Richie, is statue-still apart from his nostrils, which are quivering ever so slightly. He pivots his head to look at me again.

– Can you stop looking at her like that? Neema says.

And the room is quiet now. Somehow, the music has stopped as well. *Where the hell is Vinnie when you need him?* Frank shuffles over.

– Jesus Christ! Finn laughs out loud and I see spittle fly out of his mouth. – You guys are fucking crazy. What do you think I'm going to do, eat her? With the utterance of the word 'eat' he lurches forwards into my face and bares his teeth.

I instinctively step back and stumble into the wall. As I steady myself, I see Neema's tiny hands reach up to push

Finn away, and his fingers wrap around her wrists and pull them up in the air. Now, while laughing loudly, he is holding her up off the ground by her wrists.

– Put her down now, Finn, you're being a prick, says Richie.

But Finn is laughing now, maniacally, and staring at Richie, as if to taunt him. – Oh, is this your girlfriend? he says, and turns to Kesh, whose face is tense.

– Put her down, Richie shouts, and I can hear the anger in his voice now. I feel the same hot rage, and go to pull at Finn's arms to make him release her, but someone is holding me back, pulling me away, and now Richie has swung at Finn, but it's hard for him to make contact with his face because Neema's squirming body is dangling right in front of him.

I look down and see the blur of her ankle boots as they drum into his shins; she is kicking as hard as she can, and Finn is jerking his face away from Richie's punches and Kesh is shouting, – Finn, drop her *now*, but one of Richie's punches must have landed, because Finn is bellowing in pain and dropping Neema, who falls to the floor and then stumbles back into me.

– What the fuck are you playing at, Finn? Kesh's face is twisted into rage as he yells at Finn. – That's my sister.

Gwen is here now, scooping Neema and I into her arms and herding us away, towards the door. As we move around the bed, there is an almighty crash behind us and I turn to see Kesh crumpled on the floor against the wardrobe door, Finn standing over him.

267

– You fucking prick! Neema shrieks, breaking free from Gwen's hand and launching herself at Finn, punching and pummelling him with her fists. He pushes her away and she's straight back, trying to stamp on his toes with her heels.

– Watch it, little girl, Finn says.

Just at that moment, Vinnie walks into the room. – FINN, he shouts, and runs towards Finn.

Richie is clasping his hands around Neema's waist from behind and pulling her away from Finn, past Vinnie and Gwen and me, towards the door, as she kicks and screams, and Kesh and Finn are full-on fighting now. Finn has the front of Kesh's T-shirt scrunched up in his hands and uses it to throw him on to the floor by the end of the bed. 1 see Kesh's face flushed with fear, his hands up in defence as Finn jumps on top of him and pins him down with his thighs.

Vinnie is trying to pull Finn off Kesh now, shouting, – Finn, what the fuck are you doing?

But Finn's face is clenched in concentration, sweating cocaine and rage, his long legs clamped around Kesh. I realise that I am shouting and so is everyone else, and just as Kesh's leg kicks out and connects with the desk, where a glass lamp falls and smashes on the ground, Gwen's voice finally cuts through the noise: – I'm calling the police!

Finn's hands are round Kesh's neck as Gwen continues. – Everyone, get out now. Finn, let Kesh go. NOW.

Finn starts to laugh and clambers off Kesh, pulling himself violently out of Vinnie's grip.

Kesh pulls himself up to standing, spits on the carpet and pushes past us out of the room. Vinnie looks to me, shell-shocked, and shouts – What the fuck just happened?, but Gwen is pulling me by the hand, and we are in the corridor now, walking fast behind Frank and Kesh, and it's deathly quiet out here, so much that I can hear myself breathing, and Gwen too. Gwen, who is still holding my hand and shaking her head in disbelief, I presume, at what just happened. A set of eyes peep out of one door and then retreat, the door closing quickly as we pass. Kesh lets out a low growl, clenches his fingers into a fist and goes to punch the wall, but pulls his hand flat at the last second and slaps it instead.

Gwen whispers loudly, – Just keep moving.

We do. The corridor is dark and long, and no other words are exchanged until we turn the corner at the sign for the lift. That's where we see Richie and Neema. They are locked in an embrace by the lift. It is not the supportive hug of a friend. It is clinging, caressing; her hands are around his neck and he is hunched over, his face buried in her hair, whispering something into her ear. I have stopped walking. So has Kesh. I'm aware of his presence just in front of me. Aware of the silence.

Gwen is speaking words into the space between us and Richie and Neema. – Oi, you two, come on. No dilly-dallying, let's get out of here.

As they both turn, the looks on their faces answer every question in my head. Neema's face crumples; her eyes are circular panic. Richie steps away from Neema with his hands on his hips, turning his back to us, shaking his head slowly.

– What the fuck have I just seen? says Kesh quietly, and I turn sideways just in time to see his fingers folding into a fist once more. – Am I going to have to go for you, too, Richie? Is this for real?

Neema moves her hands up to cover her mouth. Richie swings around. His voice is placating and soft. – This is not how you were supposed to find out, Kesh.

– Oh really? Well, tell me, when is the *right* time to tell me that you're fucking my little sister? Who else knew this was happening? Kesh swings around to stare at us. He sees my face and keeps moving to the others, as if whatever expression I am wearing says I'm definitely as shocked as he is.

Frank shrugs. – Don't look at me, mate.

Gwen stays silent. Kesh has stepped up to her face now. – You knew about this?

– No one told me, she says, calm as anything. – I just guessed.

I stare at Neema as her hands drop from her mouth. Her eyes move from Gwen's face back to Kesh's as he turns around to face his sister. Richie doesn't say anything. He holds his arm in front of Neema as if to protect her.

The lift pings softly and the doors slide open. – Come on, Gwen says, and ushers me towards it. I grab Neema's hand as I move past her and pull her in with me and Gwen. Frank sees his chance and slips past Kesh to jump in too. Richie turns to give Neema a reassuring look. His skin is pale

270

against the brown velvet curtains. His eyes look frightened as the doors close him out.

We don't speak in the lift, or in the foyer. Gwen hails a taxi, and as we pull away from the hotel, she starts to talk.

– Fucking Finn. That guy needs help.

Frank turns his head to her. – He's a fucking psycho. The guy had so much bugle in him, he was lethal. He would have smashed Kesh's face in, Gwen, I swear.

– I think Neema would have smashed his face in if she was allowed, Gwen offers with a smile, and we all look to Neema. She is blank, expressionless, apart from her eyes, which look haunted, staring out the window as the streets flash past. When the taxi stops outside the house, Frank and I say goodbye to Gwen. Neema climbs out of the car and unlocks the front door in silence.

We step in behind her, and Frank closes the door. I turn to him and say – Night, Frank.

– Night, he says in a soft voice, and I can tell by how unsleepy his eyes are that he wants to stay up and chat. Part of me really wants to, because this is the first time it's felt like we could ever be friends again, but my legs take me up the stairs behind Neema instead.

Our bedroom is particularly messy tonight. There is make-up all over the floor around my bedside table. The faint smell of hairspray lingers in the air. She doesn't turn on the light, and neither do I. The moon is up, and shining soft light through the skylight. I sit on my bed watching her, hunched in the semi-darkness, peeling off her tights. I am still fully dressed. I bend down to the floor and pick up some clothes, and begin to fold them slowly on my lap. An image of Kesh arrives in my head, screaming into Richie's face in that muted hotel corridor. Kesh doesn't seem like the fighting type, but the amount of cocaine he'd consumed said different. I've never seen Richie's face so utterly crestfallen before. There's a new Richie who I need to learn about, one who's been right there under my nose, hiding behind the jokey exterior: earnest, knowing, the type of guy who tucks a girl's hair behind her ear.

There's a new Neema, too: a Neema who attacks men in a blind rage, who keeps swollen secrets from her best friend. She is standing now, pulling on her pyjama bottoms, plaid pink. I can't see her face properly, and I wonder if she's crying. I wonder if she's thinking what I'm thinking, but I don't ask. I don't say anything at all.

I can't describe the feeling I have now, but I know that it's tethered to a feeling I got after my da told me he was moving in with Flatface. It's a feeling of trying to stay afloat in stagnant water while everyone else moves with the current. It's a feeling of life leaving me behind.

I keep focusing on Neema's shape as she climbs into bed and lies flat on her back, her arms by her sides. The moonlight pours through the skylight. It reaches as far as her waist. I can see her hands and they look so small. I can't even hear her breathe.

CHAPTER 26

HAS IT COME TO THIS?

London is a metalscape made of sleeping giants, flesh made of brick, bones made of steel, blood made of hot liquid glass. Each underground station is a giant's face; the huge cavernous stairwells are their gobs, the jagged steps of the escalators their incisors, swallowing us up and snoring us out.

MIND THE GAP.

I join the flow of commuters moving towards the escalators of Angel Tube station, and as I place my foot on the moving metal, I take a big breath and clamp my mouth shut.

Richie never came back to Mill Road. He's staying with Shane in Peckham. Kesh arrived home the next afternoon, and has spent the last few days holed up in his bedroom, blasting music out into the hall. Frank went cold again once he sobered up, grunting out monosyllabic replies to any attempts at conversation. He's been out of the house a lot.

Neema has been sitting curled up on the sofa in a haze of weed smoke, staring right through the television. I've never seen her so mute, so defeated.

I'm wedged between people on the steps above and below me, part of a long line of limbs, clinging on and tensing up for the day ahead. A man in a suit walks up the steps to the left of me, clutching a briefcase in one hand, pulling himself up by the handrail with the other. He's either a show-off, or a lunatic, or extremely late for a meeting. Maybe that's everyone in London.

This morning, Neema padded downstairs in her slippers, silent as a cat. I followed her into the kitchen, where she stood over the counter blinking into an empty cereal bowl.

– Orla, I'm moving out of the loft, she said, still staring at the bowl. When I didn't respond, she dragged her eyes to meet mine. – Into Richie's room. He's not coming back. Everyone has said it's okay.

Everyone has said it's okay.

– Fine. Do what you want, I said, turning to walk out the door, but I stopped then. – Why didn't you tell me about him?

Her voice was quiet but firm. – Because I didn't think it was fair to ask you to keep it secret from the others.

– You mean you didn't *trust* me to keep it secret from the others.

– No, Orla. With Kesh, it's all so sensitive. Richie was so

274

paranoid he would find out without us getting a chance to tell him in the right way.

– Well, Richie should have been more careful in the hotel corridor, I said, stepping back into the room and leaning against the counter just in time to see the edges of anger in the shift of her expression. – How long have you been together? I asked.

She opened her cupboard and took out her cereal. – Since July.

– Fucking hell, he didn't hang about.

– It wasn't all him. It was both of us. We were both in it. She was still clutching the cereal box. Holding it by her bowl.

– You kept it from me for nearly six months, I said. I couldn't hold her gaze, so I went to the window and pushed it open, emphasising the word 'six' with the pull of the handle. The icy breeze slipped in, chilling my face.

– Orla. I'm sorry that you feel like I, like, let you down in some way, but it's not that. She started pouring her cereal then. As if this was just an everyday conversation. As if she could eat and get on with her day.

– Let me down in some way? Neema, we share, or we shared, a fucking bedroom. I told you everything about my life. I confided in you about my dad, and cried at you over Moses. And all that time, you were sleeping with Richie. Did you not *want* to tell me?

And that was the truth of it.

Why doesn't she need me like I need her?

*   *   *

275

I'm halfway up the escalator now; pressure pushing outwards from my chest. The circle of light from the ticket hall at the top is growing larger as we ascend. I take my travel card out of my handbag and hold it in my hand, ready.

Neema had an answer immediately. – It wasn't that easy. There are other people involved. The whole future of the band is at stake now. It's not all about you and me, Orla.

We locked eyes just as the soft strum of an acoustic guitar drifted through the walls from Kesh's bedroom.

Smashing Pumpkins – 'To Sheila'.

It arrived as if to soundtrack the wave of hurt that crashed through me in that moment, forcing me to turn away from her and blink rapidly out the open kitchen window as she talked behind me, quieter than before.

– I was going to tell you. I kept wanting to, and Richie would say to wait a bit longer. We argued about it.

I turned and met her eyes. – And Richie should be the one to decide how *we* communicate?

Her face went tight at first. She got her milk from the fridge and poured it on her cereal. Walked around me to get a spoon from the drawer. Then she looked quizzical, as if she was trying to figure out a puzzle in her head. – You know what, Orla? If you're not willing to let this go, there's nothing I can do about it.

– Oh right, so put the blame back on me again. This is all my fault, is it?

– No. But it's your choice how you react. And once again, you've made it all about you.

And with that, she stuck her spoon in her bowl and walked out, face cool as anything, the edge of smugness in her smile, as if she'd solved the puzzle and it was easy.

– See you later, she said.

– Neema, I called after her, and she turned around. – When you couldn't sleep, I said. It was because of all this, wasn't it?

She said nothing and walked away.

My chest is on fire as the escalator eases into the ticket hall at the top. I cling on to my travel card and rush towards the turnstile, nearly tripping over the man in front of me because I'm looking at the slot to put it into, and I don't see his stupid feet with his stupid polished work shoes, and I pretend I don't hear him cursing under his breath as I slip the card in and pull it out, and now I can breathe again. The air is full of fumes as I walk out on to Upper Street, but I swallow it down me, big lungfuls of it, until my heart has slowed down into a regular rhythm and I don't feel light-headed anymore. *She's paying extra money to be further away from me.* I've never made it all the way to the top before.

– Hello, The Castle.

– Oh, thank God.

– Anna?

– Orla. Da rang just now. He was all teary. The baby's after coming early. He wanted us to know. They've had a baby boy. He came four weeks early, and he's in an incubator.

Pause.

– Orla?

– Yeah, I'm here.

– Have you been to bed?

– Yes, I've been to bed. Fuck's sake, Anna.

– Orla. Listen. I don't want to be that person who tells you what to do, but I think you need to come home.

CHAPTER 27

A PLACE CALLED HOME

There's a baby crying on this plane. I swear, the sound of it would drive you demented. It's relentless. I'm squashed into the middle seat, near the back. The cabin is packed with the Irish in England coming home for Christmas, all preened and plucked, suitcases and wheelie bags packed with presents, ready to see old friends and have big, happy, hearty family reunions. One of the kids behind me has been kicking the back of my seat for the whole journey.

I see my first glimpse of Dublin lowering down from the top of the window as the plane tips sideways to find its course into the airport, Dalkey Island emerging from the sea, verdant green, the Sugar Loaf and Bray Head poking up behind. Big, shining brown streaks of sand appear from low tide on the beaches on the south side. The striped red-and-white Poolbeg towers signal the entrance to the city from the sea. I wait to feel some sort of emotional release, but it's hard over all the whingeing and noise.

The two musketeers are coming to collect me. I'm trying to muster up enthusiasm about this because I am looking forward to seeing them, but I've never flown or got the boat into Dublin without my lanky da standing there, waiting for me with his grave resting face, as if he's contemplating something profoundly serious. I used to love watching it change when he saw me. He always looked surprised before he smiled, as if seeing me was some sort of serendipitous event as opposed to a planned meeting.

– Orley! It's the unmistakable shrill voice of my ma. I find her in the throng, waving furiously at me. As our eyes meet, I see her face crumple slightly and her hand travel up to her heart, where she lays it flat against her chest. *Oh God. Am I that much of a fright?*

Anna is waving furiously beside her, but in a completely mocking way, with a stupid face on her. She walks up to me and takes me by both shoulders in an overdone Irish-mammy performance, shaking her head in wonder.

– Ah, would you look at ye, she says.

– Jeeeeesus, Anna, I say, laughing.

Now my real ma has me by the shoulders. – You're very thin, Orla. And very pale.

I roll my eyes while hers travel over my face. – It could be that you've dyed your hair, the paleness, she says, as if she's talking to herself.

– Nice to see you, too, Ma. I get a look at her, too. She is revved up on adrenaline, but there is a new *something* about her. Her hair is dyed a honey-blonde colour and cut into a neat bob with a long, swishy fringe that seems to accentuate her cheekbones. She looks sharper, more vivid somehow. She has been borrowing Anna's make-up. Or maybe she buys her own these days. She wears a red-cotton biker jacket over skinny jeans, with some black leather high-heeled ankle boots. Her legs look lean and toned.

– Ma. That exercise bike is working out very well for you.

– Come on before the traffic gets awful, my ma says, hooking her arm into mine and walking me towards the exit. Her boots make a clean clip-clop sound on the shiny floor of the terminal. She is wearing perfume, something new and unfamiliar to me, something citrussy and sweet. Her face, being thinner, makes her look older somehow. Or maybe it's the make-up.

Anna is wearing leggings and trainers and a baggy old rugby jersey, probably borrowed and never returned from an old boyfriend. She hooks her arm into my free one and starts singing the lyrics 'The Hills Are Alive' from *The Sound of Music*.

– How was your flight? says Ma, cutting her off.

– Packed, I say. – Loads of whining kids.

– Jesus, Anna says. – That can't be good for a hangover.

– And who says I'm hungover? I say.

– I just presumed, with your rock 'n' roll lifestyle, that you lived in a permanent state of excess, she says deadpan, eyebrows raised.

– No. No hangover, I lie, because I *am* hungover. After staying in Fahy's for the lock-in, after swearing I wouldn't. After drinking an entire shift's-worth of Guinness in two hours. Ciarán got his banjo out, Gerry tapping out the rhythm of the songs on his beer mat with his chubby little fingers. Walking home at 2am with my fists clenched, searching for predators, I slipped on the ice at the top of Mill Road and went down hard.

– Well, we're looking forward to hearing all your news, says Ma, as if there is some big revelation ahead.

– Ma, there is no news. Just the same old shite over there.

We climb into my ma's little car, Anna squeezing into the back and Ma leaning forward over the wheel as if someone has got a knife to her back.

– Ma, you're after missing the exit, says Anna, sticking her head between the two front seats.

– I'm not, Anna, it's over there, says Ma.

– Well, you can go around the whole thing again, I suppose, says Anna. – We're not in a hurry. Do a few laps of the car park, why not?

And my ma tuts and rolls her eyes, and Anna sits back and folds her arms huffily. She is rangy and tall, my sister, five-foot-eight to my five-foot-nine, with long brown hair that she bleaches the life out of, just like her mother and I used to do, except Anna straightens hers on top of the bleach, so it looks like straw. She told me once that one of her friends said we looked like Wurzel Gummidge's twin sisters. She thought it was hilarious.

– So what's going on with the baby? I say, because no one's mentioned it yet and that makes me angry.

Anna says, – I texted Dad last night. He said he's out of the emergency department and they're taking him home today.

Ma says, – They don't call it the emergency department in Ireland, Anna. What, do you think you're in *ER* or something?

– Alright, Ma, Anna says, all affronted.

There's a silence, and then Ma speaks. – Four weeks early is worrying. But that's the risk when you have a baby at her age. She's lucky.

I contemplate 'lucky' Flatface as Ma drives out of the car park and on to the M50. We drive in silence for a while, and when I see Three Rock Mountain looming in the distance I feel something dislodge inside of me. I don't think I make a noise, but when I glance over to my ma, she is already looking at me, a quizzical expression on her face.

– Is it good to be home, Orley? she says.

I don't know yet, so I say, – It's been such a long time.

Ma indicates left off the ring road and drives us down into south-Dublin suburbia, past the grocery shop I used to work in, past the side streets where Da used to teach me how to drive. I swallow down a swell of anxiety at the thought of him.

This is my second Christmas coming home from England. This time last year, I had been away in Cheltenham for a term, and Dad had only moved out of the house a few months before, to a flat down by the university. Anna said it was depressing as fuck. I went to the pub on Christmas Eve and got hammered, so the next day was more something to get through than something to enjoy, but I remember Dad arriving all cheery on Christmas morning, with a bag of presents and a bottle of Baileys in his hand, and Ma all dolled up, in full hostess mode, apron on over her dress, fussing over the food and not looking anyone in the eye. I watched them closely, waiting for signs of reconciliation. He helped to prepare the salad for lunch. Later on, he sat between Anna and me on the sofa as we all opened our presents. Then Anna and I went to watch a film, and left him and Ma in the kitchen. He popped his head round the door and said cheerio, told us not to pause it, he'd see us soon. In my head, he was always coming back.

I haven't seen him since.

Ma indicates and turns into the estate, and there are all the same pebble-dash semis, some with Christmas lights strewn across the windows, most with Christmas trees on display through the blinds. One house on the corner has a large plastic Santa and sleigh-and-reindeer display on the drive, and over-sized plastic light-up Christmas presents dotted around the front garden.

– Did you manage to get a tree? I say.

– Well, Dad offered to buy one and bring it over— Anna begins.

Ma interrupts. – Uncle Brian very kindly picked an extra one up for us.

We pull up at the kerb outside our house. I see a glimpse of the tree now, through the living room window. It's in the usual place, in the far-right hand corner of the room.

– Well, here we are, Orla, says Ma.

Anna pushes me away from the boot of the car. – Let me get your case, Your Highness.

So, I let her, and I follow Ma into the house. The second I step over the threshold of our front door, I'm confronted with my reflection in a large silver framed mirror. – Jesus, you should have warned me about that, I say. As I turn away, I see that the hall is painted a new colour, light pink. – Woah, everything is so different.

– Well, says Ma, not trying to hide the sarcasm in her tone. – A lot has happened since you were home last, Orla.

– We told you we were painting the house, remember? says Anna, coming in behind with the suitcase. – In the summer.

I walk into the living room from the hall, and it is a light green colour now, set off with a big grey rug. The fireplace and mantelpiece above it have been painted bright white, and there are new ornaments on there, metallic abstract shapes and silver picture frames holding photos of Anna and me as babies and little girls. There is a wide ornamental bowl thing full of shiny stones on the corner shelves, where Da's record player and record collection used to live. The shelves have been painted white. I see now that there is not one trace of my father left in this room. I'm silent as I follow Ma and Anna into the kitchen.

– We got the worktops replaced, says Ma, manicured hands stroking the surface as if it were a prize pet.

– Granite, don't you know, says Anna.

– Wow, I say, trying to muster up the necessary enthusiasm. – It really . . .

– Brightens the place up no end, doesn't it? says Ma. The walls are a pale blue in here. Without sunlight, the colour is tepid. As if reading my mind, my ma turns on the lamp in the corner so everything seems softer all of a sudden.

– Wow, you even got a new kitchen table.

– It was fierce annoying. Wanted something that would give us more space, Ma says as I run my hands over the white surface of the new round table, which is tucked into the corner under the floor lamp. It does give the kitchen more space. The old table was a big, heavy wood thing, with thick legs. It dominated the room. He used to sit at the head of it, silhouetted by the light from the window behind.

– Right, we're getting takeaway tonight. It's been decided, Ma says, casting a glance over at Anna.

Anna takes the hint and brings out a stash of leaflets from the drawer by the sink. – What shall we have, she says. – Chinese? Pizza? Thai?

– You know what, I say, – you choose. Honestly, I'm easy.

– Alrighty, says Anna, pulling out a chair by the table and flicking through the menus.

– I'm going upstairs to put my bag away. Is there anything I should know? I say, trying to make a joke, but it falls flat.

– Anything you should know? Anna looks up at me and, at the same time, Ma turns around from the kettle.

I feel exposed now: they can see the full state of me, blindsided by this new shiny house that I don't recognise. I try to keep my tone light.

– Like any changes upstairs, I say meekly.

– You're in your old room, says Ma. – We gave it a lick of paint, but all of your things are still in there, in the cupboard.

I nod, unable to say anything more, and haul my suitcase upstairs, without looking in any other rooms. The landing is the same dusky pink as the downstairs hallway, and the spare room is the same light blue as the kitchen. I sit on the edge of my old bed. The bed I would throw myself on after slamming doors and thundering up the stairs, when I was fourteen, fifteen, sixteen, seventeen, flaming rage in my head, always running away from Ma. Afterwards it was like I'd stepped off a rollercoaster. I needed to lie down here in the dark and get my balance back. I hold my face in my hands as a wave of exhaustion washes over me, and I can feel the tears stinging the back of my eyes, but I push my fingers harder into my face and take a long, deep, wavering breath through my nose. Up, up, up.

In the bathroom, everything is pristine white. I was only planning to splash water on my face, but I take off my jeans and shirt and climb over the edge of the bath, turning on the shower. The water gets hot quickly, and I hold my face right up into the head of it, so it pummels my skin.

There is a photo of me as a toddler, taken just after getting out of this very bath. In it, I've got shining pink cheeks and damp hair and I'm wrapped up in a towel. He has me encased in the crook of his shoulder; you can see the faded plaid of his shirt. I used to laugh at him so hysterically that my tummy hurt from it, from his silly songs and his play-acting with the bath toys.

I put my hands up against the tiles and lean my weight against them. Then I wash my hair with some of Ma's fancy shampoo and exfoliate my face. It feels good scrubbing London off my cheeks; all that dirty air from Kilburn and Angel and the smell of Mill Road. It's a shock when I catch a glimpse of the bruise from my fall on the ice. It covers most of my hip, already purpling.

Downstairs, Anna is looking at numbers scrawled on plastic boxes and allocating the food to each of us. – You got chicken chow mein, she calls, as I close the door behind me.

– Grand job, I say, and I feel Ma's eyes on me, but I don't return the stare. Instead, I plonk a bottle of champagne and a big box of chocolates down on the table and say, – I brought these for Christmas Day.

– Ooh, they say in unison, and Ma picks up the bottle and looks at it as if she's a wine connoisseur now.

– Or, says Anna, her eyes dancing with mischief, – we could open it now. I'll buy us more, I promise.

I look at Ma. She is smiling and says, – I will if Orla will.

I shrug and say, – Is it cold enough?

Anna holds her hands over it – It actually is.

– Let's do it so, I say.

Ma gets the glasses from the cupboard and Anna says, – I'll open it.

– Is that safe? I say.

– Sure, she's very experienced at opening bottles, Ma says.

Anna twists the cork and the bottle pops, a perfect little waterfall of fizz falling out the top and into the glass that Ma holds up.

– Tilt it, Ma. Tilt it, Anna commands.

– Okay, Jesus, Ma says, rolling her eyes at me.

– How's the new job? I ask Ma as Anna hands me a full, fizzing wine glass.

– I sold a dress to a lady yesterday, all by myself. Ma seems delighted by this. She rearranges herself into her chair, holding her wine glass daintily, and I get a glimpse of what the newly separated Hillary Quinn looks like when she's speaking to her friends.

– And do you like it enough to stay there? I ask.

Ma holds her glass halfway to her mouth and looks at me in surprise. – Well, I've no choice! I can't just up and leave now after a week. I have to stick it out. Sure, I've a house to keep.

– And an interior-decor addiction to feed, murmurs Anna as she slurps up her drink. – Come on, let's tuck in.

So, we slosh our food on to our plates and share the rice around, and I'm thinking, now, of what Mam said, about keeping house.

– Is Da, like, supporting you? I ask with a feeling of dread, because I realise I haven't asked her anything about this side of the situation up to this point. I haven't checked to see if she's okay for money, if she's worried about money. I reach for my glass.

– He's still paying the mortgage, Ma says, heaping food on to her fork.

– Paying us to be nice to Flatface. Anna sniggers into her plate, but I remain still, trying to take in this information.

– Is the divorce sorted? I say in a low voice.

Mam replies, – We have agreed everything pretty easily, but I haven't got the papers to prove it, because everything takes donkey's years. It'll be months and months before it's all done.

– Have you talked to him?

– No, Ma says in a matter-of-fact tone. – No direct chat. All through the solicitors.

– What will happen to the house? I ask. Anna has stopped eating now.

– Well, if we sell it, we'll get half the money each. It all feels fair. He's not trying to do us over.

– And do you intend on selling it? says Anna, eyebrows raised at Ma.

– After the work I've just had done? Not a chance, Ma says, squeezing in a sip of the champagne before the next breath.

I nod and smile at Ma and pick up my glass. – Here's to the future, Ma. Here's to your future.

And Ma doesn't say anything; she just smiles back and we clink-clink-clink and drink.

– Maybe you'll get a toyboy now, says Anna.

Ma tuts and rolls her eyes, but says, – A toyboy. That would learn him, alright.

And I try not to stare at this woman, with her ash-blonde blow-dry and her silky-looking blouse, loosened up by champagne and happy here in this moment, with her daughters laughing with her: this woman who was, and somehow still is, my mother.

CHAPTER 28

FAMILY AFFAIR

– Why The People's Park? None of us live near here, Anna
says as she pushes the palms of her hands down her thighs,
trying to straighten out the creases in her skirt. We're
standing side by side at the water's edge in well-to-do south
Dublin, bundled up in gloves and hats and scarves, the two
piers of Dún Laoghaire to the left of us and Sandycove
beach to the right. It's a perfect winter's day: the sun is
high and counteracted by a bitterly cold wind coming in
from the sea, the sky is painted with long, wavering brush-
strokes of cloud.

– Why a park at all? she says. – Sure, the baby's fucking
tiny.

Anna insisted on driving Ma's car but we couldn't find a
space because it's the Saturday before Christmas and everyone's out on show, slapping backs, cramming shopping in,
warming themselves from the inside out with hot whiskeys.

I wanted to look at the sea for a minute before we head to the park.

– God, it's lovely here, isn't it? I say, looking out across the water, where ribbons of silver light weave through the waves. A P&O ferry crawls along the line of the horizon. – Three hours on a ferry and you're in Holyhead, I add.

Anna says, – Seriously though, Orla, there's so many parks. Why such a posh one? Ma would say Flatface has notions.

– Yeah, it's like they're deliberately taking us out of our comfort zone, I say, and I realise we are both babbling, forcing words up and out of us to maintain an air of normality. We both fall silent. I look at her, put a hand on each of her shoulders and say, – It's going to be fine. We're going to be adults about this. Come on.

Anna's hair is newly bleached and straightened, and she has it tucked behind her ears. It sucks all the colour from her face. Her mascara is too thick and her eyelashes are stuck together in big clumps. Anna, who leaves broken hearts scattered behind her like the ring pulls on her beloved tins, one in, one out, click and push them open, gulp them down, on to the next. Every time I see my sister, I wonder when the tins will start showing on her, and now, I think it's finally started to happen. I can see a little tyre of flesh pushing out above the waistline of her skirt.

She grimaces and follows me as I lead her across the road and up the steps to the bottom of the park. My breathing is shallow. I'm not sure if it's the cold or my nerves, but whatever it is, it's exaggerated by the physical evidence of my exhalations, these balloons of air forming in front of my face as we walk into the park.

Da texted me yesterday: *Can you meet us tomorrow morning at 10 at the café in The People's Park? xx*

I replied: *Okay, see you then.*

And now we're walking up the lower path towards the fountain and the café at the top.

– Oh, God. Oh, Jesus. Okay, here we go, Anna is muttering.

We walk past two old women on a bench, exchanging gifts in shiny gift bags. Two couples meet up on the adjoining paths in front of us, exchanging embraces, while a kid jumps at his father's feet with hands stretched up in the air, waiting to be lifted up. We walk side by side around the fountain and arrive at the café.

Anna holds open the door for me. I walk in and scan the room. He is standing by the till, his back to us. He turns immediately, as if he senses my gaze on him, and we lock eyes.

It's been a full year since I have seen my father. Maybe I've changed. He stares, his face set in a suspended smile, and I stare back, and now the woman behind the till is saying something to him, but before he turns to her, he gestures with his hand for to me to come over to him. My heart has dropped down and is slopping around in my stomach now, because he has changed, too. His beard is gone. He looks younger. Seeing the corners of his jaw shifts the proportions of his face completely. His mouth is wide, thin lips smiling. He's back looking at us again. We awkwardly push past the other people in the queue to get to him, and as the woman is putting drinks on his tray, he reaches out his arms and gives us a tight hug, one arm around each of us.

– Thanks for coming, he says. – What do you want to drink?

I can see Anna is flummoxed by the double hug and I say, – A Diet Coke, at the exact same time Anna says, – A pint?

We all know that she's only half-joking, but it's enough bait for Da to take, and he laughs loudly as the people in the queue behind stare at us. He leans back to the lady and says, – Can I get a Diet Coke and a . . .

– Two Diet Cokes, I say firmly, looking at the lady, and Anna doesn't complain. There is an atrociously awkward moment as she goes to the fridge and takes out the cans and we stand there waiting, not saying a word, as Da fiddles in his wallet looking for coins. I catch Anna's eyes and she widens hers at me. I know Flatface must be nearby, but I don't want to look around for her. Despite the cold, I am sweating. I wipe my forehead with my sleeve.

– Right, we're over in the corner. Follow me, he says and he leads the way. I see her there now, a dark head leaning over a pram, fingers reaching in. I see her face easily because her hair is cut into a short bob and tucked behind her ears, and there's her tiny nose and massive forehead, her lips pursed outwards.

– Carol, my da says.

She lifts her head, and her face fixes on a smile as she

stands up. She wears a black jumper, leather ankle boots and black jeans. She reaches out her arms to me and I stop and hold out my hand to her instead. Her face drops and then rearranges itself into an expression of politeness.

– Hello Orla, she says, putting her hand in mine. Her skin feels clammy. I pull away as fast as I can without seeming rude. – It's so good to meet you. And good to see you, Anna. She goes in for the hug to Anna, and Anna hugs her back.

What the fucking fuck. They've met?

I've no time to process any more than this because Da is pulling chairs over to the table for us.

– Sit, sit. So how are you both? he says, taking us in. – Orla, you look so different.

Anna is in there like a shot. – Says the man who shaved his beard off, and both Da and Flatface laugh. Flatface's is more of a nervous giggle. She flashes a glance at me and I look away quickly, turning to Da.

I see how tired he looks now as he rubs his hand over his cleanly shaven chin. He directs his gaze at me and says with a smile, – Is it really weird?

– Yes, I say, because it is really weird. This is all really fucking weird. It's the Saturday morning before Christmas and my dad has a new family. I click open my can of Diet Coke and pour it into the glass.

– Well, I guess I just fancied something new, he says, and I'm fucking itching to say, *Was a new girlfriend and a new baby not enough for you?*

But Flatface is talking. – It's great you got home for Christmas, Orla. I bet it's lovely to be home.

– It's nice alright, I reply, and I give her a look that I hope says everything that's in my head. A look that says, *Oh it's just lovely to be home, thanks, Flatface, in my old house that's turned into a show home, with an alcoholic sister and an exercise-addict mother and no father. It's fucking great.* I can't say anything at all, though, because suddenly I feel dangerously close to crying. Flatface looks a little shaky, too; her eyes are bloodshot. I see a slight powdery sheen on her cheeks and realise that her face is caked in concealer. I take a sip of the Diet Coke and pull off my big overcoat, as it feels hot in here now.

– So, my da is saying, – would you like to meet your baby brother?

And on cue, Flatface leans forward into the pram and takes out a bundle of blankets. Her lips are all pursed again, and she makes a little tutting noise at the bundle as she lifts it carefully on to her lap. I take another slug of my drink and watch my da's face soften into emotion as he watches her with the baby.

– This is Harrison, he says, pulling the blankets down to expose a tiny pink circle of face.

Of course he named him after George Harrison.

We all stare at the baby. – He's our little Christmas miracle, Da says. He and Flatface are transfixed. Then Flatface looks up at the two of us, her eyes shining and expectant, and Anna leans forward and says, – Nice to meet you, Harrison.

– Do you want to hold him? Flatface offers, latching on to Anna's enthusiasm.

Anna opens her eyes wide and hesitates for a second before saying, – Sure, why not? I don't think I'll be very good, though.

– Just take him under your left arm and then put your right arm like that . . . Flatface is moving Anna's arms to cradle the baby while Da watches on, a beatific smile on his face.

Anna is stiff as a ruler and is talking to the baby. – Okay, hello baby, Harrison, how are ye? Look at you there, with your little squished-up face. Is he asleep?

– Yes, all he does is sleep, says Flatface. – He had a stressful first few weeks of his life, so he's sleeping a lot now. And eating a lot. She says this with a little hint of emphasis on the word 'eating', which makes me think that she is breast-feeding, and I hate her then for bringing that up; even the idea of her breasts is repulsive. I see that she's nervous with Anna holding him, but she's trying to be calm, and Anna is rocking him gently and talking again.

– Ah, would you look at his hands! They're so tiny. Look, Orla.

I peer over the blanket to see a minute curled-up fist.

– He looks like he's ready for a fight, says Anna.

And Flatface laughs softly again and says, – He sure does.

I still haven't spoken this whole time.

– So, Anna continues. – How are you, Carol? Are you recovered?

– I'll be fine thanks, she says looking palpably relieved,

and my da puts his arm around to rest on the back of her chair, looking down at her as she adds, – Physically fine, but not sure I'll ever get over the stress of the birth.

My da speaks in a mollifying tone, more to her than us. – But Harrison has a clean bill of health. We had a check-up with him yesterday.

– That's great, says Anna. – Isn't it, Harrison? She peers down at his face, which is starting to move, lips squirming and forehead furrowing into itself like a little mole, and there's noise coming out of him now, a tiny mewing sound. Anna looks terrified, and Flatface is up and reaching for him, saying, – I think he's hungry.

She takes him from Anna, sits down with him and sticks her little finger in his mouth. He is screaming now, as much as a little lump can scream, and I don't blame him, to be honest, because I wouldn't want someone sticking their finger in my mouth if I was upset. I can see the raw pink of his gums, and a picture of Max on the roof of The Castle arrives in my head, all stretchy muscle and pink flesh, and I blink and take another swig of my can while my da fusses over Flatface, who is putting a bag over her shoulder and pushing her chair back to stand.

– Are you sure you'll be alright? he says.

– Yes, I'll be grand, she says brightly as she tucks Harrison back into the buggy. She turns to face us, tucks her hair behind her ears and says, – I'll just take him for a walk around the park and try to get him back to sleep.

And we nod and Anna says, – Okay sure, yep, and we all watch as Flatface manoeuvres the pram out of the shop. I can see that Da wants to jump up and help her, but something is holding him back, so she holds the door open for herself as she pushes the pram through.

And now it's just us again.

Da is the first one to speak. – So you've had a good time at home, Orla?

– It's been okay, I say, glancing quickly at him and looking away.

– And how's your job at the music studio? Are they giving you a chance to learn?

– There's a guy there who's an engineer who is going to teach me.

– Right. Well, it's great that you can learn on the job, he says, moving to rest his elbows on the table and lean in to us. – And how's your mother? he asks, his gaze flitting between both of us.

Anna opens her mouth to speak, but I get there first. – You mean, your ex-wife? She's Christmas shopping by herself, in town. I'm blinking a lot and I force my eyelids to slow down.

I hear Anna muttering, – Oh, here we go.

I'm not looking at Da, but I can feel him moving to shift his weight on his chair and now he's talking again. – And how are you, Orla?

I'm not sure what to say until Anna turns to look at me, and I remember. – I'm not great to be honest with you.

Definitely not ready to go skipping into the sunset, hand in hand with your new girlfriend.

– Ah, Orla . . . he says, looking visibly pissed off now, as if I've let him down.

Something inside me snaps then. – Oh, I'm sorry to be such a disappointment to you, Da. Just as well you've a new family. Must be great to be able chop and change the people you love with total fucking impunity. I'm glowering at him now with the full force of my hurt.

I see his lips go to move and then stop. He rubs the newly smooth skin around his mouth and chin. His shoulders drop on the tail end of his sigh. – I didn't realise you were so upset.

– Well, there I am again. The inconvenient daughter.

– You're not an inconvenience, Orla. You know that.

I am buoyed by anger now. – Have you ever thought, in this whole shit-show, about how this must be for me and Anna?

He looks to Anna, and I do too. She is staring at the ground as if she can't bear to look at me. She looks up at Da briefly, then shakes her head and shrugs.

– Of course, I've thought of you two. You hardly answer the phone, Orla, so as far as I'm concerned, you don't want to talk to me.

– Oh, for fuck's sake, I say, rolling my eyes and pushing my chair backwards to stand up. It scrapes along the polished cement floor, a big, ugly sound, causing heads to turn at the neighbouring table.

– Orla, what are you doing? Anna says, looking up at me.

301

– Yes. Please, Orla. Please sit down and let's talk about it, Da says.

– I don't want to talk, I say and I pull my coat on and I look at Anna as if to say, *Get a move on.*

A dam has burst in my head and I'm frightened of the feelings that are coursing through me now. I wasn't prepared for them.

Anna is standing now. She says, – Well, I guess that's that then. Say goodbye to Carol for us. She leans forwards to Da and he reaches his arms around her neck and lays his cheek next to hers.

– Happy Christmas, he says, and holds her face and looks into her eyes. He looks at me then, with a hard-done-by expression on his face, as if he's been wronged. – And to you, Orla.

We walk out of the café into the cold of the morning, and I immediately turn back on myself to walk out the top exit of the park. I don't want to run into Flatface again. We walk past Glasthule DART station and take a left down to the seafront, past the grand houses with their perfect wreaths and twinkly lights in the windows. Anna walks in front. I stomp my heavy boots on the pavement and try to tether my thoughts to the rhythm of my footfall. Flashes of Anna and Dad's faces cheek to cheek, the slight closing of his eyes as their faces touched. His expression as he looked at Flatface. The irritation he showed when he was talking to me.

I am startled by the slam of the driver's door of Ma's car.

Anna has gone ahead and climbed in, and is already sitting behind the wheel, arms crossed. I climb into the passenger seat beside her.

– What's your problem? I say, looking across at her.

She's not good at being in a mood, Anna. She stares over the steering wheel, out to sea and sky, and mutters, – So much for being adults.

– Anna! What is your problem? I repeat. She blinks rapidly and turns to me.

– My problem is, you were a fucking bitch.

– What did you want from me, Anna? I'm not going to lie about the way I feel for their sake.

– Could you not see how fucking tired they were? Could you not see that they were trying?

– Can you not see that he has abandoned us?

Pause.

– And why didn't you tell me that you've already fucking met her?

– Because I knew you'd react like this, she says.

– Oh, I'm sorry for being angry that my little sister and my da's new girlfriend are fucking new best mates and no one thought to tell me.

– Fuck off, Orla.

I stop then, because the look on her face isn't pained. It's pissed off. She's pissed off with me.

– How are you not angry at him? I ask.

She speaks immediately. – I'm sick of being angry. Her

hands are on the wheel. She turns to me. – Being angry all the time turns you into a *prick*. She turns the key in the ignition and starts to reverse the car. She stops suddenly, the car jolting, and rummages in her handbag between the seats to find a box of cigarettes. She lights one, then offers the box and the lighter to me. I follow suit, lowering my window to blow out the smoke. She meets my gaze in the rear-view mirror as she reverses the car some more.

– Stop watching me, Orla.

I stare out the front windscreen instead and say, – But what about Ma? What's going to happen to Ma?

She's straight in with her answer as she uses both hands to lock the steering wheel to the right. – Are you fucking blind, Orla? Haven't you seen her? He's fucking set her free. All their friends have sided with her. She can go and get pissed again now.

– What do you mean, she can go and get pissed again now?

– You never heard them arguing, Orla.

– But she's drinking too much!

Anna pulls out on to the road and drives along the coast. – That's rich coming from you, she says as she indicates right, – And *that's* rich coming from *you*, I say. Jesus.

We pull up at a set of traffic lights, Anna heaving the handbrake up so it creaks. In the silence, I say quietly, – What were the arguments?

Anna sighs, a long, slow sigh. – They were always about her boozing. Ma shouted to him one night that she thought he fell in love with her because she was fun. And he said that fun is different from embarrassing, and she screamed at him to fuck off and slammed the kitchen door on him. I preferred screaming to when they didn't talk at all, though.

– Hang on, so this was the summer before last?

– Yep.

– Why didn't you tell me about the arguments?

– I don't know. You didn't live at home, and when you did come home you didn't seem that . . . available. She revs the car over the top of the hill and through the lights. – Anyway, you probably won't remember but I spent most of the summer at Marty Murphy's house. I only went out with him so I had somewhere to go. Then you fucked off to Cheltenham and Da fucked off too, as if he was waiting for you to leave or something. And don't get me wrong – she glances at me briefly – it was fucking miserable when he left, but it was better than before.

I look at my sister in profile as she drives us up the hill at Baker's Corner. She looks tired, and I realise that I feel it too, that post-adrenaline-rush heaviness. Or maybe it's guilt.

– Sorry, Anna.

Her voice breaks a little as she speaks. – Orla, Ma's trying really hard now. She's trying to be happy.

I say nothing as Anna pulls the car around the corner, past the church with the sign that says Our Lady of Perpetual Succour, towards home.

305

CHAPTER 29

IN TOO DEEP

– I'm not getting a hangover at six o'clock on Christmas Day, Anna says, standing over the kitchen sink as she twists the corkscrew into the bottle.

We have been drinking solidly and steadily since midday, before, during and after the enormous Christmas lunch served up by Auntie Sue and Uncle Brian. We were given a warmer welcome than usual: big hugs and exclamations of how great it was to see us, and I realised, as they made a fuss of taking our coats and giving us drinks, that maybe they had had a chat beforehand, maybe we're a sympathy case now, these three lost women, this family torn in two.

After the meal, Brian ordered everyone into the living room to relax, and his youngest daughter, Siobhán, said, – Oh, yes, of course, because we weren't relaxing, were we Da, stuffing our faces with all that beautiful food.

– Siobhán, go on before I make you do the dishes, he said,

the dome of his bald head sticking up from the paper crown he was wearing. He looked at me in mock exasperation and shook his head, as if to say, *What will we do with her?*

I tried to reciprocate his look with some humour in my eyes, but tears welled up instead. He put his hand on mine then, and I couldn't handle the pity on his face, so I looked back at our clasped hands resting on the holly-print tablecloth.

– Anything you need Orla, he said. – We're here. His wedding ring had a dull glint to it. A scar cut perpendicular across the main vein on his hand. It looked like a small letter 't'.

– Jesus, I'm knackered, says Ma now, walking in the door of the kitchen and kicking off her ankle boots.

– Ma, we have to do presents, says Anna.

– I know. Pour me a glass; we'll do them now, and then we'll decide what films to watch. God, I have to say it's nice not having to worry about cooking Christmas dinner, she adds, looking at the pristine counter tops.

I say nothing. Normally, Da makes a big deal of cutting the turkey and making the gravy. He drives us round for the family socials, and then in the evening, he puts records on while we do presents. *Abbey Road*, or Simon and Garfunkel's *Bridge Over Troubled Water*. The first piano chords of the titular song feel instinctively Christmassy to me, like a hymn almost. There's no music this evening, and I feel its absence loudly. I wish I could get rid of this panicky feeling in my throat.

I curl up on the sofa and text Neema.

Happy Christmas . . . xx

Two kisses from me. Two desperate kisses. Has she moved her stuff out yet, I wonder. *Everyone has said it's okay. They all fucking knew before me.*

My phone pings. Her reply reads: *Orla I don't celebrate Christmas, remember!? Hope u and ur family have a good Christmas. See u when u come back. X*

Ma puts on the lamps. The Christmas tree lights glow in the corner. The tearing of Christmas wrapping paper sounds abrasive against the silence. Ma murmurs as we hold up make-up and underwear and pyjamas.

– I thought it would go nice with your eyes.

– Now, I have all the receipts.

– Don't worry if you don't like it.

Ma's present pile is small. She doesn't look bothered when she sees it. She comes from a big family: she's used to not being fussed over. She opens the nice body wash and the scarf from Brown Thomas and thanks us. There's an envelope at the bottom of the pile.

Anna is excited now, leaning forwards in the armchair. – Open it, Ma.

– What's this? Ma says, picking up the envelope, looking excited, and I feel a surge of love for her then, her little feet criss-crossed over each other in her black tights. Anna and I exchange glances. We argued a lot over this present. Anna wanted to buy her something for the gym, but I put my foot down.

We watch closely as she pulls out the voucher for Sheridan's Travel and gawps at the amount. – Three hundred pounds? Girls, this is . . . She struggles to find the words and keeps staring at the piece of paper. – So, it means I can go any-where?

– Anywhere you like, Ma, I say. – You could go on a cruise, you could go on a sun holiday, you could use it for a hotel in Ireland and have a little holiday by the sea here.

– Or you can go to London and see Orla, offers Anna and I nod.

My Ma's eyes are shining and she shakes her head. – Girls, I don't know how you got this money together, it's very generous.

– Don't worry about that, Ma, I say.

But she's still on at it. – You haven't spent all your savings on this, have you?

– *No*, Ma! I say. – I've got two jobs, remember? I'm okay.

– And me, says Anna. She holds up her wine glass, as if it's proof of her all-round okayness and for some reason Ma and I hold up ours too. Anna says, – To Ma! To your new adventures!

We all stand up then and clink our glasses, and Ma reaches up and gives each of us a hug and a kiss on the cheek. When we sit back down, Ma says, – Now, listen, your father would like to talk to you girls today. To wish you a Happy Christmas.

– Since when were you the go-between, Ma? I say.

– I'm not. He texted me this morning to wish us a good day and asked if he could call tonight.

Anna says, – Sure, why not? I'll call him now before the film starts. And she's up and off to the hall.

Ma and I look at each other. – She's keen, I say, trying to keep the humour in my voice.

– She misses him, says Ma, sitting back into her armchair, clutching her wine glass with two hands. – Especially on a day like today.

And there is the first admission of any hurt I have seen from my ma in this whole fucking ordeal.

– Do you miss him? I whisper, stealing a quick glance at her before looking back into the fireplace.

She sighs. – It's taken time to get used to it. But it's for the best, Orla.

I meet her eyes and they are unblinking. She is calm, serene, tranquillised by the wine. I feel my bottom lip quiver again.

– Orlaaaaaaaa! – Anna shouts from the hall.

Ma looks at me expectantly, and when I don't move, she speaks softly. – Orla?

My eyes are stinging with tears.

She continues. – You don't have to talk to him now, love.

And I'm up off the sofa, running past Anna holding out the phone to me, her face all gormless and confused, up the stairs two at a time and into my old bedroom, where I slam the door and throw myself on to the bed.

I stop crying when I hear the click of the receiver as Anna puts it back on the phone. *Nice cosy chat they had. He'll be going back to Flatface – telling her that I wouldn't speak to him, with that hard-done-by expression on his face. That weird new face of his.*

I roll on to my back and take in the room. I hate this pale blue colour; it reminds me of the townhouses in Cheltenham, all insipid pastel greens and lilacs and pinks. I was so excited to leave Cheltenham. So excited to try again at living in England. My clothes are spread out over the bedspread. They all reek of smoke; the smell is so strong it fills the room. Pat has a set of clothes that she only wears in the pub, so that the rest of her clothes are free from the stench. I can't do that, because there's as much smoke in Mill Road as there is in Fahy's. Smoke and secrets. There's enough of them over here, too. I hear the low murmur of voices as Ma and Anna chat downstairs. I used to always know what they'd be talking about. Now, I can't make out the words.

CHAPTER 30

INDEPENDENT WOMEN PART 1

– Get that, will you, Orla? says Ma.

I'm upstairs, pushing the last of my things into my rucksack and I think, *Can you not bleeding get it yourself?*, but I bite my tongue and run downstairs. When I open the door, my da is standing there. His chin is down at his chest, his eyes are on me, beseeching. He clutches his car keys in his hand. I blink at him.

– I've come to take you to the airport, he says.

When I don't respond he adds, – If you'll let me.

I hesitate and look down at my feet, and then say, – Give me a sec.

Ma is sitting at her make-up table when I burst in her bedroom door.

– Did you know he was coming? I ask.

She looks at me, mascara brush in hand, and nods. – Are you okay?

I don't know. I don't know what I am. I try to convey this
to her with a shrug and an exhalation of breath.

She stands up and gestures with her arms for me to come
to her. – Let him take you, Orla. Ring me when you get to
the house.

I hug her. – Thanks for having me, Ma.

When she pulls away, there are tears in her eyes. She holds
her palm against the side of my face. – Jesus, Orla, you're
not a guest. I know it feels different here, but it'll always be
your home.

– Are you going to come down and say hello? I ask.

She presses her lips together and shakes her head. Powder
has already gathered in the cracks of the wrinkles around
her eyes.

Downstairs, Da is chatting with Anna.

– Here, I'll take that, he says, – taking my bag and bringing
it out to his car. The same car, I notice. At least that hasn't
changed.

– Well, Sister Orla. This is where we part. I shall pray for
you in Jesus' name and . . .

– Shut up, Anna. I lean in to hug her. I hold her tightly
for a long time and talk into her neck. – Take care. Come
and see me anytime. Write me letters. Call me from work.

Da is back now. – Right, he says, – see you soon, Anna.
When he leans in to hug Anna, I go and get into the car.

We don't speak as he starts the car and pulls away from
the house. Anna stands on the step waving as we drive off,

and I wave back at her, feeling a tug in my stomach as I lose sight of her, and a tug in my heart for Ma sitting at her make-up table upstairs.

Then it's just the two of us. I steal glances around the car. There's a plastic bottle of water in the side pocket of the passenger door. A scrunched-up old tissue, and what I think is the wrapper of a Cornetto ice cream. It smells different in here. Of something synthetic. I can't place it. It must be her perfume.

– Music? he says, and pushes a CD into the player before I can get a look at it. It's a song I don't recognise. As the sound of a drumbeat fills the car, he looks flustered, his eyes flitting back and forth to the CD player. – What is this? I ask.

– Oh, it's a Bruce Springsteen album. Carol loves him. I keep my expression neutral. He looks at me and then back onto the road. Then he asks – how was your Christmas Day?

– It was weird, to be honest. Not bad. Just a bit strange.

– Mine too, he says.

Well, hang on and let me get my violin out, Da. I concentrate hard on looking out the window as we drive along the M50, away from the mountains, towards the north side of Dublin. He drives the same way as he always has, two hands on the wheel at all times, taking care to stay within the speed limit. It used to mortify me as a teenager. People would drive right up his arse to try and make him speed up or get out of the way, but he never seemed to care. *It's their problem, not mine,* he'd say, as I sank down the seat in shame.

Bruce serenades us with his gruff, all-American voice. I want to ask Da if he likes the Bruce Springsteen album, but I don't.

After a while, Da says, – Are you happy to be going back?

I blink and say, after a pause, – I am and I amn't.

When I don't elaborate, he says, – Well, which bits are you looking forward to?

I think of Frank, hurt and pissed off with me. Gerry with his rheumy eyes, lost and intoxicated. Neema, disgusted with me. Neema, who has her life all mapped out and paid for, law school to law firm. I think of Biff at The Castle, barking orders at me. Damian's laugh when he remembered my demo. *Metamorphosis*. It's all so bad. I can't believe I even asked him to listen it. I feel the back of my eyes sting with tears and stare out the window until I can speak, – I'm looking forward to being able to learn Pro Tools with Max, the engineer at The Castle.

– Great, that's great, says Da, and I hear the relief in his voice that I've given him some morsel of my motivation. – Are they nice to you in the Irish bar? he asks.

– They are, I say immediately. – The regulars are gas. They love taking the mick out of me.

He laughs, more than he should, and says, – I presume you give it back.

– I give as good as I get.

– Is there live music there?

– Only for special occasions.

315

Da indicates off the M50 and takes the turning into the airport. – And are you writing any of your songs over there?

I sigh. – I've written a few, but it's hard because there's always so many people around the house, and I have to borrow Kesh's guitar.

He says nothing here, but he's smiling. He catches me looking at him and changes his expression to serious again.

– Right, let's get ourselves a parking space, he says.

When we're parked, he hops out of the car and goes to the boot for my rucksack. He puts the rucksack down on the footpath and goes back to the boot. He takes out a guitar case. His guitar case. The one with the stickers on it. I close my door and stand there looking at him as he walks over to me and puts the guitar case in my arms. I feel the weight of the guitar inside.

– You don't have to borrow Kesh's guitar anymore, he says, smiling.

I can't get used to this newly revealed smile of his, the wideness of it over his chin, how it feels more complete when you can see all of his face move with it.

He puts his hand on my hair and strokes me awkwardly, like a pet, then leans in and kisses me on the forehead and bends down quickly to pick up my rucksack. – Right, let's get you inside.

I quickly wipe my eyes as I let him put the rucksack on me, then I pick up the guitar case in one hand and my handbag with the other, shifting the weight on my feet so

I'm balanced. Only then do I meet his eyes. – I've got it, Da. I can manage. Good luck. With Harrison. Bye. I feel my throat tightening as I turn to walk away. I can't wave at him when I get to the airport's entrance, because my hands are full. Instead, I nod and smile, and keep that brittle smile on my face all the way to the plane. It's only when the plane accelerates forwards into the air, and I feel the force of the velocity pushing me backwards into my seat, that I let the tears come. They fall all the way to Stansted.

CHAPTER 31

CAN'T GET YOU OUT OF MY HEAD

Maybe the place where you grew up becomes incrementally less like home the more you visit it. Every time you come back, something else has changed, until you are a stranger to the place entirely. If that's the case, then surely it should work the other way round. Every arrival to London, for me, should feel incrementally *more* like coming home. Landmarks, smells and sounds. Senses engaged. It should feel like I'm clicking into place.

– Hello, I call out as I shut the door behind me. The house is cold, but the air in the hall has that smell that it takes on when the radiators have just come on. A kind of mouldy, earthy smell, as if there are old socks stuffed behind the radiators that haven't been touched for years. I can hear noise from the kitchen and I call out again, – Helloooooo?

– In here! Neema's voice calls from the direction of the kitchen, and immediately I feel a shard of hurt slice through me, because I don't want to be summoned, I want her to run to me, arms spread wide in welcome.

I leave my bag in the hall and walk to the kitchen. I see Kesh first, standing over the sink, washing dishes. Neema is crouched down behind the open door of the low food cupboard, loading it up with things from a big canvas bag. She peeps up from behind the door. – Hiya.

And I say, – Hi. You're just home, are you?

– Yeah, we got back a little while ago. Just unloading Mum's food. There's a fucking mountain of it.

Kesh laughs a soft little laugh at the sink. They are in harmony again. His hair is cropped close; in his round-necked jumper, he could be a dentist or a teacher. He always takes out his piercings to go home. I smile at him, and he says, – How was your trip home?

I pull in my breath and say, – It was good! Yeah. A bit strange. Different, like.

– Did you see your dad? Neema asks, leaning out from the cupboard to look at me, a packet of crackers in her hand.

– Yes. He gave me his guitar.

– Oh, that's nice, says Kesh as Neema pulls herself up on the door. I raise my eyes to meet hers, but she flits them away again, back to the bag of Tupperware boxes in front of her.

– How are your mum and sister? she says.

– They're good. And as I say it, I see it clearly for the first time. My ma and sister are doing well. They're trying

319

to make it work. They both want to move on, and I came home and dragged them backwards.

Neema is at the fridge now. – We haven't found any mice yet, she says, and then turns around. – Have you seen that, though? She points behind me to the ceiling of the gear room. I follow her eyes to a huge crack across the ceiling plaster, from one side of the room to the other.

– Oh God. What room is above there?

– The bathroom, I think? says Kesh. – And Richie's, I mean your room, Neema.

– I'm going to call the landlord, Neema says.

I turn back to them and ask, – Is Frank back?

– No, not for a couple of days yet, Kesh says.

I nod and speak to the floor. – I'll go and unpack. See you in a bit.

I haul my rucksack and guitar case up the stairs one floor at a time. The loft door is open enough for me to see the corner of Neema's bed, stripped bare. I stand outside for a moment. My breathing is loud, quickened from the effort of the stairs. I wait for my heart to slow down, then I push open the door and walk in.

Durga is gone from the wall, four dark circles where the Blue Tack used to be. The chair is empty of Neema's mirror and her make-up bags. The stacks of clothes and plastic boxes under her bed are all gone. There's no note, no gesture left to make it easier. I sit down on her bed with my rucksack still on my back and cradle my head in my hands. From here, my side of the room is chaotic as usual: empty mug on the floor, CDs and clothes sprawled everywhere, an ashtray under my bed.

I rub my face with the flat of my palms, pull off my rucksack and drag the guitar case from the floor on to my lap. I pull the buttons sideways to release the metal clasps. As I lift the lid of the case, the musty scent of the bottle-green velvet encasement fills my nostrils, and immediately my head is flooded with memories.

I'm off to do me songs.

The sound of his fingers moving along the fretboard. His long, sock-clad feet tapping the carpet on either side of my legs.

I've never really examined the guitar on its own before, out of the context of the house in Dublin. It's a Fender. The fretboard is black walnut, the wood stain blended from black around the edges to a lighter brown in the middle. There is a capo fixed on to the fret board, some plectrums tucked in behind the string at the end of the neck. Of course, he thought of everything. I carefully lift the guitar out and sit down on the edge of my bed to rest it on my lap, moving my body around it so that it fits into me.

Da always said it was an easy guitar to play. Something about the neck. Da, who never made it as a singer, but had a nightly audience with his daughter instead. Da, who only ever sang other people's songs, but who encouraged me to make up my own as soon as he taught me how to play.

I thought I had forgotten them all, but something about holding this guitar is bringing them back to me now. There was the one about my friend Gillian. A whole song about the eyes of this guy from fifth year, Dermot. I was obsessed with him. One of my favourites to sing was about swimming in the sea. I move the fingers of my left hand through the different shapes of the chords on the fretboard as I remember it: 'Like the water in the sea, will you always carry me,' it went, or something awful like that.

I tap the drum of the guitar with my fist and listen to the reverberations of the sound. I learned about frequency in Cheltenham. The ricochet of the strings' vibrations around the drum of the guitar making the noise.

I wonder if he put new strings on it. They'll fall out of tune quicker if they're new. Da is able to tune a guitar to a fairly good standard without a tuner. I used to enjoy that ritual at the start of every evening: the twang of each string, the way he pulled each note into place.

Something happened when I hit puberty. It was like each member of our family was the note of a chord, and I fell out of tune. The amount of times I was a wet mess on the floor of my bedroom as a teenager, sobbing my heart out to music, letting it unravel me like a knitted jumper, just a big ball of loose feelings on the carpet. I just couldn't really be around Da. Eventually I stopped trying with him altogether. I let it all out on Ma, the whole Niagara Falls of emotions. Pounded her with blind rage and resentment and confusion and anxiety and general hormonal chaos. Horror-movie screams. Doors slammed so hard they broke off their hinges.

Da made me keep on at the songwriting, though. That was our only communication in my mid-teens. Him nagging me to play. Me huffing and puffing, but always doing it in the end.

I look down at my hands, feeling the throb from the strings cutting into the skin of my fingers already. I wonder why he gave his guitar away. Maybe he's too worried about disturbing the baby. Or maybe Flatface doesn't like him playing. *That would learn him.*

I take a moment to decide on the first chord to play on his guitar in London. It feels important somehow, to get the right one. I choose G. When the sound of the guitar fills the little loft room, it is gentle but firm.

If my da was an instrument.

It sounds like an arrival.

— Hello, The Castle.

— Hiya, Lorley.

— Hi Ma. How's it going?

— Just on me lunchbreak. Gail's out. Thought I'd try you. She'll kill me when she sees the bills.

— Well, we can be short. Happy New Year!

— Same to you. You are twenty-two in 2002. It's got a nice ring to it. Did you have a party for New Year's?

— There was a giant rave in the Millennium Dome that I wanted to go to, but I had to work at The Castle. They were having their own party. Oh, Ma. I bought a bike!

— A bike? In London? Have you lost your mind?

— No. It'll save me a fortune.

— Well, don't you dare be getting on any bike without a helmet. And a tabard: One of them luminous yokes. And lights! You can't forget the lights.

– Oh, shite, I forgot about lights.

– Orla, do not tell me you are cycling around London in winter with no lights.

– Okay, Ma, less of the drama. I'm alive, amn't I? I will buy lights. The bike is lovely though. Bottle green. And I have a basket on the front.

– Like a little Mary Poppins. Was it expensive?

– Seventy-five quid. I bought it off this session saxophonist guy who put a message up at work. He threw in the lock for free.

– Very good. And how's work?

– Same old. Max has started teaching me Pro Tools. Just for an hour here and there, when we're not busy.

– That's very nice of him, isn't it?

– Yeah. Feels good to be learning something.

– And what about the bar?

– Same as usual. How's Anna?

– I think she's getting itchy feet. She keeps bringing home Sheridan's Travel magazines for me, but ends up stealing them.

– She should go travelling. I'm sure she has money saved by now, no?

– God knows. She doesn't contribute to the house, so I hope it's going somewhere useful.

– And you, Ma? Any sign of you using your vouchers?

– Well, I was thinking I could come and see you at Easter. If you'll have me, that is.

– Of course, Ma. If you can't stay in the house, for whatever reason, maybe we could splash out and get a hotel?

– *And why wouldn't I be able to stay in the house?*

– *Well, you would. It's just not a very nice atmosphere there at the moment.*

– *Why not?*

– *Well, the house is falling apart, for starters. It's mouse infested. And there are big cracks in the ceilings. And Neema's got the hump with me.*

– *What's happened?*

– *Just stupid stuff. Fall-outs and people snogging each other.*

– *And are you involved in any of this?*

– *Yes. Unfortunately. But I've got a date on Thursday with a guy in a different band.*

– *Ooh, that's exciting.*

– *Yeah.*

Pause.

– *Ma, you'd better go, or you'll be in trouble.*

– *Yes. Orla, just stay in touch, will you? That's all I ask. And don't forget to eat.*

CHAPTER 32

DO YOU REALLY LIKE IT?

Gwen is waiting for me at a table by the window when I arrive.

– It's fucking freezing, I say, rubbing my hands together frantically, trying to get the feeling back in them.

– You're losing weight, babe, Gwen says, squashing her cigarette into the ashtray and standing up to give me a kiss on the cheek.

– I don't think I am. I'm just not wearing big flappy jeans. I can't because I'm on my bike.

– Well, whatever you're doing, it suits you. Drink that. It'll warm you up. She points at the glass of hot port opposite her on the table, cloves pressed through the slices of lemon.

It was Gwen's idea to meet up. We're in The Hawley Arms in Camden, which is nearly full already, hot air steaming off the patrons and fogging up the windows. Leonard Cohen's voice drifts from the stereo speakers above the bar, adding to the cosiness of the room. We clink glasses.

– How's life in the music industry? I ask.

– Well, *Pop Idol* is ruining the charts. And your lot. Westlife. They're like fucking cockroaches.

– I apologise on behalf of Ireland, I say. The hot port is warming after my cycle from The Castle. I sip it down and ask, – And Redstar?

– Same as usual. Finn's gone to rehab.

– Too right, I say.

She swallows an inch of her pint, leans forwards with a smirk and says, – So, I hear you're getting your leg over with Vinnie.

– How did you hear about that?

She taps the side of her nose with her forefinger and gives me a knowing look. – Nothing gets past me.

My eyes flit to my rucksack on the ground by my feet, full of dirty clothes. I stayed over at Vinnie's house last night. Yesterday, he sent a definitive order by text: *Oxford Arms tonight. 8pm. X*

As if he knows when I don't have shifts at the pub. As if there was no doubt in his mind that I would come.

– I'm not staying long, I said on arrival. He handed me the wrap of coke as a greeting. He wore a shirt and looked different. More manly. His hair wasn't shaved as short as usual, his widow's peak was more defined..

He left the pub three times with different people.

– Am I your drug-dealing accessory? I joked when he came

back the third time. – Or is this whole thing just a strategy for you to get me to buy you drinks every time you leave the pub?

– Ha ha, he said rolling his eyes as he climbed on to the stool.

I yawned then, and he sniggered, eyebrows raised. – Am I that exhausting?

– Yes, you're exhausting, I said, giving him a sleepy smile and placing my hands on his thighs so I could lean in to kiss him.

Now, Gwen offers me a cigarette across the table and I take one. She's wearing a see-through blouse; I can see the whole outline of her black bra underneath it. Her hair has been freshly dyed and blow-dried into a scarlet sheet with a dull shine catching the light from the bulb above.

– You look very glamorous, I say, trying to change the subject.

– Had a meeting with the head of XFM today, Gwen replies.

– I hope you told him he needs to play 'Holding', I say.

– Oh, he knows all about it. How's things at Casa Shiva, anyway?

I take a sip of my drink. – I'm not home very much. Kesh and Richie made up on New Year's Eve. But Richie's moved out for good.

– And Neema and Richie?

– Not happening, as far as I can see.

Gwen looks taken aback. – What do you mean, 'as far as I can see'? Have you and Neema fallen out?

I wonder if Neema will have noticed that I didn't come home last night. Neema, who has been going through the motions of being my friend in the house. Politely moving around me in the kitchen, joining in the group conversations in the living room, but always managing to be in her room when we are alone together in the house. We used to make two of everything. Two cups of tea or coffee, two sandwiches, two biscuits. Always two portions. We don't anymore.

I sigh and smile. – No. I just wouldn't want to speak for her, you know? She's quite a private person.

Gwen narrows her eyes at me and says, – Mmm. And how about you and Frank?

– Me and Frank are cool now. I think he might be dating someone new, but he's keeping it very mysterious, I say.

She leans forward and says, all conspiratorial, – So, what's Vinnie like?

I sip my drink and think for a second.

He brought me to see a band at The Barfly. The band were screamo, extreme noise. Vinnie stood with his face screwed up in appreciation as the lead singer thrashed around the stage. I went to the toilet to do a bump of his cocaine, and then sat in the cubicle for a while after, reading all the tiny inscriptions on the back of the door.

Afterwards, we walked up Camden Road together to his flat. It was freezing. It took him longer this time. I scratched his back so that he would think I was getting carried away with it all, and then waited for my turn. It was even better the second time round, knowing what was coming, the anticipation of it. I cried out when I came. The sound of it surprised me. I hardly slept from his snoring.

– He's funny. Great in bed, I tell Gwen.

– Interesting, she says, smiling. The teeth on either side of her incisors are pointed, like fangs. – Boyfriend material?

– I don't get the vibe that he's looking for a girlfriend.

– Good. Neither do I, from what I've heard, she says.

– What have you heard? I say.

She swallows another gulp of beer and sizes me up, as if deciding whether I'm able to handle what she's about to say.

I shift my weight on my seat. – I'd rather know, Gwen.

She sighs. – He's after a friend of mine from Polydor. Shagged her a while back. He's been sending her loads of flirty texts, and they're back at it again.

I nod and take a big gulp of beer to give me time to re-arrange the expression on my face into one of nonchalance. – Shame, I say. – I've never met anyone who could do the things he does in bed.

– Well, it doesn't have to stop you, she says, eyebrows raised.

– I guess not.

I'm hot now. I stub out my cigarette and take off my jumper, aware of Gwen watching me.

– Anyway, how's old pervy Biff over at The Castle? she asks.

I think of Biff this morning. Stopping on his way out of the kitchen, just to tell me that he had never seen me in leggings before. Taking his time to peruse my legs fully.

– He told me this morning that I have legs like a man who lifts weights, I say.

– So, same as usual, she says, lighting another cigarette. She picks up the box and chucks it over the table at me.

I take one, take her lighter and ask,– Do you know Max? The engineer in there?

– Yeah, met him a few times, seems like a nice wee man.

– He is. He's teaching me how to use his music-production programme. Pro Tools, it's called.

– On his own time? Is he looking to get laid?

– Gwen. He has a girlfriend. Like, a long-term one. I think they're engaged.

She nods, not making any effort to hide the scepticism on her face. – Take what you can get. But don't be too trusting.

– I just can't see how else I can progress. It's great to have a job, but it's depressing because I want to be one of the people making the music. Damian said I need to hone my sound.

– Did he, now? Do you want to sing it as well as make it?

– Yeah. I've been writing and singing songs since I was a kid.

She taps the ash off her cigarette and leans forwards over the low table. – How come you never told me that?

I shrivel under her stare. It's accusatory. Nearly angry.

– I thought you knew I wanted to make music.

– I did know that. But wanting to produce music as a woman is fucking futile. Being a songwriter and a singer isn't. I didn't know you'd been writing songs since you were a kid, did I?

– Well, I stopped for a while when I was in college, but I have a guitar again now and I've been writing new songs, I say, squirming a little. After the disaster of what happened with my demo tape and Damian, the thought of anyone new listening to my songs is intimidating. But I already know they're better than my demo from college. They feel lived-in, as if they've been around for ever. I've been experimenting with my guitar playing so that it feels more dynamic underneath my singing, and I've been writing lists. Lists and lists of references for how I'd like the music to sound around the words.

– Well, can I hear them? Gwen interrupts my thoughts.

– My songs?

– No, your farts, Orla. Yes, your fuckin' songs.

– I've no way of recording them for you.

– You live with a fuckin' band. Get one of them to do it. Or ask your new best mate Max. She stands up to go the bar, then stops, turns and points her fingers at me, and says, – And don't tell the boys I said this, but I wouldn't be making any creative decisions based on Damian's opinions.

And she's off, flicking her hair over her shoulder and claiming her space between the men at the bar.

CHAPTER 33

KNIVES OUT

My fingers are numb and my thighs are burning by the time I pull my bike up the front steps of Mill Road. I like cycling, even in the icy dark of February. I'm not brave enough to shout back at the drivers yet, and I don't like the buses and the trucks roaring past me, but I love the freedom of pushing myself around the city with my feet. By the time I've reached my destination, my head is empty of where I've come from and there's space for new thoughts. I had an idea just now, for a song, about how my cycles are like the space between the beats of my life. The beats are the places I zigzag around in this city: Fahy's, The Castle, Mill Road. I need the cycles between them to breathe, to ready myself for what's next.

I'm humming a potential melody for the song as I drag my bike into the hall, but I stop when I see legs and an arm through the doorway of the living room.

– Hello, I call gently, taking off my helmet.

– Hey.

And I start, because it's Richie's voice. I switch off my bike lights, which are still flashing, and walk in to the living room. The whole band is there. Damian is sitting on the far sofa, his arms stretched out on either side of him. He's dressed flashily, with a buttoned-up denim shirt and silver Nike trainers. He looks pissed off that I've interrupted them. I haven't seen them all together since their big London gig.

– Hi guys. Hi Damian. Richie. You're here. I walk in and bend down to hug Richie. He stands up and hugs me back, then sits down again quickly. He's self-conscious, I realise, which is not a usual way for him to be. I unwrap my scarf from around my neck. Kesh is conscientiously building a spliff. Frank meets my gaze. I smile at him gratefully.

– We're just having a bit of a . . . meeting, says Kesh, catching my eyes briefly before looking back to his spliff.

– Okay, I'll leave you to it. I close the door behind me and run up the stairs to Richie's old room. I knock gently on the door. Neema answers it swiftly, and I realise, when her expression changes, that she thought it would be Richie knocking for her.

– Sorry, I say instinctively.

She holds open the door for me and for the first time since she's moved in here, I walk in and go to sit on her bed. She is wearing a black V-neck jumper, a tailored skirt and black tights. Richie's posters are still on the wall: AC/DC, Black Sabbath, a trippy, colourful print of Howard Marks smiling with a lit joint in his hand. She's stuck her poster of Durga on the wall over the bed, which is neatly made up with her ivory quilt, incense burning on the table adjacent. She's on edge.

– What's it like down there? she asks.

– It's all very formal and weird, I say. – What's going on?

– I think they got bad news.

– What kind of bad news? She is still standing behind the closed door, as if she is expecting someone to walk in.

– Bad news from Redstar. Richie told me the single isn't selling at all.

– Oh shit. 'Holding'?

– Yeah. It's bombed. It means they don't get any more marketing money. And it doesn't look good for them being able to release another single off the album.

– So, what happens now? I ask.

She walks towards the bed. – I think the problem is, nothing happens. If Redstar aren't seeing any signs of growth, they'll have to rethink the whole investment. Bottom line, it's a business.

I imagine Neema speaking like this in law school, hands clasped and resting on a desk, an expression of tired resignation on her face. This is the version of Neema that Amanda gets.

– So, they'll have to find another label?

She slides on to the bed beside me and leans up against the wall. – It might come to that, yeah. She screws up her face then, and says, – Fucking Gwen.

– What did Gwen do?

– Blew smoke up their arses for the last two years. Told them they were the greatest band in the fucking world. Told them how amazing they were, and how much Redstar all loved them.

– Neema, I think Redstar genuinely did love them. It felt like that when I was in the office with them, I say, thinking of the Redstar staff I worked with back in September. I wonder what they say about the band now, when they are lunching at Quinn's. I wonder what this will mean for my relationship with them all.

Neema is talking. – Well, let's hope they love them enough to keep them on when they're not selling records. Kesh already has about twenty songs written for the next album.

The front door slams downstairs. Neema sits forward and looks at me, holding my gaze for the first time in weeks.

– That will be Damian leaving. Let's go down.

All three boys are in the living room. Frank is sprawled out on one of the sofas, staring at the ceiling. Kesh is curled up in the armchair, his hand holding up his forehead as if it's a dead weight. Richie is at the stereo, fiddling with the CDs. When he looks up at us, his face is grief-stricken.

Neema and I sit down on the sofa opposite Frank. I wear a worried expression and aim it at Kesh in the hope that it will prompt him to say something.

He speaks from under his hand. – Redstar have dropped us. No one speaks.

337

Gwen must have known when I saw her at the Hawley Arms.

Neema leans forwards and talks with her whole body. – What did they say? What was their reason?

There is a long silence. Nobody moves or answers. The ground under our feet tremors slightly as a train rumbles along the track at the end of the garden.

Eventually, Frank drags his elbow away from his face and says, – They just said we'd come to the end of our contract and they're not going to renew it. They've loved working with us, blah, blah, blah. Just bollocks.

– And they couldn't tell you themselves? They had to get Damian to do it? Neema says, incredulous.

No one speaks again, so I do. – I mean. You guys can get another deal, right? You've got new songs ready to go.

Frank starts to kick the leg of the coffee table.

Kesh says, – Damian's got the demos. He's bringing them to some other labels this week.

– And are you feeling hopeful? I say, and my cheeks burn as I catch a flash of a look from Neema that says, *What sort of a stupid question is that?*

– Am I hopeful? Kesh lifts his head, laughs bitterly and then freezes, suspended in thought. – I'm not, actually. He says it as if he's just realised it right there, in that moment. – Not for Shiva, anyway.

Frank stops kicking.

Kesh says, – We need to think of a new approach.

– Right, I say, nodding enthusiastically, thinking that that sounds like a Damian line to me. I carry on, concentrate on making my voice sound calm and assured – I mean, think of all the massive bands who started out at different labels and then moved. I'm sure it takes a while to find the right fit. There's so many moving parts to it, aren't there?

Richie stands behind Kesh, chewing his thumbnail. – I wonder if anyone else got dropped, he asks the carpet.

Kesh says – The new A&R guy, Steve, never liked us. From the minute he got the job, he was looking for ways to get rid of us.

– Have you spoken to Gwen? I ask.

Kesh shakes his head, and there is another interminably long silence. Frank sighs, sits up, leans forward over the table and starts to build a joint. We all watch him for a while. I sneak a look at Neema. She is watching Richie fiddling with the CDs.

– Have we got any booze? says Frank, breaking the silence. Richie shakes his head.

– I'll go and get us some from the off-licence, I say, slapping my thighs and standing up.

– I'll come with you, Neema says.

We make a big fuss of taking orders and wrapping up warm and saying loud goodbyes to counteract the deathly silence of the living room. Once we're outside, we walk briskly, stuffing our hands in our pockets. Neema has a good strong pace on her, her shoulders pulled back, her face set into an expression of rage and pushed forwards into the wind, as if she's trying to start a fight with it.

– Do you think Kesh'll start a new band? I ask her.

She answers the footpath ahead. – Definitely. He won't want this to look like failure.

– Will Frank stay?

– He's so laid-back, I think he'll stick around unless he gets a better offer.

We walk in silence for a while, heading towards the lights of the High Road.

– And Richie?

– He's loyal to Kesh. And when I don't say anything, she adds, without looking at me, – Are you still seeing Vinnie?

– I'm supposed to see him this week. But Gwen told me he's shagging one of her mates.

– Oh my God, she says, shaking her head in disgust. I feel a kick of anger in my stomach, which shifts quickly into hurt.

The wind is stronger on the High Road, and we brace ourselves against it as we walk to the nearest set of traffic lights. We stand in silence, as London buses trundle past us. When the green man flashes, Neema puts her arm through mine and pulls me close to her. We walk across, like this, holding on to each other. We don't let go until I have to break away to open the door of the off-licence.

We take it at a slow pace back down the hill of Mill Road, weighed down on both sides by bags filled with cans and bottles. The wind bends the branches of the trees above us and rattles a squashed can along the kerb. After about a hundred yards, we stop simultaneously as the wind howls around our heads.

– We're going to be blown away at this rate, I say, laughing, but Neema's face is set into a serious expression.

She turns and shouts against the wind. – I was really angry with you after Frank, you know. Then she glances at me quickly, over the collar of her furry coat, and starts walking again. I follow her, but she's looking ahead and she's talking again, and I'm straining to hear her. – You can kiss whoever you want. And you can sleep with whoever you want, and you can eventually marry whoever you want. And you kissing Frank felt like you were rubbing my face in it, because I can't do any of those things.

When I catch up with her, she tucks her chin into her chest under her collar. After a few moments, I say, – I didn't think about it that way.

– What? she says.

I swallow and speak again, louder this time. – I didn't think about it that way.

– Well, you don't *have* to think about it that way, she replies, not looking at me.

– Neema, I say, and I stop to shelter from the wind behind the thick trunk of a plane tree. Its roots have pushed through the concrete paving slabs by my feet, breaking them into pieces. The wind sings through the branches above. She stops, too, and when she turns to face me, her mouth is tight and her eyes blink frantically, as if she's taking photos with them, *shutter-click, shutter-click.*

– I really didn't know Frank liked me, I say.

She nods at her feet. When she looks back at me, her expression is grave. – It was the carelessness of it all that bothered me. You just . . . She's searching for the words. – You spill yourself all over people.

– I was . . . so fucked, I explain.

She puts her bags down on the pavement and stretches out her fingers to relieve the cramp. Below her, through a basement window, I can see faces illuminated in the blue light of a TV screen.

She turns to look through the window too as she talks. – I didn't understand why I was angry until I was home at Christmas, getting all that shit from my family. When she turns back to face me, she has to raise her voice against the wind once more. – You don't have to think about anything but what *you* want.

– But I don't *know* what I want, Neema. My life isn't nearly as sorted as yours. You're so together. You have your career all mapped out. You're going to be a . . .

– Orla.

– What?

– You have no fucking idea.

A car drives past on the road, muted bass rumbling from inside. She looks me square in the eye before she picks up her bags and starts to walk again. – You've come over here from Ireland and just fit right in. I have to work so fucking hard just to be accepted, and I was born here, she says over her shoulder.

I pick up my bags and fall into stride beside her. I'm yelling against the wind. – I'm sorry. I'm so sorry that you have to deal with all this bullshit.

– I know you are, she says and looks at me, nodding, but she's irritated still. We walk side by side in silence, struggling against the wind. She finally speaks as we're walking up the steps to the house.

– And as for me keeping the Richie thing secret, don't take it personally. My whole life in London is a secret. With this, she opens the front door of number 74, and we step inside.

We walk back into the living room just as Richie is snorting a line. Black Sabbath blares from the stereo stack in the corner. Richie springs upright, wincing, and shouts, – Jesus, that's rough, as he squeezes his nose.

– Can't afford bugle, so we cracked into the speed, Frank shouts from the sofa, his eyes wide and unblinking. He's clearly had his line already. Kesh takes his turn next. He's wearing a hoodie with the hood up. He doesn't react at all to the speed. He doesn't say anything at all as Richie goes again and I hand out the cans.

Neema says, – I think I'll make dinner, does anyone want some?

There's a huge crash, and we all jump and turn to see

Kesh's hands, curled into fists, slammed down on the coffee table. Glasses have been knocked over, and an ashtray is upside down on the floor. Kesh is crouched on the edge of the armchair, his face in shadow from his hood.

– I can't fucking do this. I can't just sit around here like this, he shouts, then springs up and runs out the door, across the hall, and into his room.

We all stare at each other. Neema bends down to pick up the ashtray that fell on the floor. Richie goes to the stereo and turns the music down. Then Kesh comes out of his room again and turns towards the front door.

– Where are you going? calls Frank, standing up, but Kesh doesn't stop. He runs out of the door, leaving it wide open.

We all run out to the hall and down the steps on to the street to see the back of Kesh, as he sprints towards the High Road.

– Kesh! We're all shouting at him, but our voices are lost in the wind. He doesn't turn around, he's gone so fast, from a silhouette to a speck to nothing.

– Oh, God, says Neema. – He could do something really stupid.

– He'll be okay, I say to her, putting my arm around her and guiding her back inside. – He just needs to rage a bit.

Back in the living room, we sit down again. Richie is bug-eyed. He licks his lips over and over. Frank swallows rapidly.

Neema is on the armchair where Kesh had been sitting, talking, as if to herself. – His whole idea of himself is tied

344

up in being signed to Redstar. His whole identity. It's how he justifies all his choices. I'm going to call him, she says, jumping up and going to the hall, where she picks up the home phone from the carpet and starts to dial. There's silence for a few moments, then Neema walks in, looking utterly dejected.

– What? I say.

She holds up Kesh's phone. – I heard it ringing from his room.

Frank picks up his can of beer and starts to drink, his Adam's apple jumping up in his throat with each slow swallow, until the can is empty. Afterwards, he burps loudly, picks up his lit cigarette from the ashtray and smokes it.

Richie has been watching him this whole time. Finally, he says, – We're going to have to get jobs. In the looming silence, he carries on, – Otherwise, we can't pay the rent.

We all sit around and watch the film *Gladiator* on the TV. Neema sits on the sofa next to Richie. I watch them from the corner of my eye, Neema with her legs curled up underneath her, Richie with his long legs crossed at the ankle, both of them leaning into each other like magnets. When Russell Crowe is involved in a particularly gruesome scene, Neema moans and puts her hands over her eyes, and Richie puts his arm around her and pulls her in close to him.

By the end of the film, I'm crying my eyes out.

– Y'alright there, Orla? Richie asks me from across the room, his eyes bloodshot from the speed. I try to gather myself, but instead I hiccup, and then everyone laughs at me.

Afterwards, I'm in the kitchen, squeezing beer cans into the already overflowing bin, when a voice says, – You had a good cry there, Orla. Frank puts a handful of glasses by the sink.

My face is all swollen from the tears. I nod and smile, and he smiles his thin-lipped smile back at me.

– I never saw that film when it came out last year, I offer as my excuse.

Frank does his usual thing: filling the sink with warm water and putting all the dishes in to soak. As he goes to leave the kitchen, I reach out and grab his arm gently, and then let go of it quickly as he turns to me. – Frank. I'm so sorry about, you know, everything.

He looks at my shoes and then at my face and then beyond me, into the kitchen behind me. I turn around to see what he's looking at. There are two mousetraps in the corner by the fridge. The tiles over the sink are covered in mould. The cream paint is brown with grime, and covered in marks and chips.

– I wish we didn't live in such a shit hole, he says, then sighs and turns around. – Night.

I watch him as he walks out through the gear room. My eyes glide up towards the roof. The crack in the plaster has stretched nearly the whole width of the ceiling. Small fresh cracks zigzag out from the main crack now, as if the roof is an ice floe and spring is in the air. I look down then. The boys' Roland sixteen-track recorder sits on a table wedged up

346

against the wall, alongside a pint glass with cigarette butts inside it. Two barstools cluster around the table, and amps, speakers, guitar cases and various other flight cases fill all the space around them. In the silence, I listen out for the scratchy noises that mean mice, but I hear nothing.

Kesh's old four-track tape recorder is under the table. I lean down and pull it out, and turn it around a few times in my hands. I wipe away the thick layer of dust on the buttons and faders with my sleeve. Then I walk back into the living room. Everyone is gone. I look down at it again, Gwen's voice in my head, *You live with a fuckin' band.* I walk up the stairs to the loft room, tiptoeing past Neema's bedroom, where I hear low voices and music from behind the door. Up in the loft, I kick some shoes under my bed to make space to sit cross-legged on the floor and pull the four-track recorder on to my knees.

– Sister Orla.

– Anna.

– Just in case you're not flattened under the mountain of cards and roses you received today, Happy Valentine's Day.

– I forgot it was Valentine's.

– As if. Da didn't even send me a bar of chocolate like he normally does. Did you get anything from him?

– Nope. I think not getting a chocolate bar from Da on Valentine's is the least of my problems.

– How are you getting on?

– It's all go here. Shiva got dropped by their label.

– So, they can't be a band anymore?

– Well, they don't get paid to be a band anymore. They all have to get jobs. Kesh freaked out. Went missing for two days. Poor Neema was worried sick.

– Jeeesus. Where did he go?

– *Just found some fuckheads to get wasted with. He looked dead when he came home.*

– *Christ. And have you and Neema made up?*

– *We're getting there. I hardly see her though. The house is so miserable, I'm trying to stay away as much as possible to be honest.*

– *Don't blame you.*

– *Oh, I recorded some of my songs at last. Did it myself on Kesh's four track.*

– *What do they sound like?*

– *It's just me and the guitar. Just skeletons of songs. Now, I have to get them heard by people who will actually help me.*

– *When do I get to hear them?*

– *I'll send you a tape, maybe?*

– *Do, do, please. Are you still seeing that fella in the band?*

– *Yep. How's your love life?*

– *Nothing to tell, is there? I'm going to Galway this weekend with a work team, so we'll see.*

– *Have you seen the baby?*

– *I'm seeing them next week for a walk in the park. According to Da, he's started to smile, so that makes all the sleepless nights worthwhile.*

Pause.

– *How's Mam taking it?*

– *She's decided she only drinks at weekends now.*

– *Oh. Well, that's good. So, the two of you are getting on better?*

– *It's not as bad as it was before Christmas. I think the baby news messed with her head and now it's all out there, she's calmed down a bit.*

— What do you think he looks like now?

— Who?

— The baby.

— I'd say he looks like a baby, but bigger . . . Oh, Uncle Hugh had a heart attack.

— Jesus. is he alright?

— He's home now.

— Wow. Tell Da to tell Hugh that I was asking for him, will you? When you're speaking to him?

— Sure. Any other messages you'd like me to impart?

— Shuddup, Anna.

CHAPTER 34

BIG EXIT

I cycle along the canal on a freezing Sunday evening at the end of February, past Primrose Hill and London Zoo, where the nets of the aviary rise over the wall. Frank says you can hear the lions roaring from their enclosure, but I haven't yet. The Constitution pub is in the arse end of Camden: you can get to it if you cycle along the canal. I come on at Primrose Hill and whizz along the waterside, through Camden Lock, speeding up under the bridge of the main road, wary of the addicts who slope around in the shadows. At the pub, I lock my bike, remove my bike lights, and put them in my bag.

Vinnie sits in the corner.

– You look different, he says with his head cocked sideways as I walk towards him.

– Do I? I say. – Maybe it's my hair. I touch it as I say it. It's long enough now to pull up into a loose bun on the top of my head. I worry that my helmet squished it down, so I undo the hair elastic and twist it up into a bun again.

He's watching me. – What's happening? he says with a small smile.

I shrug. – Not much.

– Still cycling? he asks, looking at my helmet.

– No, I just like carrying this around. If you turn it upside down, you can put things in it, I say.

He looks at me with an exasperated expression.

– I guess I'll get a drink then, I say. – What are you having?

– I'll have a whiskey and Coke.

I sense his eyes on my back while I stand at the bar. I feel light and calm from my cycle, all fizzy with endorphins. I order his whiskey and Coke and a bottle of beer.

– No pints? says Vinnie as I return to the table.

– No, it feels a bit heavy after my cycle, I say, and clink his glass. – Cheers.

– I heard the news about Shiva, he says. – Too bad. They had all fallen out, right?

– Where do you get this shit from, Vinnie? I say, swigging from my bottle.

– A couple of people.

– Right.

– Kesh, man. He always thought he was so much better than what he was. Vinnie shakes his head from side to side as he talks, as if to physically carve into the air the wrongness of Kesh.

Kesh, who I'm sure was sniffing speed last night before he went out to work the night shift at his new job at Sainsbury's with Frank. He had a crazed look in his eyes, as if they were locked open by the drugs. Frank looked sketchy, too, come to think of it. I could see that he's lost weight, even though he was wearing two jumpers because he had to work in the fridge section.

– Stop talking about Kesh like he's dead, I tell Vinnie.

– He writes better songs than fuck-loads of other signed and successful bands I could mention.

– Ha. Like who?!

– Like Plane Trees, for a start. I laugh alongside this sentence, to imply that I'm half-joking.

– I knew you were going to say that. As if. We're going to record album number two next month. He swigs down the last of his pint and lands it down on the table, so it makes a sharp crack.

I raise my eyes to him and say, – Let's not get into this argument.

– He's . . . fragile, anyway. Takes everything too seriously, he says.

It's my turn to roll my eyes. – He's a frontman, Vinnie, d'uh. That's his job. Anyway, it's not a fucking strongman contest, despite what your dickhead frontman thinks.

After our second drink, Vinnie offers me a wrap.

– I can't, I say.

– Alright, he says with an air of nonchalance, and then adds, – Why not?

– It just keeps me awake all night, and I need to sleep. I have a double shift tomorrow.

– Fair enough, he says. – Well, let's get on with it then, shall we? And he stands and holds out his arm for me.

I hesitate for a second before downing my beer, standing, and linking my arm in his.

– Night, Ben, he calls to the barman, and Ben nods and smiles with an amused expression on his face. I wonder how many girls Ben has seen Vinnie usher out of this pub.

Outside, the icy air hurts my face. In the darkness, I knock into Vinnie with my bike.

– Fucking hell, Orla, he says.

– Sorry! I say, – this pavement is too narrow. Fuck, it's cold.

We walk with our heads bowed, against the wind. In his room, I jump into his bed under the covers to try and get warm. I'm still fully clothed. He jumps on top of me and kisses me hard, and I try to relax into it. I feel shy as he takes my clothes off, and I pull the blanket back over me once I'm in my underwear. He shuffles on top and probes at me until he's inside me.

– Ow, I say. – Wait a second. I try to manoeuvre my legs so that I'm more comfortable. He starts again, speeding up to those frantic double-time movements as I focus on the big polystyrene ceiling rose above us, and the dusty green lampshade hanging from it. As he comes, he drops his whole weight on my body for a few seconds, and then pulls himself up from the bed with a groan. Without speaking, he grabs a towel and leaves the room. I hear the sounds of the bathroom door on the landing closing and locking, the piddle of his urine in the toilet, the flush and then the gush of the shower as he turns it on.

I lie diagonally across his single bed. My T-shirt and bra are still on, but I'm naked from the waist down. I rest my hands on the shallow hollow of my gut, where my skin is soft and warm. I pull my legs up so my feet are flat on the bed, and then stick the foot of my right leg up in the air so that I can see the full length of my weightlifter's leg. The contour of a new line of muscle runs from the inside of my knee to the inside of my thigh. My bicycle is making its mark. I trace the line with my forefinger, then lower my leg back to the bed and move my hands to my hips and then down to rest between my legs. A dull ache throbs from my groin. I move my hands back up to my belly, and pull on the soft flesh there.

A draft of cold air blows in from under the curtain, causing me to shiver. Across the landing, Vinnie starts to hum in the shower, loud enough so that I can hear him over the water. I lie still and listen for a while. An image of Neema appears in my head, eyes glistening, the wind whipping her hair around her face in the darkness on Mill Road. I sit up suddenly and find my underwear and jeans, and pull them on quickly. Then my socks and trainers. I

355

get my handbag with my wallet and phone and keys. I pick up my coat, which is lying by the door, then walk out of the room and along the landing, past the bathroom. Downstairs, I heave my bike through the doorway and close the door gently behind me.

CHAPTER 35

GRACE

St Patrick's Day falls on a Sunday, so I can work the whole day at Fahy's. The bar is full from noon. Pat even puts a chalk board outside on the pavement that says *Live music all day*, and props the door open as if it was July and not a cold, overcast day in the middle of March.

The band are set up in a circle near the doors of the toilets under the windows. Ciarán alternates between banjo and mandolin, another fella is on his fiddle, and a small man with a sunken face plays the concertina and the tin whistle.

Pat has got her busy face on her, where her eyes flit from side to side underneath her frown. She's roped in her cousin to help behind the bar.

– If you need to go up to check on James, I'll handle it, I say to her.

– I've Nuala up with him tonight. She'll call down later.

Gerry and Mayo Dave are here. Mayo Dave looks slightly

bewildered, but Gerry's face is lit up in the merriment of it all. He wears a green tie knotted neatly in the collar of his shirt. They have moved positions to sit at the back end of the bar, looking towards the front door, so they have a good vantage point of the whole room.

– Gerry, you might have to be helping us behind the bar before the day is out, I tell him.

– You'll have to get him a box to stand on, says Mayo Dave, and Gerry rolls his eyes, but there is humour in them. He scans the bar, watching a group of young people roar with laughter at a table across the way.

– You might be better off with some big fellas who can deal with the people in bad states later on, he says.

All day, Pat and I rush, serving Guinness mainly, but people become adventurous as the day progresses, and as the noise increases, the bad states show themselves. I steal bites from the sandwiches I made the night before, chewing furiously while pouring a pile of shots for a crowd of men in the corner. I watch the man carry them over on a tray.

– Pat, they could be trouble, I say.

She's beside me now and I don't have to look at her; I can just feel her presence, her arms in a blur of movement around me. She looks over at them as she pours a pint. There's four of them sitting down and one man leaning on the table with his fists, like a gorilla, shoulders hunched forward, swaying gently from left to right. He looks angry with one of the other men. He lurches forwards to shout into his face, nearly toppling the pints on the table as he does so.

– Steady, I hear one of the other men saying, taking hold of his arm.

– Is no one going to eat a meal today? I shout to Pat.

– They wouldn't see the need at this stage, she says, and then adds: – Orla. Serve, gesturing at an expectant man in front of me before lifting her head to accept the order of another man to her right.

The bodies are two-deep at the bar as the band starts up again, with their jigs and reels, cutting through the shouting and the din. Ciarán is in his element, his pints lined up in front of him, his face set in concentration, his head dipping forwards at the end of a refrain before he starts again. I recognise some of the melodies. I like how they climb and climb, with bigger breaths on the tin whistle, bigger stomps from the boots on the floor. When the band finish, the drinkers of Fahy's are united in clapping and cheering for them, and the players, red-faced from the effort, nod into their pints and exchange words with each other before launching into the next song.

It's around nine o'clock when the residents of Mill Road arrive. Kesh and Frank and Richie and Neema are all spruced up for a night out in Fahy's.

– Welcome to the madhouse, I say, embracing each of them, hugging Neema extra tight. It's been such a long time since we've been out, in the same place, intentionally. I guide her to the back of the bar. – You'll have to start standing, I'm afraid. Gerry and Dave, do you remember Neema?

Mayo Dave nods and tips his pint, but Gerry turns to shake Neema's hand, and then the others'. They manage to get a table for their second drink.

It's nearly midnight when a fight finally breaks out. The gorilla man is so pissed, he can't stand up straight. He's snarling all around him, and he bumps into a fella walking past him with his shoulder, sending the fella flying. The fella comes back over to him and shouts in his face, and suddenly everyone is up off their stools, shouting, and the men disappear in a tangle of bodies, limbs flailing, fists punching, stumbling, as other drinkers try to pull them apart, and then Pat's cousin is there ushering them all out. He turns to look at Pat, who, right on cue, rings the bell for last orders. The bodies fall away, the gorilla man grunting and spitting on the floor, his opponent being looked over by a friend. People finish their drinks with resigned reluctance. I go to the Mill Road table, take their empties and say, – Don't go anywhere. They sit quietly with their drinks as the bar clears out and it's just the few of us left.

Pat and her cousin busy themselves locking the door and pulling the blinds. Pat's friend, Nuala, comes in from upstairs, and looks around the pub for Pat, giving her a nod. The band have been joined by a younger man, who is helping them move their instruments to the back of the bar. I go to get the brush to start sweeping up the glass.

Half an hour later, I'm sitting on a stool in the back corner with a pint in front of me. One table holds the Mill Road lot, and another few hold the Fahy's lot.

– Well, cheers, all of you, I say, holding up my glass, and they all do the same. There's a satisfied silence as we all sip and swallow in unison. – Jesus, I say, that is what we call sweet reward.

– You worked hard for that one, Orla, Gerry says, looking at me. He's squeezed into the table behind me with Mayo Dave and Nuala and Pat, who has finally sat down and is nursing a small glass of sherry. Kesh, Frank, Richie and Neema look relaxed now. Settled into the darkness of this place, like the pints of Guinness on the tables around them.

– Makes it all the sweeter, Gerry.

– That was a grand old day after all, says Gerry, looking to Pat for affirmation.

– It wasn't the worst of them, that's for sure, says Pat.

– I bet you've seen some rowdy Paddy's Days in here, Pat, I say.

– I've had to throw a fair few fellas out on their ears, she agrees.

I turn to the Mill Road lot and say, – Pat here has no qualms about chucking fellas out. She does it herself. Look at the size of her, I say and they all dutifully sit forward and take in the size of Pat.

Pat says, – It's nothing you wouldn't do yourself, Orla.

– Christ, I hope I don't have to, I say, laughing, and turn back to the Mill Road crew. Neema sits opposite me, next to

Richie against the wall of the banquette. – So, how's school? I ask her. Her expression darkens immediately.

– Getting more full on. I passed my latest exam.

– Course you did, I say. But a pained expression lingers on her face, so I ask, – Are you worried?

– I'm always worried, she says with a small smile, as if I should know this. As if it's a given.

Richie says, – Well I'm off on tour on Thursday. Got me roadie kit all ready, he says, rubbing his palms together. – Gaffa tape, Sharpies, Maglite, all me checklists.

– Are they sound? The band?

– Yeah, they're not too bad, you know. They get on it, but they're pretty professional, like.

Neema says, – I think you'll make a great roadie.

– Thanks, he says and gives her a warm smile, which soaks into her face and up to her eyes, making them sparkle. Kesh flips a beer mat up from the edge of the table and tries to catch it.

– How's Sainsbury's? I say to him.

Kesh has shaved off his hair. His head is a bony box. His cheekbones hang under his eyes. He says, – Fridge section again all last night. My fingers were actually blue by the end of my shift.

– Jesus. How was it for you, Frank?

Frank's sleepy eyes are working hard to stay open. – I was in the warehouse, stacking boxes.

– And did you sleep all day?

– Slept till lunchtime, says Frank and falls into a yawn, as if he's just reminded himself how tired he is.

Neema says, – I really would like it if you stopped going along the railway tracks.

– What's that? asks Richie.

Neema explains. – Kesh and Frank climb over the back fence and walk along the train tracks to Kilburn station, so they don't have to pay their fares.

– What, under the bridge? Richie asks, and adds – Jesus, you lot, that's dangerous.

– Well, find us a better-paid job then. We don't all get paid by a law firm to live in London, Kesh snaps, glaring at Neema. He's drunk. I can tell it from the way his mouth sags open when he's not talking. Frank just shrugs.

– Could you not work in the music industry? I ask.

Kesh replies, – Nope. That's too close to home.

Richie says, – What about teaching music? Like teaching guitar to kids or something?

– Don't you need qualifications to do that? says Kesh, wiping his Guinness moustache from his top lip. And a picture of my teacher from Cheltenham, Mr Langham, flashes up in my head; how he would finish his lessons with an excruciating bow, his right arm tucked behind his back and his left arm daintily spread wide, as if we were royalty and he was our courtier.

– I doubt it, I say, – it's worth making up a flyer and posting it up at Tesco and at the church and stuff. Any news of new labels?

Kesh says. – Damian's got some meetings this week with some people. He's not answering his phone recently, though, and it makes me want to fucking turn his office upside down.

– Would you get a different manager?

– I think we should, says Richie. – I think we should go with that girl Suzie who manages Plane Trees.

– Could be a good idea, I say. – It would piss off Vinnie and Finn, too, and wouldn't that be great?

They all smile at that.

Just then, a voice fills the room. It's the younger man with the band, sitting at the end of the row. He's tall and rake thin, with heavy-set eyebrows. He must only be in his teens. His eyes are closed and his right hand holds on to his pint on the table, as if the drink is what's giving him the power to sing. His voice is wavering but pure, and made stronger by the conviction in his delivery, as if the song had to be sung now, in this place at this time, and we had to be the ones to hear it. Now, Ciarán is plucking the banjo softly and the shrunken-faced man is following the boy's voice with the tin whistle, a soft and delicate sound, and as the boy sings about a quiet street, where old ghosts meet, and a woman walking away from him, the fiddle player lifts his fiddle under his chin, and it's a confluence of sound, each instrument fitting neatly and naturally on top of the other, the tin whistle, the banjo, the fiddle and then this boy's voice, raw and yearning, leading the flow. Pat is leaning back into the soft cushioning of the banquette, Nuala tucked up beside her, watching intently.

Mayo Dave blinks slowly at the table and Gerry, on seeing me looking at him, leans over and whispers, – That there singer is Ciarán's son.

I nod and smile at the revelation. I can see the likeness in the two of them now. As the song draws to a close, I blink tears out of my eyes and clap with the rest of them, Richie putting two fingers to his mouth and wolf-whistling loudly, Kesh and Frank banging the table with the palms of their hands, and Gerry joining in until Pat sits forward and shoots a glare across the table, silencing everyone immediately. Kesh's face is twitching. I wonder what he thinks of this boy, who can command a room with such force. The boy doesn't even crack a smile when we clap, he just looks to his father, who nods his head in approval and then looks around at everyone else, as if to say, *Who's next?*

– Orla, calls Neema from the other side of the table. – You sing. She's looking to everyone else for back-up as she says, – Orla should sing, right?

– Damn right, says Richie. The Fahy's crew watch on, bemused.

– But I don't have a guitar, I protest.

Ciarán says, – You don't need a guitar. Just tell us what you're singing. Ciarán and his son look at me expectantly, the same quick, pale eyes underneath the same heavy eyebrows. After a second's pause, I say – I guess I could sing 'Vincent'.

And I take a big swig of my pint and focus on Ciarán, who plucks softly with his plectrum and holds his eyes on me as he plays, dipping his head forwards to signal my cue to sing. I close my eyes and let the words fall out of me, and as they do, I imagine my voice sitting parallel with my da's easy baritone, a clean line of sound; we are singing together to 'Vincent', telling him how sorry we are, that the world can't take beauty like the beauty he gave us.

And when I finish, my head is empty: a cool, blank space. I open my eyes and I'm back in the corner of the bar, and I see Pat's face first, right in my eyeline, softened with emotion, her eyes glassy and faraway. Nuala is beside her, her hand resting on Pat's forearm. Gerry's cheeks are ripe little plums; Mayo Dave beside him looks dazed, the lumpy skin on his face burning red. And the Shiva lot are all smiling and clapping now, most of all Neema, who stares at me intensely, her eyes shining with certainty as she claps, and then she's looking at Kesh and saying, – You see?

– Hello?

– Hiya, Ma.

– Hiya, Lorley. You picked a good time to call. EastEnders *just* finished. How are you, love?

– Good thanks, Ma. How's the shop?

– It's been dead. It seems the ladies of Glasthule are well dressed enough at the moment.

– Ma, I sent the demo I made of my new songs to Gwen from Redstar, you know, who I worked with. She got me the job at The Castle.

– Right . . .

– And she played it to this manager she knows. I met him yesterday. He seems kind, and he's so into my songs. Anyway, he wants me to record them in a proper studio, with more music on it. I'm going in tomorrow with Max.

– Orla! We'll be hearing you on the radio next. You'll be coming home on a private jet to play The Olympia. I'll say, 'That's my daughter singing, she got it all from me.'

– Ha. And you'd be lying.

– Jesus, give me something, would you? You got your father's height, and his music skills.

– I posted him my tape. With the songs on it. I thought he might want to hear.

– He might want to hear about this new manager fella, too.

– I got your hair, Ma.

– What?

– I got Da's music skills and his height, but I got your hair.

– Ha. You did, God help you. You might have got my brains, too.

– The brains that barely passed my exams? Thanks a bunch.

– I was the same as you. Could never hold anything in.

– Maybe I did get my brains from you.

– I remember your school reports. It was always, 'Orla doesn't apply herself', 'Orla doesn't focus'. You could never finish things. It was like your head wouldn't let you stay in one place.

– Jesus, Ma, you'll have me crying in the hall here.

– It was the same at home. You'd get these notions to start things. Roller-skating, stamp-collecting, you name it, you'd go for it, all guns blazing, and after a week, you were totally over it. The only thing you ever kept up was your songs.

– Thank God for the songs.

– Well, just make sure I get front-row tickets to the shows, Orla, that's all I ask.

– Ma, did you ever want to leave Ireland?

– *I was dying to leave Ireland. But then I got that job in the pharmacy on Nassau Street, and my father wouldn't let me.*

– *And then you met Da.*

– *And then I met your father, yes.*

Pause.

– *Ma, I'm sorry for being such a wagon. When I was a teenager. I'm sorry for being so horrible to you.*

– *Where did that come from?*

– *Just talking about school and stuff. I was, so angry. I don't know why.*

– *You had to go through it, love.*

Pause.

– *Do you think I, my behaviour, like, changed things for you and Da?*

– *What are you trying to ask me, Orla?*

– *Well, I never thought, until recently, what it must have been like for you, with me, just, being so difficult. I never thought that it might have had an effect on you and Da as a couple.*

– *Ah, Lorley. You're not to be thinking us splitting up has anything to do with you. Jesus, you've enough on your plate over there in London without worrying about breaking down your parents' marriage. Ha!*

– *Okay. Well, that's good to know. You can stop laughing now.*

– *Sorry, love. It's just . . . God, if it was only that simple . . .*

Pause.

– *Listen, would you believe I've started packing already for London?*

– I would, Ma. I would believe you have about four outfit changes a day, too.

– Of course I do. You have to be covered for all eventualities.

– I can't wait to bring you to Fahy's to meet Pat and the lads.

CHAPTER 36

ELEVATION

The air in Max's studio is stuffy and suffused with a day's worth of band sweat and smoke. I tried to turn the winter heating schedule off and managed to jam the heating to being on all day. The engineer is due tomorrow to fix it, and we must suffer Biff's moaning until then.

Max is stripped down to a vest. The top of his arms are pink and fleshy. He has my demo in his hand, but he wants to chat.

– So, how are the boys? he asks, his bulbous eyes wide, making him look like a goldfish.

– Mmm. Okay. Kesh and Frank are taking a lot of speed.

Max's forehead crumples, so I add, – They're just putting off having to deal with the world, their families . . . all that.

He nods and says in a grave tone, – It's a cruel fucking world, the music industry.

– Max, can you listen to the tape now?

I watch his face closely as he pushes the cassette into

the player and presses play. As the first track starts, he nods along, eyes looking down towards the frayed carpet. – You wrote these yourself? he asks.

– Yup, I say. I'm sitting behind him, on the squishy sofa, pulling little shreds of skin off from around the base of my thumbnail.

– You've got a nice voice. Kinda husky, but still strong.

I can feel my cheeks heating up now as I try to honour his compliment with a smile. As the second chorus of 'High Places' finishes, he stops the tape and looks at me.

– You sound like you mean it, Orla. I believe you. That's the hardest bit, and you're already there. Let's start with this one. What do you want to do with it?

– I want to build up some more music around it.

– Okay, he says, – what's the brief?

– There is no brief.

– The manager didn't give you a brief?

– No. I told him my ideas, and he said to make it exactly how I want it.

He spins around on his chair and slaps his hands on his thighs, grinning. – Well, let's hear these ideas.

I laugh then, and take out my notebook and a pile of CDs from my bag. – I've got about ten years' worth of ideas right here. But I know exactly what I want for this song.

Six hours later, I'm cycling along the outer ring road of Regent's Park, the tall handsome townhouses to the left of me, the manicured border hedges of the park to the right. Dusk has fallen, but a strange burnt-orange colour remains behind the churning clouds. Rain starts to pitter-patter on my helmet, and as I cycle round the bottom corner of the park, I can see veils of it, slanting across the light of the lamp posts ahead.

Each time my bicycle approaches a lamp post, my shadow appears, hurtling past on the inside of me before disappearing into the darkness ahead. I laugh at this.

I'm passing myself out.

Then I start to sing. I'm quiet at first but with every push of the pedals I push my voice louder. The sky flashes and belches out thunder as I pedal up the hill on the west side of the park. I throw my head back, rain pelting my face, and I sing as loudly as my lungs will let me.

In Kilburn, I cycle past the beginning of Mill Road. The boys are working the night shift tonight, Neema is staying at Richie's in Peckham. Then The Eagle pub, where I lost my voice and the light fitting moved across the ceiling. Past Glengall Road, where Gerry shuffles home every evening to his lonely bed. Ahead is Quex Road, where a young Pat queued up for hours to get her National Insurance number when she arrived from Ireland all those years ago.

I lock up my bike across the road from Fahy's, the stained-glass windows glowing warm light into the dark of the High Road. Shane McGowan's voice greets me as I walk into the bar, always on the edge of a sneer, tin whistle and the dense chords of an accordion backing him up as he sings of the measure of his dreams. And there's Gerry and Mayo Dave perched in their places, Ciarán in the corner, banjo case propped up beside him, Eamonn wedged in under the telly, wet eyes. Pat is halfway through pulling a pint, her head moving fast on her neck like a little bird, as she chats. When she sees me, she says, – Jesus, you're soaked.

– I got caught in the rain.

– Have you a change of clothes?

– Stupidly not, I answer, and she's off, lifting the hatch and going upstairs. I hang up my coat and my helmet, rub the sweat from my forehead with the sleeve of my soaking jumper and say, – Well, Gerry. Dave.

– Orla. What's your news? says Gerry. – I made a song, I tell him, lifting the hatch and walking under it to behind the bar. – It needs work, but the bones of it are there.

It needs work, but the bones of it are there. The words and the beats and the spaces in between.

Gerry nods, his pint tipped to his lips. Pat arrives with an old, checked shirt of James's, waits for me to go to the toilet to put it on, then when I'm back under the hatch, she pushes a tea towel into my hands and points to the glasswasher. I pull it open and stand back as the steam rises to join the smoky haze that hangs above the bar.

Then I get to work.

ACKNOWLEDGEMENTS

There are many kind and generous people who volunteered their time to contribute to my writing of this book. My huge thanks to Nerm, Sangna Chauhan, Owen Hopkin, Tom Fahy, Reajuka Sharma, Fiona Byrne and the legend that is Margaret Hamill.

To my first readers, Tom Bell, Ronan O'Halloran, Molly King and Nikesh Shukla thank you for the encouragement and feedback.

My eternal gratitude to Bjork for allowing me to use a lyric from her song 'Bachelorette' for the epigraph. To Fintan O'Toole for the use of his words also.

To my agent Ben Dunn, I'm grateful for the real allyship and real talk. More wine and more lunches please.

Ella Gordon, thank you for believing in my writing when I don't. Your insight as an editor and as a fellow Irish gal in England has been invaluable. Namaste!

Susanna Hislop once again you have helped me through, draft by draft. I owe you so much.

My gratitude to Alex Clarke and everyone at Wildfire Publishing for their hard work and passion for this book, especially Areen Ali, Rosie Margesson, Joe Yule and Elaine Egan.

Big shouts to Oliver Sasse, Ellie Shaw and Fabia Jones Russell and the whole team at Good Life Mgmt for your guidance and support, and to Megan Carver and the team at Carver PR.

To my siblings, whose influence is all over this book. Rachel Macmanus, you're a fucking boss. Thank you for contributing to this book. Rod Macmanus thank you for laying the foundations of my love for Irish music. Davey Macmanus I'm so glad you invited me to move into that big tumble down house in Forest Gate all those years ago. Thank you for reading the book early on and giving me the insight and encouragement I needed.

And finally to my parents, who quietly facilitated my urge to get out of Ireland when I never thought to look back at what I was leaving behind. I'm looking now.